The scruff of Phillip's whiskers rasped her skin, ruffled along her nerves. Aubrey stroked the curve of his jaw, tracing his bottom lip with one fingertip. His eyes grew diamond-bright, and she shuddered when his tongue flicked out to taste her touch. She laid her other hand on his chest, shyly pleased to discover the frantic thump of his heart.

Still, uncertainty frayed the edges of her desire. "What happens if—"

"No." He tilted his head, resting his cheek in her palm. "No *what ifs*. Answer me this. Do you want me? Tonight, right now?" He asked the questions confidently, as if he had no doubt of her answer, but his eyes watched her warily. She took heart at this sign of vulnerability.

"Yes." Her heart swooped into freefall. His hands lay on the cushion of her chair, and she lowered her feet, feeling the stiffness of her joints and ruing the aches and pains of age. Spreading her knees just the tiniest bit allowed her to feel his fists like heated embers on either side of her thighs. "But—"

"No." He was stern. "If you have any doubts at all, tell me now and I'll go to my own room. If you want me to stay, you have to promise me one thing."

"What?"

"That you won't regret it in the morning. That you won't feel guilty or ashamed or any other emotion that might taint something so lovely as desire."

He was right. Desire *was* lovely, and even more beautiful when felt for someone so honest and trustworthy and genuine. He didn't deserve to be the subject of her insecurities.

She spoke slowly so he would know she meant every word. "I promise you. I will not regret tonight. No matter what happens."

"And what's going to happen, Aubrey?" He leaned closer, their breath mingling, the heat of their bodies entwining. "Am I going back to my room?"

"No," she said, and kissed him.

Turn the Next Page
(Silverberry Seduction Seasoned Romance Series,
Book Three)

By Brenda Margriet

TURN THE NEXT PAGE
(Silverberry Seduction Seasoned Romance Series, Book Three)

First edition published December 2022
Copyright © 2022 Brenda Margriet Clotildes
Digital ISBN 978-1-990697-00-5
Print ISBN 978-1-7773513-9-7

Cover Art by K. B. Barrett Designs

To the children that grow not only under our hearts
but in them.

***

This story mentions the loss of a child through Sudden
Infant Death Syndrome and deals with the search for
another child given up for adoption decades ago.

I hope I have treated these subjects with the care and
compassion they deserve.

Turn the Next Page

CHAPTER ONE

Aubrey Windt parked her car in a visitor's slot at Riverbend Seniors' Apartments and turned off the ignition. Though her father lived on the opposite side of the complex, she could feel his disapproving gaze burning into the back of her neck.

Breathing deeply, she strove to calm the anxiety fluttering in her throat. With detachment, she noted her hands gripped the steering wheel so tightly her knuckles were white. It took a determined effort of will to release the molded plastic, and she flexed her fingers to work out the stiffness.

After one more fortifying breath, she got out of her car and headed for the entrance. A moving van was parked just out front, the shadowy interior half-full of blanket-wrapped furniture and cardboard boxes of all sizes. She skirted around it, her heels clicking on the brick walkway.

Despite the fact both doors leading through the vestibule were open to allow the movers easier access, she stopped at the intercom panel and punched in her father's code. He wouldn't fuss if she showed up at his door unannounced, but it gave her just that little bit more time to prepare for the sermon waiting for her.

"Yes?" Her father's voice came brusquely through

7

the speaker.

She swallowed to clear the sudden rush of nervous saliva. "Hi, Dad. It's me."

The buzzer sounded and she walked past the large reception desk and imposing gas fireplace and turned toward the elevator. She would normally take the stairs—it was only four flights, after all—but the elevator was incredibly slow in deference to the elderly residents and was one more delay she could reasonably make.

She rode up in solitary splendour. When the doors opened, she waited just a moment more, and then stepped out into the hall. About twenty metres away, her father stood in the entrance to his suite. As soon as he saw her emerge, he disappeared. Lifting her chin, she walked briskly down the carpeted hall and inside, closing the door behind her.

"Hello." She fought to keep her voice level and calm.

Clarence Windt stood in the middle of the bright, well-ordered space, his weight resting lightly on the black metal cane in his right hand. Behind him a large window and single French door led to a small deck, the cloudless May sky outside silhouetting his tall, lean frame.

"Aubrey."

It was amazing how much meaning he could impart in the sparse syllables of her name. And infuriating how he could make her feel like a recalcitrant teenager with just his tone. Back then, of course, he'd been flanked by her mother, who had set the same high standards for their only child. Alice had died of complications from multiple sclerosis years ago, but her ghost was standing at Clarence's shoulder, disappointment etched on her face.

Reminding herself she was a mature woman with no need to defend herself, she took a seat on the sofa placed at right angles to a stiffly upholstered wingback chair and waited.

He regarded her intensely. His years in the courtroom, both as litigator and judge, had honed his ability to wield silence as a weapon, but she was used to this tactic. She simply looked at him, her face frozen in a polite expression.

He rapped his cane on the glossy floor. "So. Do you have an explanation for what happened?"

Bitter satisfaction curled through her. At least she'd won that small battle. "No." She couldn't help it. Her gaze flickered away from his and she took refuge in smoothing the navy-blue material of her pencil skirt over her knee. "My team and I worked hard to win. The voters chose Monica."

The sense of disconnect she'd experienced Saturday night as the votes were coming in hadn't yet dissipated. If she stabbed herself, would she feel it? No wonder her spine ached, as if metal clamps were screwed onto each vertebra.

Everyone on her staff, both paid and volunteer, had worked their asses off to get her re-elected. *She'd* worked her ass off, too. Not because she believed in herself. Because *they* believed in her, and she hadn't been able to say no.

That was the source of her searing guilt. She'd *wanted* to lose. Hiding that blasphemous thought had taken every last dreg of her energy throughout the grueling campaign.

"That's a weak excuse." Her father took the few steps necessary to reach his chair and lowered himself into it. A wince of pain creased his cheek, but she didn't react. He needed a hip replacement and was refusing to get one—because Clarence Windt was invincible and gave into no one and nothing. Ever.

"Whatever you choose to call it, there's no changing what happened." Thank god Monica Corban's win had been decisive and there was no hope of a recount. "I'm not the only Member of the Legislative Assembly who lost their seat. The voters wanted a change in

9

government, and they got one."

"Bah." Clarence waved a hand in disgust at this democratic opinion. "Not saying the party didn't make mistakes, they did. But you won the by-election by a wide margin, and you had more than three years to build support. You should have been able to get re-elected."

Should have. Could have. Didn't. She bit back the facetious response. He wouldn't appreciate her attempt at humour. "I won the by-election on the coattails of Oliver's success and sympathy at his death." There were still moments when she missed her husband so much she could barely breathe. And other days when she used that breath to curse him for dying so suddenly.

"Of course you did." Clarence's agreement didn't make her feel any better. "The voters needed to know what you'd done for them since then. You threw away the chance to make a real difference by taking their support for granted."

"I took *nothing* for granted." Damn it. She'd let him needle her into a show of emotion. She flattened her tone once more. "I did my best, every day, every hour, every minute. It's not my fault it wasn't enough."

"It was a debacle from start to finish. Luckily, voter memories are short. When you run again in four years you'll know better."

Her vision dimmed and her gorge rose. "Run again?" she croaked.

Phillip Church stood in his aunt's new apartment, smiling broadly as Marjorie Strahl commanded the burly movers she'd hired with the ferocity of a drill sergeant. Or, rather, like the cardiac surgeon she'd been, barking out orders in the operating room.

God, it was good to have her back in town.

Riverbend was a relatively new complex, and his aunt had been on the wait list for several months before a suite had come available. While it catered to seniors, it didn't provide nursing care or assisted living. Not that Marjorie needed such help. If he knew her at all, she'd be running the place before long.

She planted her hands on her hips and glared at him. "What are you doing, standing around? There's a truckload of things to bring up."

Her steel grey hair curled around her face in a fresh perm—an old-fashioned style she refused to give up—and she wore a flower-print house dress with an elastic waist. She looked like a rounded, cozy granny, but anyone who took her at face value did so at their own peril.

He laid his hands on her shoulders and kissed her forehead. "Have I told you how happy I am you've come home?"

She pushed him away, though her eyes twinkled with pleasure. "Yes. Now go get more boxes."

"Yes, ma'am." He saluted and she huffed in feigned irritation.

Carrying the hand truck, he took the stairs down the two flights, pushed open the heavy steel door at the bottom, and turned left into the hall. The elevator closed as he passed, and he caught a glimpse of a woman in a white blouse and navy-blue skirt. An impression of mature vitality and no sign of a walker or cane had him thinking *visitor* not *resident* as he strode to the moving van parked at the main entrance.

He loaded the hand truck and used the elevator to return to Marjorie's apartment.

"Put those in the bedroom for now." She pointed at a door next to the gas fireplace.

He went where instructed and stacked the boxes in a corner. It really was good to have her home again. She was mother as much as aunt to him, taking on the role of guardian after his parents drowned in a canoe accident when he was eight. His own twin sons had been preschoolers when she'd taken a position in one of the major hospitals in Vancouver. During the years she'd practiced her medical career there, they'd kept in close contact, with frequent visits and phone calls. She'd retired a decade ago but remained in the Lower Mainland. As time passed, he'd started to worry about her being on her own, especially so far away. Not that he'd ever say such a thing to her face. At eighty years old, she was as fiercely independent and terrifyingly competent as ever.

He rolled the now empty hand truck back to the living room.

"Where is my area rug?" Marjorie demanded of one of the young movers.

He stifled a chuckle when the other man hunched a shoulder as if warding off a blow. "Still in the truck, ma'am."

"We should lay that down before we put the sofa in place, shouldn't we?" Her voice had a slight quaver of age to it, but she was no less forceful for that one small weakness.

The mover's hunted expression made Phillip grin. "I'll get it. Be right back." He took the stairs to the main floor once more. Inside the truck, he hefted the rolled-up carpet onto his shoulders. It was heavy and awkward and he staggered down the ramp, concentrating more on staying balanced than where he was going.

"Watch it!"

Even if he hadn't heard her voice just days ago while watching the election results on television, he was certain he would have recognized it from only those two words. Still, the unexpectedness of hearing it, here and now, made his heart beat in a ragged rhythm and he drew in a breath. He tilted the carpet down and rested it on end, wrapping his arms around it to keep it steady.

Aubrey Windt, his first ex-wife, stood before him, sleek and sophisticated in a navy-blue skirt suit, her silver and blonde hair smoothed back into a tight bun, her face scrunched in a scowl.

CHAPTER TWO

"Hello, Aubrey." It took an effort to speak evenly, so disconcerted was he by her appearance. Not just the suddenness of it, but the contradiction between his memories and the woman standing before him.

She recognized him that same instant. Her expression flattened, any hint of annoyance gone. "Phillip. Hello. What are you doing here?"

So much for casual small talk. "Marjorie is moving in today." He patted the carpet he was supporting. "What about you?"

Her mouth tightened. "Dad lives here."

Despite the years between their marriage and now, he could read the signs. It seemed that whatever else had changed about Aubrey, her uneasy relationship with her father hadn't.

"I hope he's doing well." It was the polite thing to say, even if resentment still burned over how the old curmudgeon had manipulated Aubrey's life—and Phillip's own.

"He is, thank you." Her gaze flickered over his shoulder then resolutely came back to meet his. "And your family? Jeanette, isn't it? And your boys? That was your son who interviewed me on Saturday, wasn't it?"

And hadn't that been a shock, seeing his son standing next to his first wife. His boys had no idea he'd been married to anyone other than their mother. His marriage to Aubrey had been so brief and so long ago, it hadn't seemed necessary to mention it. Maybe he should have done so when Asher had joined the local news team, especially since Aubrey had been a Member of the Legislative Assembly representing one of the Prince George ridings at the time.

Too late now.

"It was, yes." He could have guessed she'd connect the dots. Prince George was a tight knit community, despite its size, and Church wasn't that common a surname. "Both boys are well. Jeanette, too. She remarried last year."

That cracked her polished facade. Her expression softened. "Oh. I hadn't heard of your divorce. I didn't mean—"

He waved off her implied apology. "It was a mutual decision. No hard feelings either way." Unlike when his marriage to Aubrey had shattered.

He wondered if he should offer his condolences on the death of Oliver O'Keefe. He'd never met her second husband. Would it seem too forward to mention it now, years later? He decided to stick to a more recent loss. "I'm sorry about the election."

Something bitter sparked in Aubrey's eyes, but she merely said, "Thank you."

The Aubrey he remembered had been a chatterbox, heedlessly and impulsively saying whatever came to mind. She'd favoured long, loose flowing skirts and scoop-necked T-shirts. The woman before him now exuded restraint, her expression as tightly buttoned-up as her white blouse. Was it possible the warm, loving woman she'd once been was still inside, hidden behind the shiny, hard-shelled exterior? Curiosity tugged, and he opened his mouth to extend their conversation, but she broke the short silence first.

"I should be going. Nice seeing you again." She brushed past him with staccato steps.

He turned to watch her hurry across the parking lot. It appeared *she* had no wish to talk about old times.

Shouldering the carpet once more, he headed into

the building. Aubrey didn't have to worry. Even though Marjorie and Clarence were living in the same complex, there was little likelihood they would see each other again. And if they did, a polite nod would suffice. No need to actually *talk* to one another.

The thought made him sad.

Aubrey unlocked her car door and slid into the driver's seat with a gasp.

She risked a glance in the rear-view mirror and saw Phillip disappear into the building, the bundled carpet hoisted onto his broad shoulder. Thank goodness he was gone. She could take a few minutes to calm herself before driving away. Seeing him again, and so unexpectedly, had sent her pulse into the stratosphere. Especially with her heart still pounding from her altercation with her father.

She'd sat and listened to Clarence with nauseating dismay as he'd laid out his plans. "For now, you'll return to Wakim, Wing and Wright. You were one of their best corporate lawyers. I'm sure they'll be happy enough to take you back. Then we'll start planning for the next election."

Everything after that had been muffled, incomprehensible murmurs. Her ears rang as blood coursed so rapidly through her veins she swayed with dizziness. Her denial was a whisper. "No."

He didn't stop talking. Maybe he hadn't heard her. Maybe he *had* and he was ignoring her the way he always did.

"No." Not a whisper this time. Clarence stuttered and stopped and she felt a rush of resentful gratification.

"What did you say?" His bushy eyebrows rose imperiously.

"No." Her voice gained strength with every word. "No to everything. I am not going back to the law firm.

I am not going to start planning for four years from now. I am *not* going to run again."

That got her father's attention. "I know you're upset you lost." His tone was as conciliatory as she'd ever heard it. "But you'll get over it. Things will be different next time."

"There won't *be* a next time, Dad. I hate politics. *Oliver* was the one who wanted to be in public office, never me." If he hadn't accepted a ride with a pilot friend only to crash into a mountain on their way to Victoria, she wouldn't have even *considered* running. She'd only done it because she felt she owed it to him, to his legacy.

"Aubrey—"

She sprang to her feet, propelled by a desperate determination. "I'm sorry, Dad. I'm sorry I disappointed you by losing, I'm sorry I can't fulfill your dreams by running again. But they are *your* dreams, not mine. I'm fifty years old. It's time I lived my life for me, not for anyone else."

"Fifty-two." Clarence couldn't stand inaccuracies.

"Yes, fifty-two." She bit off the words. "That's not the point. The point is I'm through with doing what everyone else thinks I should do. I'm going to do what *I* want to do for a change."

"And what is that? What on earth is *that*?"

She stared down at her father helplessly. His pale grey eyes stabbed her, demanding a response.

"I don't know." Panic had welled up, but she'd forced herself to tell him the truth. "I honestly don't know."

That had gone over well—*not*. Her eyes burning with the threat of tears, she'd walked out on him midway through a sentence. She'd probably pay for that later in cold silences and disapproving glances, but she couldn't let him see her cry.

Then she'd almost been knocked to the ground by a perambulating carpet—though it had been partly her own fault for not paying attention to where she was going—only to realize it was being brandished by Phillip Church.

It had been disconcerting enough on Saturday, having to act like she didn't know who Asher Church's father was. She'd tried not to stare as the young man had asked his questions, but hadn't been able to stop searching his features, seeking Phillip in the shape of his jaw or the colour of his eyes. Thank goodness she'd known ahead of time who had been assigned to her—it had given her time to prepare.

Not like today.

Staring blindly through the windscreen, she breathed deep and slow, replenishing the oxygen that had whooshed out of her lungs at her first face-to-face in more than thirty years with her first husband.

He looked exactly as she remembered. Maybe he'd gotten a little heavier, but he carried it well. And yes, his dark hair had gone grey, but it was a sexily stunning silver. Even the way it receded at his temples added an air of wisdom to the sharp intelligence that had always shone from his eyes. And the creases and wrinkles around those eyes when he'd smiled at her—

Aubrey squeezed her lips tight. Enough. Phillip was in her past and would be staying there. Even if she wished for something as platonic as friendship—not that she did—he would never welcome her back into his life. She'd burned too many bridges.

Judging herself finally calm enough, she put the car in reverse, carefully backed out of the slot, drove slowly through the parking lot, and took a left turn onto 20th Avenue.

She had nowhere to go and nothing to do, for the first time in as long as she could remember. No one waited for her at home, not even a goldfish, and she couldn't bear the thought of going to her condo and staring at the walls. She'd end up rehashing her conversation with her father, and she was not in the mood for any further flagellation.

Driving aimlessly, she cruised up and down the streets of one of Prince George's oldest, most attractive neighbourhoods. The city had boomed during the 1960s, and the *get-'em-up-quick* mentality had resulted in acres and acres of characterless square boxes marching side by side. But not here. This area was one of her favourites, with mature elms arching over the streets, quirky old homes in random shapes and sizes, and large lots.

After Oliver's death and her win in the by-election, it had been pointless to keep the elegant home they'd shared. She'd worried his daughter Sophie would protest. She'd grown up there, and it was Aubrey who had moved into the house after she married Oliver when Sophie was ten. But once her initial shock passed, her stepdaughter had agreed it was the best thing to do. "I haven't lived there for years," she'd said, "and now I'm in Toronto, there's no reason to keep it. You'll be spending half the year in Victoria when the Legislature is sitting, after all."

Aubrey had invested fifty percent of the proceeds from the sale, as well as the main portion of Oliver's life insurance, in Sophie's name, and then used the remainder as down payments on modern, efficient condos in both Prince George and Victoria. She'd revised her will to leave everything to her stepdaughter, a child she'd been blessed to help raise and a young woman she was proud to love. Then she sold anything she didn't need to furnish her two small homes and called it a day.

Recently, the chilly soullessness of her residences had become the outward symbol of her inward restlessness. Selling the one in Victoria would be the work of a moment—she'd probably make money on the transaction, real estate prices having gone up substantially over the last few years—but that didn't solve her Prince George problem. She'd been sleeping badly for weeks now, and her home was not the refuge it should be.

She needed a change—and as she turned the corner onto Cedar Street, fate handed it to her.

The real estate agent's sign—*Immediate Possession Available*—caught her attention. Pulling to the curb, she turned off her car and leaned over the passenger seat, peering through the side window. She still couldn't see well enough, so she got out and rounded the hood to stand on the sidewalk.

If there hadn't been a sign, she might not have even seen the house it advertised. A huge, completely out of control hedge hid all but the curled and tattered shingle roof from view. Buried in the scraggly shrubbery she could see greying wooden stakes, hinting at an ancient picket fence. No driveway led to the house—this area had backyard access via alleys—and the only break in the towering green wall was a narrow passageway through which a crumbling concrete path led.

Stepping cautiously through the arching foliage, she took her first good look at the house itself. Two bay windows bowed out on either side of the front door, which stood at the top of a flight of five semi-circular disintegrating concrete steps. A screen door hung drunkenly from one hinge, the bottle dash stucco was scabrous with missing chunks, and paint peeled from the wooden window frames in long, brittle strips. Along the foundation more rampant flora sprawled, hiding what Aubrey assumed would be yet more neglect.

She tiptoed down the side of the house, doing her best to keep her heels from spiking into the relatively clear and level area that might once have been a lawn. A window up near the peak of the roof suggested a second storey, and a jutting extension at the back was probably a newer addition. Not that it was in any better shape than the rest of the structure.

Unlike the houses on either side, there was no garage. A tightly packed, deeply rutted dirt rectangle had evidently sufficed as a parking space. At some point, a fence had separated the back yard from the alley, but it had given up the job years ago, the rotting posts and weather-eaten boards scattered on the ground and obscured by dead vegetation. The yard was a jungle of thistles and grasses and weeds. Since it was only mid-May in northern British Columbia, the new greenery hadn't taken a firm hold yet, but the growth of previous years was evident in the knee-high tangle of dried stalks and stems.

Circling to the other side, Aubrey pulled out her cell phone and without giving herself a chance to second guess her gut, called the real estate agent. Though the woman listed on the sign tried to play it cool, Aubrey could hear the eagerness in her voice, and her willingness to meet strengthened the impression that the house was an albatross she desperately needed to unload.

Steeling herself to the fact that the interior was probably even worse than the unloved exterior, she waited for the agent to arrive.

She was buying this house. It needed her, and she needed it.

CHAPTER THREE

"This **is the house** you bought?" Natalie Minton's brown eyes widened in shock behind her thick-framed glasses.

Aubrey couldn't blame her friend for her appalled reaction—the house *was* a disaster—but a surge of protectiveness warmed her chest.

"It was a steal." She did her best not to sound defensive. "The real estate agent has been trying to move it for months."

"I can believe it." They were standing just inside the enormous hedge and the house rose before them in all its ramshackle glory. Natalie blinked, her stare locked on the sight, mouth hanging open in horror. "It's like a car accident. I can't look away."

It took a lot to faze Natalie, and she felt a whisper of unease. Had this been a horrible mistake? Too late now, she supposed. "The previous owner had a hate on for all the developers bulldozing old houses and putting up modern monstrosities." Natalie tore her gaze away long enough to flick her a wry glance. "I know, I know. Those are his words, not mine. The agent said he had even filed suit against the city to force them to stop giving permits for those kinds of projects. Not that he had a hope of winning, of course."

"He sounds a little...well...crazy." Her tone hinted that Aubrey might share that craziness.

In fact, she did sympathize with the previous owner. Prince George had a few protected heritage homes, but others, while providing architectural diversity, had no historical value. Nevertheless, tearing them down simply for profit did feel wrong.

"It's not that bad." Natalie snorted but made no further comment. "Sure, it needs a good cleaning, and the yard is a shambles. But the house inspector says the foundation is sound and the electrical and plumbing is safe, even if it is old." She didn't mention that he'd warned her certain renovations might require bringing everything up to code, no matter what the cost.

"Have you told Clarence yet?"

She flinched. "No. I still have that pleasure." Her father wouldn't understand the impulse that had led to her purchase. If she was lucky, he would just look disapproving. The way her life had been going lately, she didn't think she'd get off that easily.

"And you take possession when?"

"A week. But I'm keeping my condo here for now." She had already accepted an offer on her Victoria home, and its sale would fund the house purchase and a start on the renovations. She was lucky to be in a financial situation where she didn't need to sell her Prince George apartment yet. While she planned to move to Cedar Street as soon as the house was clean and habitable, she thought it might be necessary to have a refuge after the serious construction work had started.

"Good idea." Natalie grinned. "Well, when you told me you were leaving politics, you said you wanted a project. I think you found one."

"What about you?" Natalie wasn't only a friend. She had managed Oliver's last campaign, and he had always spoken highly of her. When he died, Aubrey had inherited her for the by-election, and when she had won, she had convinced Natalie to leave her position at the Prince George Public Library and run the riding office. They'd worked well together for three years, but Aubrey's election loss meant Natalie was out of a job, too. One more heaping helping of remorse to pile on her plate. "Have you started looking for a new position, yet?"

A dead leaf had attached itself to Natalie's sleeve when they'd pushed their way through the hedge. She plucked it off and crumbled it with slow, deliberate motions. "Not seriously. I have a few feelers out, but I need a break after the campaign. I'm sure something will come together soon." Scattering the remains of the leaf at her feet, she slapped her palms together, putting an end to the conversation. "Let's get going. I can't wait to introduce you to all the Silverberries. You're going to fit right in."

They had been on their way to Aubrey's first Silverberry Book Club meeting, but Natalie had insisted they swing by her new purchase first. As they climbed back into Aubrey's car and headed toward the Southridge neighbourhood, where the host lived, she returned to the topic of politics. It was like a hangnail. She couldn't stop picking at it.

"Thanks again for supporting my decision." She pulled into a left turn lane and halted for a red light. Telling Natalie she was quitting political life hadn't been nearly as nerve-racking as telling her father, but she'd still been anxious. It had dawned on her that the younger woman was the only friend she had—and *friend* might be pushing it. Sure, Natalie had made frequent attempts over the years to get Aubrey to join after-work activities, but maybe she had just felt sorry for her widowed boss.

She hoped the fact Natalie had extended yet another invitation, even after the debacle of the election, proved she wasn't wrong about the friendship.

Natalie chuffed out a breath. "Stop saying that. You have to do what's right for you."

"It's just that, if I can't give it my whole heart and soul, I don't think I should do it at all."

"I get it. I really do. You don't have to explain again."

She could feel Natalie's gaze on her profile as the

light turned green and she led the line of traffic behind her onto the highway. "All right, no more apologizing. Moving on. Tell me more about this book club of yours."

"It was started by Helen Mansfield after her first husband died," Natalie said. "You met her once. Her and her second husband Nathan. It was a few years ago at a charity golf tournament, just before Oliver announced he was running for office."

"I don't remember them. Sorry." She had met so many people during Oliver's campaign.

"No biggie. I'd be more surprised if you did. Anyway, I've been going to the club for a couple years now."

"How did you find out about it?"

"Helen's daughter and I became friends at university. I even lived with them for a short time. We lost touch, as you do, but when she heard about my divorce, she called to see how I was doing. She suggested I join, as a distraction."

Aubrey's opinion of Natalie's husband had never been high, but it had dropped to the bottom of the barrel with his treatment of Natalie. As far as she was concerned, the divorce had been a blessing. But she couldn't say that to Natalie, not even two years later.

"What kind of books do you choose?" She powered past a lethargic logging truck in the right-hand lane. She'd read enough heavy, meaningful, *important* books to last a lifetime, foisted on her by her parents, her professors, even Oliver. She hoped this club's taste leaned toward more frivolous stories. Life was too short to read any more depressing books.

Natalie chuckled. "We're not your average book club. But I don't want to spoil the surprise. We're almost there."

"Ready to go?"

Phillip looked up from his computer screen, eyes

aching, and squinted at Dexter Seymour, standing in the doorway of his office. "Is it that time already?"

"It's *past* that time." Dexter smacked the door jam. "Meet you out front."

He saved the work order he'd been revising, shut the lid of his laptop, and hooked his gym bag from beneath his desk. It had been a busy Monday, and he vaguely remembered various staff calling their goodbyes as they headed home for the day, but he hadn't realized it was almost six-thirty. He strode through the deserted office to the washroom, changed into his riding gear, and made sure the security system engaged after stepping out the front door.

Dexter waited in the parking lot. He'd already unloaded his bike from the rack on his SUV as well as Phillip's from the box of his truck and stood patiently, gripping both sets of handlebars, helmet fastened under his chin, a small backpack strapped to his torso. His stocky body was encased in tight bike shorts and form-fitting shirt in an eye-watering array of colours.

"You look like a bag of Skittles." He should have been used to his buddy's clothing choices by now, but Dexter continued to shock him.

"You're just jealous 'cause you can't pull off my style."

He snorted his denial of this arguable statement and clipped on his own helmet and backpack. Dexter gave Phillip's bike a shove and he snagged it as it wobbled toward him. In one continuous motion, he stepped onto the pedal, kicked his leg over the seat, and led the way out of the parking lot.

They cycled past the large wooden sign that guarded the entrance to Twin Rivers Landscape and Maintenance. Lately, the thrill Phillip felt when he read the name of the company he'd built from practically nothing had faded. He was still proud of what he'd accomplished over the last thirty years. It just no longer gave him the sense of satisfaction it used to.

What a depressing thought.

"Sawmill Trail today?" Dexter came abreast on the narrow road. Twin Rivers' office and yard were only metres from the main highway heading west of Prince George, but in behind was a huge wilderness park that could be accessed from the narrow side road edging Phillip's land. Mountain bikers and hikers shared the miles of trails crisscrossing the area with moose, bear, bobcat, and deer, and it was a favourite with both of them, in part because it was so convenient.

"Sounds good. You lead."

For the next forty-five minutes Phillip pumped over terrain rutted with roots and muddied with snow melt, staying far enough behind Dexter to avoid the worst of the grime spraying off his tires. It had been a cooler spring than normal, and small patches of rotten snow were still visible in the shadows. The trail climbed and dipped under towering forests of pine, spruce, and fir, through open meadows of grass and shrubs, and past amber pools edged with reeds and weeds. They powered up one final hill and came to their destination, a scarred wooden picnic table overlooking two interlinking ponds.

"Feel better?" Dexter leaned his bike against a tree next to Phillip's and they sat on the tabletop, their feet on the bench.

"What do you mean?" He chugged water from the bottle he'd taken from the clamp on the bike frame and ripped open a granola bar. He'd have a proper supper later but needed something to tide him over.

"You've been cranky as shit lately."

Trust Dexter to notice. "Is that your medical opinion, Dr. Seymour?" Dexter was a psychiatrist who worked mostly with youth, but that didn't stop him from analyzing his friends. Or in this case, the ex-husband of his sister, the father of his nephews, and his best bud since high school.

"Yup." Dexter took a swig of his own water. "Ever

since Marjorie moved back to town, in fact. Is everything okay with her?"

"She's fine. It's great having her here." He swallowed the last of the granola bar and crumpled the wrapper in his fist. "Asher's planning to leave town."

"What?" Dexter straightened out of his slouch, eyebrows raising in surprise. "Since when?"

"Since a couple days ago." The shock of it still rippled under his skin.

Two and a half decades ago, when Jeanette had told him they were expecting twins, he'd been thrilled and terrified. Thoughts of two tiny toddlers speaking their own secret language and wreaking double the havoc had amused and alarmed him. From the moment Asher and Zeke had taken their first breaths, however, they could not have been more different, and their differences had only grown with them. They didn't actively avoid each other, but the magical bond twins were reputed to share was missing from their relationship. He worked hard to keep them connected through their shared love of sports, both as fans and athletes. If Asher left town, he'd miss his son like he'd miss an arm. But what worried him even more was that the boys would lose one of the few links they had—proximity.

Dexter was waiting for more details with his usual calm expression. Phillip ran a hand through his sweaty hair. "We were all at Marjorie's, having a little housewarming celebration, and he dropped the bomb. You know he's always wanted to work in sports broadcasting, more than news. He only took the reporting job here because there are so few opportunities in television. But now he's got some experience he wants to go for sports full out. I always knew he'd move on someday. I just hoped it would be later, rather than sooner."

"Does he have a job lined up?"

"Not yet, but he's been applying all over the place. It

won't be long before he gets an offer." Asher was an excellent reporter and anchor, and Phillip didn't think that just because he was his father. He'd heard it from Asher's bosses, viewers, and colleagues, too.

"Is that all that's bothering you?" Dexter prodded gently.

He rose restlessly and stepped to the edge of the lookout. He could leave it at Asher and Dexter wouldn't insist on more. He knew when to push and when not to. Instead, he said, "I think I'm going through a mid-life crisis." He shook his head and turned back to Dexter, still sitting on the picnic table. "Crisis is too strong a word. I'm bored. I love my company, but it practically runs itself. The boys are grown and don't need me. Even Jeanette has moved on."

"Robert treats my sister right. Not that you didn't, but she's happier with him," Dexter agreed. "Your sons are adults you can be proud of. And you've surrounded yourself with excellent employees at work. So, what's wrong?"

Damn psychiatrists, asking leading questions. He shifted his weight from foot to foot and shrugged. "Not that I needed to create a dynasty, but I suppose it's always been at the back of my mind that someday one of the boys would take over the company. Asher found his passion for broadcast early, so I knew he was out, but I thought Zeke might take an interest. It's become obvious over the last couple of years that won't happen. He has no desire to be a boss and is happy as a machinist at the pellet plant. Which is perfectly fine," he hastened to add before Dexter could comment. "I guess I just started wondering what that means for me. What the future holds, not just for the company, but my own life."

The image of Aubrey the day he'd met her at Riverbend flashed before him. She'd looked so poised, so controlled, so *frozen*. So un-Aubrey-like, as he remembered her, at least. Was she feeling the same thing he was—trapped in a holding pattern, needing to break out?

Without stopping to consider consequences, he said, "I saw Aubrey the day Marjorie moved in. Her father lives in the same apartment building."

"Ah."

He narrowed his eyes at Dexter. "What does that mean?"

"Nothing."

"Don't get all shrinky with me. Spit it out."

Dexter's brown eyes gleamed with amusement and the smile so much like his sister's and his nephews' split his face. "Don't forget, I was a third wheel through high school, and then, when you got married right after graduation, through your marriage. I know what you guys were like together. I know you loved Jeanette, but it wasn't the same as with Aubrey."

"We were kids. We didn't know what love was." Passion, yes. Lust, definitely. But love? The steady, solid kind of love that survives tears and tribulations and desperate days? Obviously not. At least Aubrey hadn't. As soon as things had gotten tough, she'd fled home to her overbearing parents.

The ghost of the pain he'd felt during those turbulent times stabbed him, searing despite the passage of decades. Many marriages didn't survive the trauma that had fractured his with Aubrey. He shouldn't be too hard on her.

Didn't mean he couldn't wish it had worked out differently. If it had, though, he might not have his sons. Playing the *what if* game could lead to madness.

Irritated with himself, he strode to his bike. "My turn to lead. Try to keep up, okay?"

The woman that opened the door to Natalie's knock appeared to be about sixty years old, with unapologetic wrinkles, pixie-cut grey hair, and a trim build. She wore jeans and a button-up blouse in bright florals, a teal feather boa, and a silver crown from which sparkling silver balls swayed.

"Natalie! You've brought your friend! How lovely. Come in, come in. I'm Helen." She stepped back, crown boinging and bouncing.

Aubrey blinked. She'd half-expected to remember the woman once she'd seen her—she didn't—but she certainly hadn't expected *this*.

"This is Aubrey Windt," Natalie said. "She wants to know what kind of books we read."

Helen threw back her head and laughed boisterously. Aubrey watched in fascination—and awed respect—as her host waved the martini glass in her right hand without a drop of the red liquid escaping. "Don't worry, Aubrey. We'll let you know all our secrets soon enough. Come on in and meet the others."

She led them to an elegantly appointed living room—cream walls stretching to a high ceiling, white mantle above the modern gas fireplace, dark beige sofas, eclectically framed prints, photos, and artwork. A colourfully patterned area rug kept the space from being monochromatic, as did the jewel-toned throw pillows.

There wasn't a book in sight. Not even a bookcase, or a stack on the low, square coffee table.

Numerous gazes swung toward Aubrey and a qualm of nerves coiled in her stomach. The sensation reminded her of her first days at university, the law firm, even the Legislature. Knowing she was being assessed and appraised, worrying that she'd be found lacking.

"Everyone, this is Aubrey Windt, our newest member. Say hello."

Dutifully, like students answering a teacher, a chorus of greetings rose from the people scattered about the room.

"Nathan, sweetheart, will you make sure Aubrey

meets everyone while I get her a drink?" Helen asked. "Wine, tea, fizzy water? Or will you join me in a Red Shoe Martini?"

It was barely seven on a Monday, but Aubrey had a feeling she might need a kick to help her through the evening. "I'll try one of your martinis. Thanks."

The other woman nodded. "Your usual white wine, Natalie?" At her agreement, Helen swept out of the room, leaving a humming silence in her wake.

Aubrey turned back to the group. A man about Helen's age approached, his pale blue eyes surrounded by crinkly laugh lines created by a wide grin. "Don't worry." He patted her shoulder. "You'll get used to my wife. Helen's a dynamo. The rest of us are much lower key."

"Speak for yourself, Nathan." The comment came from the man on the sofa where Natalie had taken a seat. He wore royal blue slacks with a knife-edge crease, a sweater vest over a paisley print dress shirt, and a bow tie. "I am very high maintenance, and you know it. If you need proof, just ask Bennett."

"Aubrey, meet Terrance." Nathan directed his next remarks to the other man. "You may be high maintenance, but you're also lazy. No one would ever call Helen lazy."

"I resent that remark," Terrance said placidly. "I'm not lazy, I'm a maestro at proactively conserving my energy reserves by the considered delegation of meaningless tasks."

"Trust a university professor to use a dozen words when one would do. Welcome, Aubrey. I'm Lynn." The woman who offered her hand was about Aubrey's own height—five-six—and dressed with a casual elegance she envied. Whenever she tried to wear yoga pants and a tunic, she came off sloppy, not lithe yet dignified as Lynn looked. "I voted for you in both elections. Sorry about the recent result."

"Thanks." It was the only acceptable response, of

course, even if the condolences were unwelcome. Aubrey hadn't revealed the true extent of her relief at her loss to anyone and never planned to.

"I'm Penta." The last woman in the room approached Aubrey. She was short and plump and wore a sweatshirt bearing the logo of a local high school over capri-length jeans. Aubrey wondered if that explained her slightly harried expression. Was she a mother of teens or a teacher? "You'll love this club. We all do. It's the best night of my month."

"I'm sure I will." Aubrey felt like an automaton, spouting all the right responses without feeling the corresponding emotions. She *wasn't* sure she'd love the club, but she couldn't say that. She'd quit politics so she could quit hiding her true feelings, yet here she was, mouthing platitudes while her insides knotted. Where was Helen with that drink?

CHAPTER FOUR

Thankfully, Aubrey didn't have much longer to wait for her liquid courage. Helen swooped back into the room, gave Natalie her wine and handed Aubrey her glass, just as a knock sounded at the door. "That will be Stephanie." She dashed back out, the bobbles on her crown waving, boa fluttering.

Overwhelmed despite the friendliness of everyone so far, Aubrey joined Penta on the sofa opposite Terrance and Natalie and took a sip of the sweetly tart concoction. She couldn't detect any alcohol and vowed to limit herself to the single drink. Those were the dangerous ones, after all.

Helen's light, cheerful voice mingled with one in a deeper register, and a moment later she reappeared in the living room entrance with another woman in tow. The newcomer was tall, with broad shoulders narrowing to a slim waist. Her height was emphasized by the classic lines of her deep rose sheath dress and owed little to the low-heeled pumps in a matching shade.

"Hi, everyone." Her reserved smile lifted one corner of the wide mouth under her strong, straight nose. She waved to the room, flashing heavy-knuckled fingers tipped with pink. In her other hand she carried a black leather clutch purse. Still no books in view.

Stephanie made her way in between the facing sofas to where Lynn was perched on a large ottoman and

33

leaned down to hug her. "How's my boy doing? I miss having him underfoot."

"Oscar's great. Or were you talking about Benjamin?"

General laughter followed Lynn's response, in which Aubrey did not take part. Her feeling of being out of place intensified with the inside joke.

Stephanie settled next to Lynn and nodded regally at Aubrey. "Welcome to the Silverberry Book Club. I'm Stephanie."

"Thank you. I'm glad to be here." She smiled politely to disguise the lie and hurried to change the subject. "I'm beginning to wonder where the books come in, though."

Helen laughed and perched a hip on the wide arm of the upholstered chair where Nathan sat. She laid her hand on her husband's shoulder in a casually affectionate gesture, and he looked up at her with a glow of pride. Unexpectedly, Aubrey's throat tightened, and she swallowed the sensation away. "Now we're all here, I'll let you in on our secret. We're not really a book club."

"I was beginning to suspect something was up." She allowed herself a pang of disappointment. "Is it just a social club? An excuse to get together for drinks and conversation?" She'd agreed to Natalie's invite because she thought it would be more than people sitting around talking about inconsequential things. Not that she'd wanted anything too serious—but she had hoped for new experiences.

"No, not that either." Natalie's grin revealed her delight at Aubrey's confusion. "Tonight is our annual planning meeting. Your timing is perfect. Now you can help us decide what we'll be doing for the next year."

"Decide what?"

Terrance took up the explanation. "Our activities. Anything goes as long as it isn't illegal. And if it is dangerous, it has to be done under the supervision of a professional."

She blinked. "Dangerous? Illegal?"

What had she gotten herself into?

Two hours later, she knew most of the secrets of the Silverberry Book Club.

"It started out as a regular book club, but then we got bored." Helen had shared an intimate look with Nathan that had made Aubrey suspect there was more to that story. "We tried to mix it up by meeting in different places, even out of doors during the summer. One night during a heat wave we met at Nathan's cabin on Cluculz Lake, and instead of discussing the book we ended up paddleboarding and canoeing and swimming. It evolved from there. Now our only rule is never to have another boring meeting."

Aubrey and Natalie waved goodbye to their hostess and climbed into Aubrey's car. "So, what did you think?" Natalie asked.

"I think if *you* think I am going rock climbing you are crazy." She pulled away from the curb. The soft dark was pricked with streetlamps and the glow of lights from the houses they passed.

"It's inside at a climbing wall, fully supervised. I bet you'll enjoy it."

The thing was, she thought she might, too. Her protest was a knee-jerk reaction. As a newcomer, she hadn't felt comfortable suggesting any activities. Instead, she had sipped the fizzy water she'd switched to after her martini and listened in fascination as the eclectic group had batted ideas around like a pinball machine.

"I am looking forward to the art appreciation night at the gallery," she admitted, "and the mixology class sounds fun. Who wouldn't want to learn how to make a few fancy drinks?" The day-long hike up Mount Pope, not so much. She'd have to up her visits to the gym to get in shape for that. By *up her visits* she meant actually go.

She dropped Natalie off at home and returned to her sterile, cold apartment. She couldn't wait to move into her new house and planned to do so as soon as possible. Unlike the breathless, suffocating feeling she suffered the moment she set foot in her current home, when she walked Cedar Street's narrow-planked, creaking floors she felt energized, invigorated. It was ridiculous to believe the house had been waiting for her, but something about it simply felt *right*.

Plugging her phone into the charger on her nightstand, the screen lit up, showing a missed call from her father. She had put it on silent before arriving at the book club meeting with a sense of rebellious freedom, unable to remember a time when she'd been able to ignore the device without worrying she might miss an important call from a client or colleague.

She sat on the edge of the bed and debated whether to return it or not. It wasn't quite ten o'clock, and he rarely went to bed before midnight. He hadn't left a voicemail, though, so the call couldn't be too vital.

Sighing heavily, she tapped the screen, knowing she'd only obsess about it all night if she didn't. Setting the phone to speaker, she stretched out on her back and closed her eyes, feeling the luxurious mattress cradle and support her. Her bed was at the top of the list of things to bring to her new home.

"Hello, Aubrey." Her father's crisp, clean baritone filled the room.

"Hi, Dad. Sorry I missed your call. I was at a book club meeting." She wondered if the reason the Silverberries had never changed the name was to avoid unwanted questions. *I was at book club* would generate far fewer comments than *I was whitewater rafting*.

"I see. Well, that's fine. It was nothing, anyway."

She'd been idly wondering if it might be a good time to confess her impulsive purchase of an entire house. At this unexpected statement, however, her eyes popped open. Her father *never* called for no reason. "Is everything okay, Dad?" She stared at the ceiling but visualized his lean frame in his wingback chair, a glass of scotch—his nighttime ritual—sitting on the small table at his elbow.

"Of course." He cleared his throat, and her eyes opened wider at this almost-unheard-of indication of uncertainty.

She sat up, swinging her feet to the floor, and stared at the phone's screen as if she could see through it to her father. "Are you sure?"

"Did you know that Marjorie Strahl moved into Riverbend last week?"

She was bewildered less by the question than the tone in her father's voice. Did he sound *upset?*

"I did, actually." She chose her words carefully. "I met Phillip there the last time I was at your apartment. We talked for a while." She remembered her jolt of awareness when she'd realized who the man carrying the carpet was. She hated he still had the power to make her toes curl.

"I would have appreciated being told. I met her this evening in the hallway. It was a trifle disconcerting."

"Why?" She frowned. Marjorie and her parents had met occasionally before and during Aubrey and Phillip's short marriage, and as far as she remembered they'd been polite but neutral with each other. "I never knew you had any issues with Marjorie."

"I don't. But when someone from your past reappears after decades, it can be a shock."

Why did she have the feeling her father was talking about *his* past, not Aubrey's? "I'm sorry. I would have told you if I thought you'd be interested at all. It never crossed my mind."

A short silence followed. "Well," her father finally said, "it's a moot point now. Goodnight, Aubrey." The connection dropped.

She stared at the darkened screen. What on *earth* had that been about?

Two days later, she flew to Victoria to decide what to bring back to Prince George and arrange for its delivery. It wasn't much—a few pieces of artwork she was particularly attached to, the photos of Oliver and Sophie she had in her bedroom, and the clothes she'd kept there—but too much to carry on the plane. Then she called a charity thrift store and offered them everything remaining. By the time they'd loaded what they wanted, there wasn't anything left but a family of dust bunnies and cleaning supplies.

She left those for the new owner to deal with.

Flying back to Prince George, she felt lighter and freer than she had in a long time. The only dark cloud hovering was the fact she still hadn't told her father about her recent activities. She remedied that the day after she took possession of the house.

She parked outside Riverbend Seniors' Apartments and watched him walk toward her. His limp was pronounced, and he was putting significant weight on his cane. Apparently, his hip was bothering him more than usual.

"Where are we going?" He lowered himself into the passenger seat. "I need to be back in an hour."

"You'll see." Her palms sweat and she rubbed them surreptitiously on her jeans. "What's happening in an hour?"

"I have an appointment." His tone brooked no questions.

If she hadn't been so anxious about showing him the house, she might have prodded deeper. Instead, once he was buckled in, she exited the parking lot, taking the same route she had the day she'd met Phillip.

"Remember how I told you I wanted to do what *I* wanted for a change?" She held her shoulders tight, waiting for a repeat of his assault last week, prepared to defend herself.

Clarence huffed. "And that you didn't know what that was? Of course I do. You sounded like a hippie." It was one of his most cutting insults, but she refused to react.

"I'm tired, Dad." Sometimes her bones ached with exhaustion. "I went from university to law school to corporate law to a politician's wife to a politician without pause. I need to give my brain a break. I want to do something that doesn't require analyzing the fine print or arguing matters of policy."

"You have one of the best brains I've ever known." She would have puffed with pride if she hadn't heard the *but* coming. "But I've always had to push you to use it. Otherwise, you would have wasted all that intelligence."

And there it was.

If only her father had recognized there were careers other than law and politics that required a brain. He might have accepted her decision to become a doctor or accountant if she'd fought hard enough. But she didn't have a passion for those careers, either. After the tragedy that had ended her marriage with Phillip, it had just been easier to let her parents guide her. She'd barely had the strength to get up in the morning— battling them for control of her life had been far, far beyond her.

She turned onto Cedar Street and rolled to a gentle stop at the curb in front of her house.

Her house. It looked just as bad as it had the first day she'd seen it, yet she couldn't stop a thrill of pleasure from sweeping down her spine. "Here it is."

"Here's what?" Clarence lowered his head and peered suspiciously out the window.

"My house."

His jaw dropped. "Your *what*?"

"My house. I took possession yesterday." She

39

reached into her purse, found the keys, and jingled them enticingly. "Want to go see?"

Without giving him a chance to reply she slipped out of the car, rounded the hood to his side, and opened his door. Silently, he levered himself from his seat, getting his balance before moving ahead of her up the path between the hedges.

"Watch your step." She sidled past him and up the crumbling stairs. Propping the dangling screen door out of the way, she pushed her key into the ancient lock and twisted. "Come on in."

Still without speaking, he entered the tiny square vestibule, stepped through the interior door, and took a left into the living room with its smudged and grimy bay window. The air was musty and still, so she let the screen bang shut but left the other doors open. She went to one of the small windows flanking the fireplace and tugged. The wooden frame was caked with paint and swollen with age, but she managed to drag it open with an ear-splitting shriek. A breeze fanned her face, cooling the anxious blush heating her cheeks.

The longer Clarence remained silent, the more nervous she became. She had promised herself she wouldn't make excuses, but despite her best intentions her first words sounded apologetic.

"It was an excellent price, because, well"—she waved a hand at the dingy walls, the battered wood floor, the chipped brick overmantel—"it needs some work. But it's the worst house on the street, so I'm sure to recoup any money I put into the renovations." Not that she intended to flip it. This was going to be home for a long time, she could feel it. If her dad thought of it as an investment, though—

"Have you lost your mind?" The words were fierce, but his tone was mild, and she took heart.

"The idea of going back to an office, sitting at a desk, being at the beck and call of clients, makes me sick to my stomach." He opened his mouth, and she fluttered her hand in a wordless plea. He shut it. "Oh, I'll have to go back to work eventually. And since law is all I know, chances are that's where I'll end up." It was a depressing thought, but she shoved it away. Once she had the break she craved, she'd be fine going back to the career she'd built. She hoped. "Think of this as a sabbatical. I'll work on the house for a few months then go back ready to tackle anything."

Clarence's eyes narrowed. "When you say *you'll* work on the house..."

"I want to get my hands dirty, Dad. I want to *do* things, not just *think* them."

"You don't know one end of a hammer from the other."

"Of course I do." A glimmer of amusement lightened her nerves a fraction. "The head is the end you hit your thumb with." Clarence raised an eyebrow, but his mouth retained its straight line. She sighed. "Don't worry. I'll hire professionals for the important bits."

He surveyed the room, his posture stiff and tight, his face pinched. "I don't understand this. I don't understand *you* right now. But what's done is done."

He was taking the news much better than she had hoped. Maybe his pained expression reflected the discomfort from his hip and wasn't entirely disapproval. She pointed through an archway toward the back of the house. "Let me show you the rest. Fair warning. It doesn't get much better. But the house inspector promised it wouldn't fall in on me."

Clarence shook his head but followed.

CHAPTER FIVE

As Phillip had predicted, it didn't take Marjorie long to become deeply involved in the life of the Riverbend residents, so it wasn't a surprise when, a couple weeks after she moved in, she invited him to the communal birthday celebration that was held on the first of every month.

"But your birthday isn't until December," he'd said.

"It's not for me," Marjorie had replied in the patient tone that made him feel twelve. "I want you to meet my new friends, and this seems like as good a time as any. Besides, at my age, you have to party when you can."

Which was why he'd left work at two o'clock on a Tuesday afternoon. In years gone by, skipping out early would have made him nervous and anxious, and sent him back to the office in the evening to catch up on what he'd missed. Today, it had been a relief, and he had no intention of returning until tomorrow.

He'd tried to drum up his old enthusiasm by negotiating to takeover a smaller landscaping company. It hadn't helped. Even completing that deal today had left him feeling flat and lacklustre. His enthusiasm had been waning for a while, but since accepting Zeke's decision to have no role in Twin Rivers it was even more challenging to generate any level of excitement.

His attitude was in danger of affecting his business, and it was time he made some difficult decisions. But right now, he was in the Riverbend dining hall, seated at a table with Marjorie and two other elderly ladies, and he pushed aside his gloomy thoughts to focus on the party.

Helium balloons, attached to the back of the chair of every resident who was having a birthday that month, bopped and swayed. The guests of honour also sported paper crowns and had been presented with cupcakes adorned with sparklers. The crowd had just finished singing *Happy Birthday* and everyone was now tucking into dessert and coffee.

Phillip let the conversation between his aunt and her friends wash over him as he ate his cake. Even his usual sweet tooth was dulled, though, and he had little appetite for the treat. He really had to break out of this funk. He was starting to drive himself crazy.

His chair faced out of the dining room, giving him a view past the administration desk and lounge with its huge fireplace, straight to the main entrance. The glass doors opened and in walked Clarence Windt, closely followed by Aubrey.

He lowered his gaze before she could make eye contact. He still wasn't sure how he felt about her accidental reappearance in his life. He knew one thing, though. She still had the power to make him *feel*. The ennui blurring the edges of his everyday life vanished whenever he thought of her. Which was more often than he should, given everything else he had going on.

His attempt to ignore her was foiled by Marjorie, sitting at his side, which gave her the same view.

"Clarence!" she called. "And Aubrey!" She rose to her feet, the heavy chair screeching on the vinyl floor. "Come join us! Phillip, pull over a couple more chairs." Her lack of surprise at seeing the father and daughter made it apparent she'd met Clarence at some point during the last two weeks. He wondered why she hadn't mentioned it and felt a tug of unease. She had said she wanted Phillip to meet her new friends. Did she include Clarence in that group?

He rose, intending to follow Marjorie's direction to

procure more chairs.

"Oh, don't bother," said Imelda, the tiny, dark-haired lady seated across from him. "Mary and I will join Stan and Laura."

Clarence's face retained its calm, judicious expression—one that had made a teenage Phillip queasy with nerves—as he strode to the table, limping slightly, cane in hand. Despite Aubrey's casual dark denim jeans and teal T-shirt, she still had that perfectly put together, shellacked appearance he'd noticed the day they'd first met. But her eyes revealed an inner turmoil—wide and anxious yet somehow pinched around the edges. She looked like she was searching for a reason to refuse. Then she met his gaze, and her shoulders lifted, as if preparing for battle.

His initial instinct to ignore her dissolved.

A slow-motion flurry of activity followed as Marjorie's friends rose to their feet and rolled their walkers to another table, allowing Aubrey and Clarence to take their vacated seats.

"Well, now." Marjorie nodded with approval. "Isn't this nice?"

Phillip regarded her with exasperated affection. She did the fluttery old lady act well, though she was anything but. His suspicion that she'd insisted he come to the birthday party specifically for this contrived meeting strengthened. He sipped his coffee and waited for her to make the next move.

"It's so good to see you again, Aubrey. How long has it been?"

He repressed a snort. There was nothing wrong with Marjorie's memory. He'd be willing to bet she knew exactly how long it had been.

"About thirty years." Aubrey quirked a small smile, a pale imitation of the blazing brilliance he remembered. Was the incandescent woman that had left a burn mark on his soul nothing but grey ash?

"My, how time flies." Marjorie reached out and

patted Aubrey's hand where it lay on the table. "You look just as lovely now as you did then." She turned to Clarence. "You must be so proud of her. A lawyer, a Member of the Legislative Assembly. So successful."

"She's not an MLA anymore," Clarence said gruffly. The slight frown on Aubrey's forehead smoothed out and her eyes went blank.

The bastard hasn't changed one bit. His old instinct to protect her clawed its way out of the cave where he had entombed it long ago. "The last election was a blood bath for her party. I am sure her loss had more to do with the leadership being rejected than Aubrey herself."

Clarence's pale eyes met his dismissively. "Doesn't change the result."

He opened his mouth to defend Aubrey again but stopped at the tiny jerk of her head. *Right. Not my place. Not anymore.* Switching gears abruptly, he turned to Marjorie. "So, when did you discover Clarence was living here, too?" *And why didn't you tell me?*

"Oh, a week or so after I moved in." She fiddled with her teaspoon, her face averted. "It was lovely to find an old friend here."

"Old friend?" Aubrey's dark eyes flicked questioningly from Marjorie to Clarence.

"Acquaintance," he muttered. "Old acquaintance."

Phillip watched Marjorie as Clarence spoke, and her eyelids twitched, an odd expression flashing on her face, gone an instant later. "Yes, of course. Acquaintance," she said brightly. "Now, who would like cake?"

Was **this** *the appointment* her dad had wanted to be back for?

When Marjorie called them over, Aubrey had racked her brain for any excuse to get out of a cozy cake and coffee birthday party with Phillip. Clarence, on the other hand, had marched over as if he'd expected

Marjorie's invite.

Odd vibes were spinning webs across the table. Her knee jittered and she stilled it with conscious effort, avoiding Phillip's gaze and concentrating on Marjorie. The older woman had been a mother to him after the death of his parents when he was still a child, and she'd been warm and welcoming to Aubrey, too. It was no hardship to catch up with all that had happened in the decades since they'd seen each other last.

Still, the tension crisscrossing invisibly between the four of them was impossible to ignore, and as soon as was polite she made her excuses. Phillip rose when she did.

"I should go, too." He bent to kiss his aunt's papery cheek and offered her father a curt nod. "Clarence." It was less a farewell than a simple acknowledgment and was returned in kind. It didn't look like the two men would be any friendlier now than they had been thirty years ago.

"It was so good to see you again, Marjorie." As she spoke, she realized it was the truth. It *had* been good to see Marjorie, who had done her best to smooth the edges between the two families during Aubrey and Phillip's short marriage.

"And you, too, dear." Marjorie's smile was sweet but sharp. "I hope we'll be seeing lots of each other from now on."

Phillip stayed at her side as they made their way out of the building and into the parking lot. The sun blazed from a blue June sky and she squinted at him, feeling the skin around her eyes wrinkle. "Goodbye, Phillip." She turned to go.

"Aubrey, wait." He touched her shoulder, and she froze. His palm was warm and firm through the thin silk of her T-shirt and heat seeped deep into her body. An instant later his hand was gone and she faced him, her skin still prickling.

"Yes?" She pulled her increasingly brittle armour

46

into place. Phillip had crept into her thoughts at the oddest times in the last couple of weeks. This most recent half hour had made it perfectly plain that keeping up an impersonal facade was vital.

Leaving him had been the second hardest thing she'd ever done in her life...and he didn't know, even now, the whole truth.

"Don't think I'm crazy, but..." He trailed off and scrubbed a hand through his hair, the silver threads glittering. "Was there something weird going on between Clarence and Marjorie?"

She blinked, knee-shakingly relieved he hadn't wanted to talk about their past. Although why he would want to do so, she couldn't imagine. She pulled herself together. "You felt it, too?"

His shoulders relaxed. "Yeah. That bit about old friends and acquaintances. And then she knew how he takes his coffee, and he said something that made it sound like they'd had dinner together."

"Now you mention it..." She frowned. "My dad doesn't have dinner in the dining hall. He cooks his own meals."

"Marjorie, too. So, if they did eat together, who hosted who?"

They stared at each other. In a flash of connection, she knew he was thinking—and rejecting—the same thought she was. They were reading too much into a simple friendship. They had to be.

His eyes, a rich brown flecked with gold, gazed unblinkingly into hers. Nostalgia shuddered through her. When was the last time she'd looked—really *looked*—into someone's eyes? Locked in his gaze, the divide of years and regrets vanished, and they were eighteen again.

From the street behind her, a horn honked, the long, angry wail making her jump. How long had they been standing there, not talking?

She hurried to fill the gap. "It's a good thing, right?

Old age can be so isolating. They both need friends."

"I just don't want Marjorie to get hurt."

Her spine stiffened. "You think my father would *hurt* her?"

"Not physically, of course not. But you have to admit, he's not exactly easy to get along with. He can be downright mean, in fact."

"My father is honourable, intelligent, and respected."

"And so is Marjorie. But she's also affectionate and outgoing, while Clarence...isn't. It wouldn't be a very balanced relationship."

He wasn't telling her anything she didn't know. But *she* was the only one allowed to criticize her father. "Does Marjorie have dementia?" She was too irate to be delicate.

"No!"

"Then she is perfectly capable of choosing her own friends. Stay out of it, Phillip."

"Just like your parents stayed out of our marriage?"

She gaped like a gutted fish, pain slashing from neck to belly. "What does that have to do with anything?"

To do him justice, he looked horrified. "I'm sorry. I don't know why I said that." He took a couple steps back. "You're right. Marjorie can look after herself. Goodbye, Aubrey."

He walked away, his strides long yet jerky, as if his knees wouldn't bend at his command. She stared, in shock at his bitter comment, until he disappeared around the corner.

No matter how uncertain and restless Phillip's attitude toward his company, Twin Rivers still required his attention and commitment. During the next week, he re-focused his energies and gagged the little voice muttering in his ear, the one whining that it shouldn't be so hard to do what he used to relish. He might have fallen into the landscape and maintenance industry by chance, but he'd thrived while being his own boss, growing his business, expanding its services, and dealing with the challenges. He'd taken what had been a tiny yard maintenance company and built it into a year-round enterprise by adding residential and commercial snow clearing and janitorial services. He'd slept well at night, knowing his family was secure and his employees satisfied.

Now, coming to work in the morning felt like a chore. One he feared he was growing to hate.

Telling himself not to be melodramatic, he dragged his concentration back to the spreadsheet displayed on his computer screen.

Prince George had a short growing season, which meant residents were fiercely determined to get the most out of their yards and gardens while they could. May and June were two of the busiest months for the landscape division, what with cleaning up winter's ravages, planting annuals, and adding perennials. It was also the time when most customers approached them regarding large design jobs.

That division's days were about to get even busier. The paperwork had gone through on his takeover of one of his smaller competitors, the one he'd finalized last week. Given his current state of mind, maybe he'd be better off selling Twin Rivers, rather than buying up other companies. He thrust the disloyal thought away.

The single-woman operation he'd purchased had an excellent reputation and a solid client base. When she'd decided to follow her partner to new adventures in Whitehorse, she'd approached Phillip about buying her business. Despite the apathy he was fighting, the decision had been a no-brainer, and negotiations had moved rapidly. Now the jobs she'd contracted for had to be added to his team's to-do list.

He began reviewing each of her current projects. Minutes later, he came to a halt at the sight of a familiar name.

Aubrey Windt.

It gave him a twinge to see her maiden name there before him in black and white. When they'd married, she'd taken his surname. He remembered the swell of pride the first time he'd introduced her as Aubrey *Church.* They'd been so young, so foolish, thinking their love was strong enough to survive her parents' disapproval and Marjorie's apprehension, their lack of money and an unexpected pregnancy. And maybe it would have been—if Samantha hadn't died.

She would have been thirty-four now. Maybe married with children of her own. Or a dedicated career woman. More than likely, some combination of both. He closed his eyes and sucked in a lungful of air. The pain would never go away, he knew that now. But most of the time it was a quiet, dull ache that he could accept for weeks, even months, at a time. Then something would cause it to sear into icy flame and he'd have to sit quietly for a few minutes to get his breath back.

He opened his eyes and read the details under Aubrey's name. She wanted a quote for landscape design. He clicked to the photos she'd sent, and his eyebrows rose. They gave evidence of a jungle of weeds and overgrown hedges and falling-in fences.

Thoughtfully, he tapped his fingers in a rapid tattoo on his desk, and then picked up his phone. Carla, his landscape manager, answered with a brisk hello.

"Have we given a quote to Aubrey Windt yet?" He fidgeted with his computer mouse as he spoke. "She's on the job list from Flora-licious Gardening."

"Let me check." There was a short pause. "No, not yet. I'm scheduled to do a site visit this afternoon, in fact."

"Do you mind if I handle it?" He searched for an acceptable reason for this unusual request. It had been years since he'd been out in the field, so to speak. "Aubrey's an old friend, and I'm going stir-crazy sitting in the office all the time."

"Fly at 'er, boss," Carla said agreeably. "I could use the extra hour. Thanks."

He hung up and leaned back in his chair, swivelling gently. He was going to see Aubrey again. This time he'd be prepared, which hopefully would stop him from saying anything too stupid, as he had the last time.

It took him a little while to recognize the warm feeling rising in his chest.

Anticipation.

CHAPTER SIX

Aubrey squirmed out of the cramped corner, raising her head slowly to avoid braining herself on the low, slanted ceiling, her knees and hips creaking. She was only fifty-two, for god's sake, but after a week of intensive cleaning, clearing, packing, and unpacking, she felt one hundred.

The aches and pains didn't diminish her satisfaction, though. Arching backward to relieve the stiffness in her spine, she surveyed the results of her most recent labours, a smile creasing her face.

The house on Cedar Street had three levels. The basement was a dingy, musty cavern reached by a set of narrow, steep stairs that might more honestly be called a ladder. She hadn't done anything down there yet, though she had explored its murky depths, discovering a few random items left behind by the previous owner. The main floor had captured most of her attention the first few days, with its living room, dining room, tiny kitchen, ancient three-piece bath and two small bedrooms.

Today, she'd tackled the top level—an open space with sloped ceilings and tiny windows on either end that faced east and west. It meant a lot of ducking down and bending awkwardly in order to access all the corners where spiders had spun their sticky webs. She'd been forced to crawl on her hands and knees to reach all the nooks and crannies.

She couldn't do anything right now about the

rippled, stained carpet and needed to clean the windows from the outside, but even so the improvement was noticeable. The sun cast a warm glow through the glass on her right, and it occurred to her that the space was big enough to make a wonderful master suite. One end could be sectioned off for an efficient yet luxurious bathroom, though bringing plumbing to the upper floor wouldn't be cheap. Still, a vision of cream-coloured walls and slate-grey trim and a bed mounded in colourful pillows tucked under the eaves danced before her.

Her phone dinged and she dug it out of her back pocket. It was a reminder that the woman from Flora-licious Gardening was expected in ten minutes. That gave her enough time to have a quick wash and get a drink of water. Her fellow MLAs wouldn't recognize her today—face devoid of makeup, hair covered by a scarf, outfit a faded T-shirt and jeans she'd bought from a thrift store specifically for getting grimy.

Since it was pointless to change just to walk around the yard with someone who would probably be wearing a similarly grubby uniform, she made her way down the narrow stairs and, after a quick stop in the bathroom to remove the worst of the dust from her face and hands, headed for the kitchen. Refilling her water bottle from the tap, she crossed through the dining room, out the front door, and took a seat on the top step.

The hedge blocked most of her view of the street. She knew it had to be tamed, but she rather enjoyed the sense of privacy and secrecy it gave the front yard. Unlike neighbouring gardens, there were no mature trees on her property, although a few rotting stumps indicated that hadn't always been the case. The lot was long and narrow, with the house placed close to the street and just over a metre from the properties on either side.

Leaning back on her hands on the gritty stoop, she raised her face to the sun, closed her eyes, and let her imagination create arches covered in flowering vines in those narrow gaps, through which meandering brick paths led to a sheltered oasis of scented peace in the back yard.

The low growl of a pickup truck grew louder, and she sat up. Through the jungle-like hedge she glimpsed a white vehicle come to a stop at the curb. A door clicked open and slammed shut, followed by a beep indicating the driver had engaged the locks. She rose, scratched an itch on her nose, brushed the butt of her jeans in a futile but automatic gesture, and waited for the woman from Flora-licious to come through the leafy tunnel.

Instead, the person who appeared was Phillip.

She frowned down from her vantage point at the top of the stairs. "What are you doing here?"

"The quote for your landscaping."

She shook her head, not in denial, but in confusion. "What?"

"As of yesterday, Flora-licious Gardening has merged with Twin Rivers Landscape and Maintenance." He smiled, a half-grin that tickled her belly. "I don't imagine you were told the purchase was in the works when you booked this appointment."

"No, I wasn't." She'd deliberately contacted a landscape company *other* than Phillip's—and the glint in his eye told her he had guessed that much. He had caused enough of a stir in her life recently, and she hadn't wanted to create any further opportunities that might force them together. But she couldn't simply send him on his way. That would reveal exactly how discombobulated she was by his presence.

"Well, you're here now." She didn't care that she sounded ungracious. She was the customer. He could lump it. "You might as well take a look."

Crushing a sudden compulsion to run back into the house to change, put on make up, and comb her hair, she joined him at the bottom of the steps. In opposition to the grass-stained, grubby gardener she'd envisioned, he wore a spotless pale blue collared shirt and tan trousers. His firm jaw was smoothly shaved, his hair brushed back from his forehead in neat waves. He studied her face, and his dark eyes crinkled at the corners, his smile widening.

Had she scrubbed all the dirt off? Her arm twitched but she resisted swiping a sleeve across her forehead. "Just so we're clear, I'm only looking for ideas and a ballpark figure. I plan to do extensive renovations to the house, and it seems pointless to do much with the garden until contractors are done trampling through it."

"That's probably a good call." Unruffled by her rudeness, he looked up, over her head. "I assume new shingles are on the list?"

Relieved he'd removed his attention from her, she shifted so they were standing shoulder to shoulder and lifted her gaze to the roof as well. "Yes. And new siding. And probably windows."

"You've got yourself quite the project here."

His tone was polite, but she bristled in defiance, clenching her teeth. "That's the point. I want something to *do*. I'm done with being stuck in an office, for a while anyway." Why was it so hard for people to accept that?

"Hey, don't get me wrong." He bumped her shoulder with his and for an instant she was seventeen again and they were standing in the hallway in school, too shy to admit their attraction and reduced to unspoken cues. "I love these old houses. I'm glad you're going to show it care and attention instead of tearing it down."

"Oh." Maybe he did understand. If so, he'd be the first. Rattled by his approval—and his casual touch— she spun around and waved a hand at the hedge. "Anyway, about the garden. I think Steve has to come down."

Phillip choked. "Steve?"

She hadn't meant to let the nickname slip out. Heat

rose in her cheeks. "You know, from the kid's movie. My stepdaughter Sophie loved it. The one with the animals who don't know what a hedge is."

"Ah, yes. Steve." He chuckled. "Other than the fact Steve's out of control, do you like the idea of a hedge in the front?"

Remembering her earlier sense of solitude and peace, she shrugged. "I like how it screens the yard from passersby, but there's an old picket fence buried inside it so I don't think it can be saved. Besides, it does nothing for street appeal. I want the front to be open and welcoming. The back will be the place to build a private retreat."

"I see." He turned to the house again. "The shrubs along the foundation?"

"There's one or two I'm hoping you can save, but you're the expert. If it's easier to pull them out and start again, I'll take your word for it."

During the next half hour, they toured the yard. He talked pergolas and flagstone paths and lattice screens, and suggested numerous trees and shrubs and flowers, the names of which she promptly forgot. His enthusiasm for the house and lot was obvious, and she slowly relaxed, more relieved than she wanted to admit that *someone* shared her vision of what could be.

Phillip watched the self-consciousness slide from Aubrey's shoulders as she showed him around her home. For the first time since they'd met at Riverbend, he felt like he was seeing the *real* Aubrey, the one he'd fallen in love with as a teenager. An Aubrey that had been soft and loving and enthusiastic—not hard and proper and restrained.

"Do you plan on building a garage?" They'd circled the house once, and then returned to the back yard. The best that could be said was it gave him a clean slate to work with. Nothing growing was worth salvaging, although he intended to reclaim the weathered and battered boards of what used to be a fence along the alley. Ideas were already bubbling, and the thrill of creativity, long missing from his workdays, was deeply welcome.

"Yes, but not where the parking area is now." She pointed to the opposite side of the lot. "I'm thinking there, with a breezeway leading to the back door. Then there'd only be a few feet open to the elements."

The house was a blocky L-shape, with what appeared to be an addition poking out the back. "If you can't have an attached garage, that's not a bad compromise."

"That's what I thought. I'm not sure what to do in the space we have to leave between the it and the next property, though. It will be so shady and awkward."

"Let me think about it. I'm sure I can come up with something." He took more photos of the neglected space, his mind filling with colourful images. It was as if a rusted shut faucet had forced itself open, allowing concepts to pour forth in a cataract of inspiration. Adding a few last thoughts to the note he'd started on his phone, he tucked it into his pocket. "I think I've seen what I need to." He couldn't wait to get started on the design, his fingers positively itching with excitement. "I should probably get back to the office."

Aubrey stood in a shaft of light, shadows from the neighbour's trees dappling the peeling wall of the house behind her, and all thoughts of a hurried return vanished. A messy ponytail was gathered at the nape of her neck, with the rest of her hair covered by a floral scarf. Tendrils escaped around her face and clung to her damp temples. The smudge of dirt he'd noticed when he'd first arrived still shadowed the bridge of her nose, and she'd added another along her jaw sometime during his tour. The V-neck of her T-shirt dipped between her breasts and, for the instant he allowed himself to look, he saw sweat beading the pale skin there.

"Right." He swallowed, knowing it wasn't just the June sun beaming down that flushed heat along his spine. "Time to go." But he didn't move.

Silence hummed between them, past and present flowing and fusing. The Aubrey before him shimmered between the innocent, open girl he'd married and the guarded, wounded woman she was now.

"Would you like a drink of water?" She waved vaguely over her shoulder, as if a spout had magically appeared behind her. "I'm sorry, I should have offered sooner. It's so hot out, and you don't have a hat. Or maybe iced tea? Or a beer? But if you have to get back to the office I understand. You are working, after all."

She clamped her mouth shut, a slightly wild expression in her eyes. *She feels it too.* His satisfaction at this revelation set his pulse racing. The self-assured political campaigner held no interest for him. This rather flustered, harum-scarum female, though—she intrigued him.

"Iced tea would be great." The office could definitely wait.

What am I doing? Aubrey berated herself as Phillip followed her up the rickety wooden steps that led to the back door, through the addition that served as a mud-slash-laundry room and into the kitchen. *He was leaving. You were in the clear. Why did you invite him in?*

Because you didn't want him to go, her inner voice explained patiently.

After her initial surprise and nervousness had abated, she'd enjoyed showing him around and talking about her plans. He'd been open to all her ideas, given constructive feedback, and never once laughed at her for thinking she could manage a project like this.

After Natalie's amused horror and Clarence's

critical reception, Phillip's reaction had been a balm to her soul, and she wanted to bask in it a while longer.

"Have a seat." She waved him toward one of the pumpkin-coloured vinyl swivel chairs surrounding the square, faux-wood dinette table tucked into a corner. "I'll get our drinks."

He sat down gingerly. "This is, uh—classic." He patted the indestructible laminate top.

"It's hideously ugly, is what it is. You don't have to be polite. The 1970s have a lot to answer for." She reached down two tall tumblers and opened the ancient avocado green fridge to retrieve the jug of iced tea. "The last owner was the first owner. He lived here for fifty years, I was told, and passed away several months ago. Whoever cleaned out the house abandoned that monstrosity and a few other bits and pieces, like the equally hideous sofa in the living room. I'm happy enough using what was left here for now since it's no use bringing over my own furniture until I'm done renovating." Carrying the glasses to the table, she placed Phillip's in front of him and took a seat opposite. "Except for my bed. I love that mattress too much to leave it behind, so I manhandled that over."

"You're living here?" He sipped his tea, licking a stray drop from his lip.

She swallowed and dragged her attention back to the question. "Yes, mostly. If I have to spend a night at my condo, there is still a bed there, in the spare room Sophie uses when she visits, the rare times she comes home from Toronto." Why did she keep talking about beds? Argh. "Most of my furniture, too, like I said. But I want to live here for a bit before I decide what changes to make."

His reply was interrupted by his cell phone.

Followed immediately by her own ring tone.

They dug their phones out of their respective pockets, checked the screens, and looked at each other.

"Marjorie," Phillip said.

"My dad," Aubrey said.

The phones shrilled again, one right after the other.

"You stay here." She rose from her seat. "I'll go to the living room."

CHAPTER SEVEN

Aubrey connected the call as she crossed the room and leaned against the fireplace. "Dad? Are you all right?"

"Why wouldn't I be all right?" His disgust came clearly through the speaker. "Can't I call my daughter without it being an emergency?"

"Of course you can." Maybe Marjorie's call to Phillip was just a coincidence. She could hear his calm, deep tone in the kitchen but couldn't make out the words.

Clarence was speaking. "I was hoping you had time tonight to stop by for a drink."

She resisted repeating her question. Her father never did anything without purpose. Small talk was wasted air, as far as he was concerned. So why was he inviting her over? There was only one way to find out. "What time?"

"Seven-thirty." There was no question in his tone. Obviously, he expected her to make that work.

Curiosity nipped with needle-pointed teeth, but she ignored it. For now. "See you then."

"I'll meet you in the lobby." He disconnected the call without further ado, and she made her way back to the kitchen, tapping her phone on her palm.

Phillip sat where she had left him, a thoughtful expression on his face. "Marjorie wants me to come over tonight."

"So does my dad. Seven-thirty?"

"Yup."

"He said he'd meet me in the lobby. Why not at his apartment?" Phillip's comments after the communal birthday party raced through her mind.

"Marjorie sounded rather secretive, too. What are those two crazy kids up to?" he mused.

She stifled a laugh at the thought of her father being a *crazy kid.* "Maybe we're jumping to conclusions. We're only guessing they called at the same moment to set up a visit at the same time for the same vague reasons. Maybe one has nothing to do with the other." She wasn't sure why she was so discomfited. Hadn't she told Phillip a relationship between his aunt and her father was a good thing? It was he who had been concerned about the possibility.

"I guess we'll find out tonight." He drained his glass in one long swallow and stood up. "Now I really have to get back to the office. I'll have the quote to you in a few days."

"Great." She walked with him to the back door. "See you tonight...maybe?"

"Probably, I think." He sketched a salute and was gone.

After some consideration, Phillip decided to arrive at Marjorie's fifteen minutes early to avoid any possibility of an awkward encounter with Aubrey and Clarence. If memory served, his ex-father-in-law was almost pathological in being neither early nor late, but exactly on time. If he said he'd meet Aubrey in the lobby at seven-thirty, he wouldn't be hovering there if Phillip arrived at seven-fifteen.

Marjorie buzzed him in, and he took the stairs to her second-floor apartment in the west wing of the complex. She'd left the door ajar and he entered to find her setting a platter of pastries on the coffee table.

"Hello!" She stretched onto her toes to give him a kiss on his cheek, smelling of talcum powder and hair spray.

He couldn't resist giving her a hug. He had a few memories of his parents, but they were dim and distant. Marjorie had guided him through his grief in those first horrible months, given him structure during his teenage years, and offered silent but sincere support after Aubrey had left him. She was both father and mother to him.

"I love you." He squeezed her one more time before releasing her.

Her cheeks pinked, flustered but pleased, and she patted her hair, though there was no way he could have mussed her fiercely styled do. He didn't expect her to return the sentiment, and she didn't. Marjorie's love was expressed in actions, rarely words.

"I have coffee ready. Would you like some?" She bustled into the kitchen. A peninsula with sink faced the dining room and living area, with a single French door leading to the tiny deck overlooking the parking lot. "Or would you rather something stronger?"

"I don't know. You tell me. Will I need something stronger?"

Her eyes widened with an innocence he didn't trust at all. "What do you mean?"

"Aubrey needs some yard work done at her new place. I was with her when you called me."

He knew instantly that Marjorie understood everything he'd left unspoken. She might have learned to keep her face impassive in her role as surgeon, but he knew her too well to be fooled by the artless expression she plastered on after a tiny hesitation.

He sighed. "I'll have whiskey."

"You always were too clever for your own good." She smacked him on the shoulder. "You know where everything is. Help yourself."

He was taking his first sip when a knock sounded on the door. Marjorie smoothed her hands over her hips, tugged down the pink-flowered blouse she wore with black slacks, and went to open it.

Clarence and Aubrey stood in the hall. Phillip glanced at the microwave clock. 7:27. What kind of grenade did it take to blast the older man out of the habit of a lifetime? And how did Marjorie fit into all this? He assumed he'd find out soon.

"Hello, dear." Marjorie patted Clarence on the arm as he stepped passed her. Somehow, the small gesture revealed more than a simple greeting. Phillip's eyebrows rose. "And welcome, Aubrey. I'm so glad you could make it."

Aubrey followed her father into the apartment. Gone was the slightly disreputable-looking woman of the afternoon. In her place was the sleek, sophisticated lawyer and politician wearing a crisp white blouse and tight charcoal-grey skirt. A silky scarf in shades of blue and green softened the monochromatic look. Her legs were bare, and he took a moment to appreciate the full curve of her calves.

She didn't appear to notice his scrutiny as Marjorie invited her to take a seat in the living room. Her focus was split between the two older people, and she didn't even grant Phillip a glance when he sat next to her on the small sofa. Marjorie fluttered about, pouring wine for Aubrey and herself and getting Clarence the coffee he asked for. It seemed he was the only person who didn't feel liquid fortification would be necessary to face whatever was to come.

Clarence had taken one of the upholstered chairs opposite the tiny gas fireplace, making a beeline for it as if it was his accustomed seat. When Marjorie was finally done with her fidgeting, she took the other chair, putting her furthest away from Phillip and Aubrey.

"All right, then." She perched on the edge and sat at an angle in order to face them more directly. "As you've guessed, we invited you both tonight for a reason."

Scant inches separated Phillip and Aubrey, and while they were not touching, he couldn't help but be aware of the tension in her posture. At Marjorie's words, she coiled into herself even tighter, as if bracing for a blow. Out of the corner of his eye he saw her head turn toward Clarence.

"Marjorie and I are getting married," her father said.

Aubrey drew a breath in so quickly she choked. "I'm s-sorry, w-what?" she stuttered through her coughing fit. Phillip braced the hand holding her wineglass, the warmth of his grip steadying her racing thoughts, though she doubted comfort was his motivation. It was more likely he didn't want red wine splattered on his trousers. Once she'd finished coughing, he released her.

"You heard me." Clarence stared down the length of his beaky nose. It was a look that had cowed her often in the past, but he wasn't getting away with it tonight.

"I heard the words." Drawing on years of legal debriefings and policy meetings with people determined to obfuscate the truth, she stared right back. "Now I need the background so I can understand."

"I knew I should have been the one to make the announcement." Marjorie's look of fond exasperation bewildered Aubrey. Her father was being an ass. Didn't that bother her? "Clarence has never understood the need to soften unexpected news."

"It's our news." Clarence switched his haughty stare to his fiancée—*fiancée*—who seemed not one whit disturbed. "We can announce it how we want."

Before Aubrey could protest this callous comment, Phillip spoke with no little hint of sarcasm. "Since you've broken the ice, shall we say, why don't you fill us in? Or is that too much to ask?" His mouth pressed into a tight line.

In the few years she'd been with Phillip, he'd never shown Clarence anything other than the respect her father demanded. He'd even admitted more than once that he was intimidated by the older man.

She didn't think that was the case any longer.

Clarence opened his mouth but remained silent when Marjorie raised her palm. "I think it's best if I handle this." Aubrey watched in shock as he subsided with barely a grumble.

"I know this probably seems very sudden to you both." Marjorie's sharp gaze swept from Phillip to Aubrey. "But I am eighty years old, Clarence almost ninety. We see no reason to delay something we've both wanted a long time."

She blinked. "A long time?"

Marjorie resettled herself on her seat and met Aubrey's confused gaze. "Obviously, Clarence and I knew each other before coming to live at Riverbend. Most recently, while you and Phillip were married."

"Of course, but—that was thirty years ago."

Marjorie nodded. "Yes. Your mother was still alive, had just been diagnosed with multiple sclerosis. I don't want you to think there was anything...dishonourable...between your father and I then. But with my medical background and your mother's condition, it was natural we would chat."

"I don't remember you mentioning anything about that." Phillip shifted and his thigh pressed against Aubrey's, but all his attention was on his aunt. "Why wouldn't you tell us?"

That forced Clarence out of his forbidding silence. "There was nothing deceitful about our omission." His words were clipped out between clenched teeth. "Marjorie was a wonderful support for me—for us— during that time."

"I'm sure he meant nothing scurrilous." Marjorie shot her nephew a look that said *You better not have.* "However, that wasn't the first time Clarence and I had met. You see, we knew each other years before then."

Aubrey's head swam. "You did? When? And why are

we only hearing about this now?" She placed her wineglass on the table in front of her. Her cheeks were already tingling with apprehension and nerves. She didn't need alcohol to enhance the feeling.

"It was in the early days of my law practice." Clarence's pale cheeks flew flags of angry colour. She knew he hated having to explain himself. "Marjorie was my secretary."

"Your secretary?" She felt like a parrot, mindlessly repeating words that had no meaning in the context they were presented.

"It was the late 1950s." Marjorie folded her hands in her lap, but Aubrey didn't miss the slight tremble in her fingers. "I knew I wanted to be a doctor, maybe even specialize. With no university in Prince George at the time, I needed to leave town, but my parents couldn't afford to send me. So, I did what a lot of women did. I trained as a secretary and took a job right out of high school, intending to apply to university as soon as I'd built up enough savings to support myself in Vancouver. That job was with your father."

"I second Aubrey's question. Why have you never mentioned this before?" Phillip raised one hand and dropped it back onto his thigh in a perplexed gesture. "You'd think the fact you worked together might have come up at least once in conversation. Why treat it like a deep, dark secret?"

The older couple shared a glance that sent a sliver of ice melting down Aubrey's spine. "You and Mom married in 1955."

"Yes. Marjorie came to work for me in March 1958," Clarence said with his usual precision.

"So that was why the three of you were friendly when Phillip and I were married?" If her suspicions were correct, her mother would *never* have allowed Marjorie back into Clarence's life. So those suspicions couldn't be true...could they?

"Your mother didn't have much to do with the day-to-day in my office. She hosted dinner parties for colleagues, of course, but Marjorie didn't attend those. She never connected the Marjorie she met in the late 1980s to a secretary I employed for a few years decades before."

That admission only fed the oily queasiness in her gut. "Why do I get the feeling you're not done with the awkward surprises?"

Marjorie rose from her chair and took the two steps necessary to stand by Clarence. He rose, too, in his courtly old-fashioned way.

"Our relationship in the eighties was purely friendship." She took his hand and held it in both of hers as if gaining strength from the contact. "But in the fifties, when I worked for Clarence"—she looked up at the much taller man and her lips curved in a small, sad smile—"we had an affair."

Aubrey couldn't speak, numb with shock. Phillip sat bolt upright beside her, frozen and silent.

"I fell in love with him." Marjorie drew their clasped hands to her breast and cradled them. "And he did the same with me. Divorce was frowned on in the fifties, and not just for Roman Catholics like your parents."

"You thought about divorcing Mom?" Aubrey hadn't been born until 1967, the long-awaited child after several miscarriages. It was a story her mother had told often. It had made her feel special, wanted, loved, even as she'd striven, usually unsuccessfully, to meet their expectations. If what Marjorie said was true, she might never have been born. She swallowed down bile.

"No." Clarence was firm yet sorrowful. "I admired and respected Alice, and I couldn't dishonour her that way."

Phillip's chin was lifted, his eyes narrowed with focus on the older couple. His hand crept from his thigh to where Aubrey's lay in her lap as if it had a mind of its own and she clung to it.

"That didn't stop you from sleeping around." His

tone was as cold as she'd ever heard it.

"Phillip!" Marjorie's voice cut the air with a scalpel-like stroke. "I am as much to blame as Clarence. You will not talk to either of us in that tone."

Aubrey stifled a hysterical giggle. The impulse to rant and rave bubbled inside her and she bit down. It was time to get out of there. She needed a chance to absorb everything she'd just heard. In private. Away from prying eyes.

Relinquishing her death grip on Phillip's hand, she pushed to her feet with caution, her knees wobbly with shock. "I have to go. I need to think about all this, put it in perspective."

Marjorie held out her palm in a *wait a moment* gesture. "We know this has been a shock, but there's one more thing we need to tell you."

"What else could there be?" Phillip straightened to stand at Aubrey's side. She heard an echo of her own distress in his voice.

Marjorie shifted closer to Clarence and squared her shoulders. "We had a child together. A son. We gave him up for adoption, but now we want to find him. We want your help."

CHAPTER EIGHT

Phillip knew things were bad when Aubrey didn't demur at his arm around her waist as they left Marjorie's apartment. Deciding the elevator was the best bet to get her to the ground floor safely, he pushed the button and waited for the car to arrive.

He sympathized with her trance-like state. He was battling his own disbelief and turmoil. And he hadn't found out he had a half-brother somewhere. A cousin was shocking enough.

She remained silent as they crossed the parking lot to the visitor stalls. When they reached her car, she paused, took a deep breath as if waking from sleep, and stepped out of his embrace.

"Thanks." Her voice was colourless, the word meaningless. What did she have to thank him for, after all?

He stuck with the expected script. "You're welcome." It was eight-thirty, and the sun was high in the June sky, dusk hours away. He could clearly see the blankness haunting her eyes, the tight lines around her mouth. "Are you okay to drive?"

She rolled her neck as if her shoulders ached. "Of course." She reached into the sleek leather bag she carried and pulled out her keys, and then stared as they danced in her trembling hand. "Maybe I need a minute."

"Why don't we sit over there?" He jerked his chin at a circular garden nearby. Metal benches surrounded an inner bed of neatly planted rose bushes with a creeping phlox border. In the outer ring, tall spikes of decorative grasses—Karl Foerster reed grass, his landscaper's mind noted—provided an illusion of privacy.

"That might be a good idea."

He took her hand and led her to the nearest bench. In the apartment, during Marjorie and Clarence's astounding revelations, he hadn't been able to stop from touching her, offering—and seeking—wordless comfort, and the feeling hadn't dissipated yet.

They sat shoulder to shoulder on the iron slats. Traffic swept by in a soothing, monotonous rush and the sound of children playing in the schoolyard on the other side of Riverbend reached them, muted and soft.

"Everything I thought I knew has changed." She spoke so quietly he wasn't sure she wanted him to hear. "I'm too old to deal with this."

That surprised a laugh out of him, and good god he needed it. "I know what you mean." He leaned back and stretched out his legs with a sigh. "Once you reach a certain age you figure the drama is behind you, especially when it comes to your parents."

"Exactly! And then something like this comes along and knocks you flat." She squirmed on the seat, twisting to face him. She'd lost the slate-wiped-clean expression that had been pasted on her face since Marjorie and Clarence's bombshell. "My father had an affair. One of the most upright, devout, *judgmental* people I know. What was he thinking?"

"They were in love."

"He was *married*. To my *mother*. I don't care if it was sixty years ago. I can't believe he did such a thing."

"If it's any consolation, I believed them when they said nothing happened when they met later." He slid his feet back underneath the bench and sat up straight as an idea struck him. "I wonder what Marjorie thought when I brought you home for the first time. She must have known who you were, who your father was.

Clarence was a well-known judge, and she was making a name for herself in the surgical field. Prince George isn't that big a city, even now. People in that echelon of society always know each other, at least superficially."

"Oh my god." Aubrey's eyes were huge and dark. "Do you think that's why my dad—" She broke off, biting her lip.

He had no trouble filling the blank. "Disapproved of me? Do you think he was jealous? I don't see why. I'm Marjorie's nephew, not her son. I think he just didn't like me. Doesn't, still."

"Son." Her eyes widened even farther, filling a face that had gone suddenly pale. "My father has a son. I have a brother."

"Yes."

"I wasn't thinking of it like that." She sprang to her feet and took a few racing steps away from the bench before spinning around. "I have a brother. Half-brother, I guess, but still. I used to dream about having a brother when I was a little girl. And all the time I had one. *And my father knew I did.*"

It was easy to see this betrayal loomed even larger than the fact Clarence had cheated on her mother. As an only child himself, Phillip had some sympathy of how she felt. "What else could he have done? It was a closed, private adoption. Once they gave the baby away, they had no legal rights to call him their own." Clarence and Marjorie had provided some of the details regarding the process, but he wasn't sure how much Aubrey had absorbed.

"I don't care. He should have told me *something*." Her expression was fierce.

To his dismay—because he never wanted to think he and Clarence had anything in common—he sided with him on this decision. It would have been pointless to tell her she had a half-brother when there was no way the two would ever be able to meet. He determined from her continued muttering and pacing, though, that she wasn't ready to listen to logic. "Well, now he has. And he wants us to help find him." He had no detailed knowledge of adoption laws in British Columbia, though he did have a vague recollection they had changed twenty or thirty years ago to make it easier for birth parents and adopted children to find each other, should both parties wish it.

"I can't do it." She came to a halt, hands on her hips, staring down at him. "I am not helping you find a child that my father couldn't be bothered to tell me about until I was fifty-two years old. This is all Marjorie's doing. My father would have gone to his grave with this secret if she hadn't insisted, I know it."

"Are you telling me you wished they *hadn't* said anything about it?"

"Yes! No. I don't know." Emotions warred on her face—sadness, rage, hope, fear. "I think this is the most selfish thing he's ever done. He's willing to ruin my peace of mind, the ingrained understanding I have of my family, to find a child he sent away without a second thought."

"That's not fair." He couldn't help the protest that sprang to his lips. "Giving a child up for adoption couldn't have been easy. You have no idea what emotions they were feeling. They did it hoping it was best for their son."

"And that's another thing." She resumed her pacing. "The baby was a *boy*. I know my father always wanted a son. How disappointed he must have been to end up with *me*. I wonder if he ever thought he'd made a mistake, keeping me instead of him."

"Aubrey—" Again, he found himself with the urge to defend Clarence. He hoped it wasn't going to become a habit. "You're not thinking very clearly right now. Your father loves you, I know he does."

She waved that away. "Oh, I suppose so. But I never quite measured up to his expectations, you know that."

He had no intention of delving into the complicated

depths of that relationship. "Don't you have any empathy for your father and Marjorie? Think about it. They were in love sixty years ago. Regardless of the mistakes they might have made, they finally have a chance to be together, and to reunite with the son they lost. Don't you want to give them a happy ending?"

Aubrey stared at Phillip. How could he be so calm and logical? Had he always been so composed in the face of disaster? She couldn't remember, and it didn't matter. Right now, it was infuriating. Didn't he see how this changed *everything?*

"If I'm this rattled about finding out I have a half-brother, what about *him?*" She pointed a finger in a random direction. Somewhere in this world was a man who shared her DNA. It was ridiculous, but she couldn't help feeling as if a piece of her had fractured off and was frantically searching for him. The yearning to find her brother pulled at her painfully. And yet—

"How will he feel when he learns he has another family?" It was as if every nerve ending in her body had rewired itself, leaving her twitchy and breathless. "Don't you think he'll be even more upset than I am, to have his life knocked sideways?"

"It's not like we'll just walk up and ring his doorbell. There are processes in place for this sort of thing. And he's sixty years old—what are the chances he doesn't yet know he's adopted?"

She couldn't blame him for the exasperation leaking at the edges of his tone. But couldn't he give her a minute—just a goddamn *minute*—to wrap her head around all this? "If he does, why hasn't he tried to find his birth parents? Doesn't that imply he doesn't want to know them?"

"Maybe he tried but couldn't find them. Did you hear what Clarence said about the adoption?"

She'd been in too much shock to pay attention to the

details, her mind running on a hamster wheel of confusion and hurt. "I heard him say it was privately arranged."

"Yes. A lawyer handled it for them. They have no idea how he found the parents. He might have gone to an adoption society, another lawyer, a government agency. They left that up to him, trusting him to take care of their child. To all intents and purposes, though, their baby no longer existed."

The air punched out of her lungs in a searing gasp. She swayed. Was *that* why she was so upset? Not because she had just discovered she had a brother, but at the fact that her father had voluntarily given away his child, when losing her own had almost destroyed her?

"Aubrey!"

She opened eyes she hadn't realized she'd closed. Phillip was standing in front of her, clasping her elbows. Sorrow weakened her knees, and she was grateful for his support. "Do you ever think of her?" she whispered.

His fingertips dug into the soft flesh of her arms. "Of course. Often."

"Can you imagine *any* scenario where we would have agreed to give her away?"

"No." His hands loosened their grip but before she could feel the loss of his touch they slid around her waist and pulled her closer. He lowered his forehead to hers and she blinked, trying to keep him in focus. She felt sheltered, cherished, safe.

It was dangerous to feel that way, especially with him, but she didn't have the strength to pull away.

"Samantha was taken from us." He spoke softly, his breath fanning her face with the faint, oaky scent of whiskey. "Sudden Infant Death Syndrome is just that, sudden, always unexpected. Things were different for Marjorie and Clarence."

"I would have done *anything* to keep Samantha. *Anything*. How could they give away their baby?"

He didn't reply. He just tucked her head under his

75

chin and held her.

God, she missed being held by a man. She wouldn't let herself get used to it, but she didn't have the strength to move away quite yet. "If you want to help find their son, I understand. But I don't know if I can. It will hurt too much." Her refusal no longer had anything to do with her father's long kept secret, and everything to do with the reminder of Samantha.

"You don't have to decide right now." His voice rumbled under her ear. "We've both had a few shocks today."

She huffed out a tired chuckle. "You don't say. I feel more wrung out than a well-used dishcloth." His arms dropped from her waist. She took the hint, stepping back and breaking their connection. "Don't wait for me. To start looking, I mean. Marjorie sounded pretty impatient, and I'm going to need time to wrap my head around this."

"You're not the only one. They've waited sixty years. A few more days won't change anything." He reached out and brushed a strand of hair from her cheek. Her skin tingled and she resisted the longing to lean into his touch. "Take all the time you need. But I know you'll do the right thing. You always do."

"Why is the right thing never the easy thing?"

He smiled and the creases in his cheeks deepened, though his eyes remained sober. "Despite your differences, you love Clarence, and I know you care for Marjorie. You'd be doing this for them, not yourself."

"What if I'm tired of putting other people first?" The admission shuddered to the depth of her soul. She was tired. But did that give her the right to be selfish? "What if I want to do what's best for *me* for a change?"

"Go home, Aubrey." He took her arm again and they walked to her car side by side. "Have a glass of wine, a hot bath, a bowl of ice cream—whatever you do to relax. We'll talk later."

She wanted to snap back, accuse him of being

patronizing, but he was only trying to help, and she was too tired to be angry. This time when she took her keys out of her purse her fingers were firm. "Goodnight, Phillip."

"Goodnight, Aubrey."

He walked away, and she watched until he reached his pickup, her hand clenched around her keys so tightly a cramp squeezed her thumb.

CHAPTER NINE

As there were few rules when it came to *what* the Silverberry Book Club did, *when* the club met was also flexible. "We try to get together at least once a month," Helen had explained, "but when and where depends on what we're doing, of course."

Which was how, on the Saturday morning two and a half weeks after her first Silverberry meeting, Aubrey found herself in the back seat of Penta's seven-passenger minivan on her way to Mount Pope. Next to Penta was Stephanie, with Natalie and Terrance in the middle row. In the SUV leading the way, Lynn was riding with Helen and Nathan.

Fort St. James, the village a few kilometres from their destination, was ninety minutes north-west of Prince George. They'd left bright and early that morning, so it was barely eight-thirty when Penta pulled in next to Helen in the parking lot at the base of the mountain.

"Tell me again why we're doing this?" Terrance's plaintive question mirrored Aubrey's own worried thoughts. "It seems rather energetic even for *this* club."

"Because you used up your veto on parachuting." Stephanie peered back between the front seats as she unbuckled her seatbelt.

Terrance shuddered dramatically. "Oh, yes. Once was definitely enough of *that*."

As the club's mission was to try new things, activities couldn't be repeated more than once a year.

Aubrey was glad she hadn't been around when they'd done tandem jumps with a local parachuting club. Listening to the group relive the experience at her first meeting had made her dizzy.

Natalie slid open the side door. "If I'd gotten my way, this is where we'd be doing our rock climbing. There are excellent routes here." One of the many shocks Aubrey had had at her first meeting was learning that Natalie was an avid climber. "All we're doing today is hiking a well-maintained trail, not scrambling up a cliff by our fingernails." She'd been vetoed on the outdoor activity, but everyone had compromised on an indoor session. Thank goodness it wasn't scheduled until next spring. Aubrey had plenty of time to grow accustomed to the idea.

She glanced at her own her fingernails as she gripped the back of the seats in front of her and crouch-walked out of the van. She'd given up on the gel polish she used to maintain meticulously when she'd been in the public eye, as the manual labour she'd been doing since buying her house wasn't conducive to a decent manicure. She was rather proud of their battered state these days.

"All right, my Silverberries." Helen clapped her hands briskly as the group gathered at the trail head. "Everyone have their water bottles?" Nods and agreeable murmurs answered her. "The trail climbs about seven hundred metres over three kilometres to the summit, so it's going to be steep. We've given ourselves plenty of time, and the weather is supposed to stay clear, so there's no need to rush. Just travel at your own pace and we'll all meet at the top for lunch."

The ascent began almost immediately, and it wasn't long before the group stretched out in a meandering line. Aubrey wasn't surprised when Helen and Nathan strode briskly at the front—the couple seemed to have endless stamina. Small gaps separated the rest, though no one was walking alone.

A breeze set the branches rustling and the muted roar of a boat engine reached Aubrey from the nearby but presently invisible waters of Stuart Lake. She focused on the lift and push of her legs, the rhythm of her breathing, and the peace she'd been searching for since Clarence and Marjorie's announcement finally seemed within reach.

Until Natalie said, from her position a few steps behind, "Are you okay? You were rather quiet on the drive out."

She couldn't deny it. She *had* been quiet, letting the conversation in the van wash over her as her mind had spun with the thoughts that had eaten away at her the last few days. "I'm fine. Just something on my mind."

"Anything you want to talk about? Is Clarence driving you crazy again?"

If she had had enough breath she would have laughed. "What do you mean again? It's *always* with my dad." Her thighs burned and her cheeks had warm with exertion. The view from the top was supposed to be amazing, and it had better be, given the effort it was going to take to get there.

Natalie remained silent as the trail wound up and around a mossy outcropping of rock, the pine needle strewn path bumpy with small stones and tree roots. Aubrey had had no reason to own hiking boots ever before but had bought a pair soon after her first Silverberry meeting and broken them in by wearing them as she tackled work around the house. She was thankful for their support and traction now.

"I know when my family is driving me insane"— Natalie's breath puffed between phrases—"it helps to vent to friends. And I'm your friend, Aubrey."

She was beginning to believe that was true, despite her worries right after the election. It had been years since she'd been able to bitch and moan without worrying it would get blown out of proportion. Her father frowned upon whining, even in private, and as a politician Aubrey had been well aware she needed to be discreet. The pressure to let go, to tell *someone* about the bomb that had detonated in her life, became overwhelming.

"I have a brother." The words felt sharp in her mouth, and she was thankful Natalie was behind her so she couldn't see her face. "A half-brother, technically. He was given up for adoption years before I was born."

"Wait, what? Stop for a minute."

She obeyed the command, her leg muscles sighing in relief as she came to a halt. The path was a little wider here, so they stood off to the side, panting slightly.

"Start from the beginning. Use small words." Natalie pushed the frame of her glasses up her nose, brown eyes wide behind the lenses.

"My father had an affair with his secretary. The baby was born in 1960, and they arranged a private adoption."

The younger woman's mouth dropped open. "An affair? He was married to your mother when this happened?"

Aubrey nodded. She understood Natalie's shock. She still couldn't believe it herself. She unscrewed the top of her water bottle and took a swallow. Penta and Terrance caught up to them but continued past when Natalie waved and smiled and said they'd only be a minute.

She turned back to Aubrey, eyebrows raised. "You're going to have to give me the full story, but I suppose I can wait a couple more hours until we get to the top. I think I'm going to need all my breath for this one."

The incline forced Aubrey to concentrate on putting one foot in front of the other, and the exertion drove all thoughts of her troubles from her mind. As they slowly made their way up Mount Pope, sweat beaded between her breasts and in the bend of her elbows and her breath came in gasps, calling for frequent rests. She welcomed the grueling effort. It was freeing and cleansing and purging.

The last few hundred metres, the path became rockier and required even more focus to avoid twisting an ankle. She cleared the treeline and reached the sloping, exposed, wind-worn peak. A wooden cupola perched at the very top, held down by thick wire guy-lines bolted into the mountain. Helen and Nathan waved encouragement from this shelter as the rest of the group scaled the final distance. Aubrey helped the much shorter Penta haul herself onto the floor in an inelegant scramble as there were no steps into the small structure, and then clambered in herself. Rising from her knees, she lost her breath once more, but for a completely different reason.

The world stretched out in all directions, the blue dome of the sky arching over variegated green forests and slate-grey water. The village of Fort St. James wasn't visible, but the enormous length of Stuart Lake stretched out into the distance, with more lakes visible to the north-east. Shadows from scattered clouds drifted over the lower peaks and valleys like leaves on a pond, and the wind whipped at her ferociously. She gripped the railing.

Stephanie stood at her shoulder. Her elegance from the first Silverberry meeting was still evident in the stylish hiking gear and understated makeup, and she appeared barely winded from the climb. "Worth it?" She had to shout over the howling gusts, her chin-length hair whipping about her face.

"Yes." Aubrey drank in the scene. "I've never considered myself an outdoorsy person. Never made the time, I guess. But this"—she waved a hand wordlessly at the panorama—"this could change anyone's mind."

An especially vigorous blast of wind bowled through

the group, causing Terrance to stagger. "All right," he said decisively. "Time for lunch. And a sip of wine. Anyone joining me?" On her way up Aubrey had noted the small area within the protection of the trees that functioned as a picnic site. It boasted rustic benches made from split logs but no other amenities. She'd been warned she would need to pack out whatever she packed in, and that there were no facilities available at the summit, not even outdoor toilets. She hadn't quite believed Helen, but she'd obviously been telling the truth.

After a cozy, convivial lunch of sandwiches, fruit, granola bars, and the wine Terrance had mentioned—he had carried a plastic bottle with enough for everyone to enjoy a toast—the group spread out again, exploring the peak and savouring the view before the trek back down. Natalie tacked Aubrey to her seat with a look and waited until they were alone.

"Okay, let me have it." She squirmed on the uncomfortable plank as if settling in for the long haul. "Why did Clarence decide to tell you about your brother now, after all this time?"

"Because he plans to marry the boy's mother." Natalie blinked, and Aubrey explained about Marjorie and Riverbend and her father's request.

"He's a smart man." Natalie fiddled with the cap on her water bottle. "Why does he need you?"

She hadn't considered that angle. Her father had never needed her help before. "I didn't stick around long enough to ask. Anyway, I don't want to do it. It was enough of a shock to *me*—what if this man doesn't know he was adopted? How would you like to be sixty years old and find out your whole life history is not what you believe it to be? But Phillip thinks we have to."

"I can't believe you were married before Oliver. How did that not come up in conversation?"

"It's no big deal." She hoped she sounded carefree and nonchalant, though she didn't feel that way.

Meeting Phillip again had been disconcerting enough without all the other revelations thrown at her in recent days. "We married right out of high school. We were young and foolish. It didn't last long."

Natalie didn't take the hint. "What was it like, seeing him again?"

She sighed and decided honesty was the only way to get out of this uncomfortable conversation. "More unsettling than I'd like to admit. My first thought was he hadn't changed a bit. Then I noticed how he had, and it annoyed the hell out of me. Why is it that men age better than women?"

"Just one of the many unfair ways of the world. Still had all his hair, then?"

"Yes. And no paunch, damn him. The least he could have done was gotten fat." It depressed her to think of the softening and sagging her body had done over the years.

"So, what are you going to do?" Natalie peered at her inquisitively. "Will you help him look for your brother?"

"I don't know." She banged her fist lightly on her thigh. "I honestly don't know."

CHAPTER TEN

"Come on, old man, let's see what you've got."

Phillip gripped the ball, tucking it into his side and leaning over to protect it. Breathing through his nose to disguise his need to pant, he watched Asher warily. His son hovered, balanced lightly on his feet, arms outstretched, blocking Phillip's path to the basket. Any evidence of his smooth, sleek reporter's persona had vanished—his dark hair damp with sweat, lips pulled back in a taunting grin. Zeke lurked just behind him, ready to steal the ball from either of them given the chance.

"I've got what it takes to beat you two punks." He faked to his left before streaking to the right. His bad hip twinged sharply but he ignored it, dribbling past a scrambling Zeke, and driving to the basket for a single point.

"What's the score now?" He forced himself to walk back to the free throw line without limping. "Twelve, nine, eight? All I need to do is make these three shots and I'm right back in it."

"Just shoot already." Zeke planted his hands on his hips.

He bounced the ball a couple times, hiding his need for a breather. Playing twenty-one with his boys took more out of him that it used to, though he could still give them a run for their money. He focused on the basket and let the ball fly.

Twenty minutes later the game ended with Zeke

holding onto his lead, beating Asher and Phillip by only a couple points. Wooden benches were scattered around the edges of the multipurpose court. He dropped onto the nearest one, holding back a groan, and leaned against the chain link fence.

"I'm glad you both could make it today." He did his best not to wheeze.

Asher sprawled loose-limbed on the bench beside him, and Zeke lay on his back on the asphalt, knees bent, head propped on his duffel bag. Asher worked Tuesday to Saturday at the television station, and Zeke was shifted four on, four off at the pellet plant, so getting all three of them together took some organizing. If Asher got a new job—*when* he got a new job—in another city, times like these would become a thing of the past. And while Phillip could afford to travel financially, it would be tough to find the time, given his responsibilities with Twin Rivers.

But that was the future. For now, he would simply appreciate a sunny Sunday with his boys, despite the serious reason he'd needed to see them.

"Always a pleasure to put you two in your place." Zeke guzzled from his water bottle.

"Just because you play dirtier than—" Asher began.

"As much fun as the game was"—Phillip cut him off before the conversation could degenerate into a slanging match—"there is something I need to talk about."

His sons looked at him, eyebrows raised in identically quizzical expressions. His heart squeezed. He wished they were better friends, not just brothers, but had to trust they'd find their own way.

"Marjorie told me something last week. Something you both should know." He'd debated the need to tell his sons and had come to the conclusion there was no point in hiding the news. He also had a selfish reason for mentioning it—he could use it as a bridge to Aubrey. It was time his boys knew about her, especially if he was going to be spending more time in her company.

Which he fully intended to do, whether she helped in the search for her brother or not. And not just because she'd agreed to his quote on her landscaping project. Aubrey was unfinished business, and it was time to put some closure on that part of his life.

"Is she okay?" Zeke sat upright in a sudden move. "She's not sick, is she?"

"No, no, nothing like that. Here's the thing—" He told them the story pretty much the way he and Aubrey had learned it, starting with Clarence and Marjorie's decision to marry, and moving on to the search for the child they had given up. Asher and Zeke took that news calmly, as he'd expected. They were less interested in the long-lost baby than they were curious about their great-aunt's fiancé and his daughter.

"You know I covered Aubrey Windt's campaign this past election." Asher pushed a lock of damp hair off his forehead. "I never met her father, of course. It really is amazing how small this world is."

You are about to find out it is even smaller. "There's something else you should know about Aubrey." He took a deep breath. "She and I were married."

His sons stared at him. Asher recovered first. "You were? When?"

"Aubrey and I were high school sweethearts." He felt self-conscious at the mushy term, even though it was nothing more than the truth. "We married right after graduation. Her parents weren't happy about it. Marjorie wasn't either. Everyone thought we were too young." *Everyone* had been right, he thought sadly.

"How long were you married?"

"Not quite two years." He wondered whether to tell them about Samantha, but figured he was giving them enough shocks for one day. It wasn't the same as Aubrey finding out about her half-brother, but there were enough similarities to make him cautious. "I'm sure you'll have questions. If not today, then later. I'll answer them as best I can."

"Huh." Zeke lay back on the ground, a small frown between his eyes. "It shouldn't matter. It's not like it changes anything with you and Mom. But it does feel kind of weird."

"I'm glad I didn't know about this before the election. It might have made things awkward." Asher shot Phillip a startled stare. "Wait a minute. Did she know who *I* was?"

He had wondered if that would come up. "Yes. We met, totally by accident, the day Marjorie moved into Riverbend. Aubrey mentioned seeing you."

"I didn't get a hint from her at all. Of course, politicians are used to hiding their thoughts."

Once again Phillip was struck by the differences between today's Aubrey and the one he'd loved so passionately as a teenager. *That* Aubrey had never suppressed her feelings—at least not that he knew of. Even toward the end, when they'd been grieving and struggling and fighting, she'd never kept secrets.

No, she'd been painfully honest when she told him she was leaving because she didn't love him anymore.

The phone he'd hidden under the sweatshirt he'd discarded before they'd started playing trilled out a text notification. He debated ignoring it, but neither Asher nor Zeke seemed to have anything more to say about what they'd just learned, already in a heated discussion about the Blue Jays' chances at winning the pennant this season. He fished it out and stared at the screen. The message from Aubrey was short and blunt.

I'll do it. We should meet.

He didn't want to give her a chance to change her mind. He tapped a quick reply.

One hour. My place. He added his address, hit send, and waited while the little dots danced.

See you then.

He interrupted Zeke halfway through a creatively profane insult blistering the Blue Jays pitching staff.

"I've got to go, guys. Something's come up."

Accustomed throughout their lives to business calls that interrupted family meals and vacation activities, they didn't question him, just gathered their gear, and headed to the parking lot where their individual vehicles waited.

"Remember," Phillip said before they went their separate ways. "If you have any questions about what I just told you, all you have to do is ask."

"It's all good, Dad." Zeke punched him lightly on the shoulder. "It was a long time ago, right?"

Which was true, as far as it went. But he wasn't sure the past was going to stay in the past much longer.

Once the thought flashed into Aubrey's brain, she couldn't believe it had taken her so long to figure it out.

Her new house on Cedar Street was just like the one she and Phillip had rented during their brief marriage. Not the neglected yard and long-ignored condition. Even then, he had used his skills to keep everything in good repair. But the coziness and sense of timelessness.

Was *that* why she'd been so drawn to it?

It was even odder that she hadn't had that thought until she pulled up in front of Phillip's building. Something about the tall, narrow rowhouse with its characterless, modern styling had sparked the revelation. Maybe because it reminded her of her own characterless condos—so neat and tidy it was like living in a magazine layout, but without as much personality.

The address he'd texted indicated the middle residence in a block of five homes in a brand-new complex. Well, new within the last two years, anyway. A tiny patch of grass was split by a concrete sidewalk leading to a glossy black door on the ground level of the three-storey building. Each storey was sided in a different colour, giving it a striped appearance she found jarring.

She eased out of the car. Her whole body ached from the strain of climbing Mount Pope the day before. The return trip had been faster but more intense than the ascent, and her shins throbbed painfully whenever she took a step. With a sinking heart she acknowledged she'd probably have to go up and down stairs inside Phillip's home. She only hoped she wouldn't groan out loud when she did.

The doorbell chimed softly when she pressed it, and the thud of feet sounded from inside. The door swung wide.

Her mouth dropped open.

"Hi." Phillip stepped back to give her room. "Come on in."

She didn't move. Did he realize he wasn't wearing a shirt? Of course he did. *Why* wasn't he wearing a shirt? Sure, he had a towel draped over his shoulders, but all that did was draw attention to his lightly furred chest and flat stomach. At least he was wearing sweatpants— grey ones that hung off his hips and drew attention to—

Her gaze lifted hurriedly. Only to snag on his neck, where water droplets glistened.

"I just got back from playing basketball with the boys." He used the towel to wipe the moisture off his skin and she followed his motions, mesmerized with unexpected lust. "I thought I had time for a shower before you got here, but I cut it a little close."

"I'm early. I can wait in the car." Her breath strangled in her throat.

"Don't be silly. Come upstairs." He gestured to the carpeted flight beside him.

He obviously saw nothing odd in being half-naked in her presence, so making any further demur would only highlight her discomfort. She slipped inside, careful not to brush against him, all too aware of the damp heat emanating from his skin.

The sight of the climb waiting for her went a good way to distracting her from her lecherous thoughts. The two steps to the small landing on the left were manageable, but she had to bite her lip to keep from moaning as she climbed the long flight to the next floor. Knowing he was watching, she tried to keep her movements light and graceful, an impossibility given the rigor in her lower limbs.

"Are you okay? You look a little—"

"I'm fine." He'd noticed. Of course he'd noticed. She was moving like a rusty robot. "Just a bit stiff. My book club hiked Mount Pope yesterday." She reached the top of the stairs with a heartfelt but silent sigh of relief and found herself in a well-lit, wide-open space with a kitchen, dining area, and living area. Another flight of stairs led to the next level, and a door just beside it revealed a bright white bathroom.

"You'll have to explain what a book club is doing climbing a mountain later. Have a seat. I'll be right back." He disappeared up the stairs with a swiftness she envied in her crippled state.

She hobbled to the nearest chair—a sleek leather beast that looked more suited to a corporate office than a living room—and sank into it with a muted moan. Once off her feet, she could more easily forget the pain in her legs and take stock of her situation.

She'd successfully avoided thinking about her missing half-brother during the return to Cedar Street yesterday. Aching with fatigue, the first thing she'd done was draw a bath in her purple-fixtured bathroom. Unfortunately, once she'd sunk into the foaming, heated water, the thoughts had bubbled up again. Accepting she would never be able to forget her recently revealed sibling, never be able to go back to how things had been before, she had decided to be a part of whatever discoveries were made. Helping with the search would give her an illusion of control.

It had still taken her a night and most of a day to get the courage to text Phillip. And she hadn't been prepared for him to suggest such a swift meeting. But now that she'd made her choice, there was no valid reason to delay longer.

She resolutely ignored the soft shuffling sounds above her head, refusing to imagine Phillip shucking off those loose-fitting jogging pants, wiping the last of the dampness from his chest, standing naked as he chose what to wear—

She banged her head lightly against the leather headrest. Enumerating what she was refusing to imagine meant she was imagining it. It wasn't *Phillip* she was attracted to, she told herself, it was his representation of a sexy, age-appropriate man. She hadn't had sex since Oliver died—not with another human being, anyway.

It had taken her a long time to recover from her grief. Because she *had* grieved Oliver, despite media speculation to the opposite, especially after she'd decided to vie for his place in the Legislature. After winning the by-election, finding partners had been fraught with complications, and it just hadn't seemed worth the trouble.

"Would you like a glass of wine?"

She levitated from her seat, pressed a hand to her chest, and swivelled around to see Phillip grinning in the kitchen. "I didn't hear you come down."

"Sorry." He lifted a bottle of wine and waggled it in her direction. "I have beer and a couple of ciders, too. Or I can make coffee or tea."

"Tea would be great." The last thing she needed was anything that might lower her inhibitions. Though he now wore black jeans and a deep green collared shirt, the extra coverage only caused her to speculate how she might get him naked again.

Stop it, she scolded herself. *There's no way he's thinking the same thing, so get your head in the game.*

CHAPTER ELEVEN

Phillip turned away from Aubrey to fill the kettle and place it on the stove. He'd used his time upstairs to get his traitorous appetite under control but found himself fighting it once again at the sight of her cradled in his usual seat. His mind had stripped off the neat and decorous summer dress she wore, leaving her in nothing but lacy lingerie, searing red against the paleness of her skin as she draped herself on the black leather.

He opened a cupboard and blindly took down two mugs. He didn't think he had imagined the flare of attraction that had heated her eyes when he'd opened the door. But it had been replaced so quickly with a vague look of panic he couldn't be sure. Taking his fantasies to this level was dangerous and delusional.

Glad he was no longer wearing soft fleece pants that would do nothing to hide his body's reaction to such erotic thoughts, he turned back to the living room, rested his hips against the counter beside the stove, and crossed his arms. "I'm glad you're going to help. I think it's the right thing to do."

She sighed. "So you've said. As there's no way to close Pandora's box—" She shrugged. He kept his eyes firmly on her face, not the gentle movement of her generous breasts under the thin fabric.

The kettle shrieked and he poured the boiling water into the mugs. "Sugar? Cream? Lemon?"

"Lemon if you have it."

93

He cut a thin slice for each of them, arranged the mugs, teabags, spoons, and lemon on individual plates and carried them to the living room. He handed Aubrey hers and took a seat on the couch, near enough to touch her, but not so near he would be tempted to do so.

"Thank you." She fidgeted with fixing her drink and he had the strong impression she was avoiding his eyes. When it was finally prepared to her satisfaction, she sat back, a wince crossing her face.

"I never took you as a mountain climber." He remembered her with her nose in a book most of the time, not intrepidly adventuring in nature.

"Trust me, I'm not." She blew on her tea to cool it, drawing his gaze to her pursed lips. "It was a perfectly easy, accessible trail, no real climbing involved, just a steep incline." She flashed him a quick, self-deprecating grin. "I was passed by a family with three children under the age of ten. They scampered by like I was standing still."

"Well, congratulations on persevering."

A faint blush coloured her jaw. "This book club that's not really a book club will be good for me. Push me to try things I'd never do on my own. But I didn't come here to talk about that."

"No." He propped his feet on the coffee table and clasped his mug on his stomach. "So, what do you think we should do first?"

She blinked, as if she hadn't expected to be consulted in the process.

"You're a lawyer." And much more intuitive than himself. Surely that hadn't changed. "You're used to asking questions, getting answers. If I was on my own, I would be able to fumble my way around. But you're the expert here."

Her blush grew richer. Was she that uncomfortable being complimented? She had to be used to people deferring to her intelligence. She'd been the top student all through high school, and he knew it had driven her parents mad when she'd decided to marry instead of attend university. "A waste of the brain God gave you," had been the gentlest of Clarence's cruel comments.

Excitement flickered in her eyes, and she settled deeper in her chair. "If this were a case a stranger had brought to me, I'd recommend DNA testing."

Phillip took a sip of his tea, watching her over the rim of his mug. His posture was relaxed and casual, with his knees bent and feet on the coffee table, but his eyes were bright with purpose. "You mean one of those at-home tests you see advertised all over the place?"

She nodded. The idea had come to her last night as she lay sleepless. "Marjorie, Clarence, and I should do the tests. If we ever find their son, he may demand proof, and having the results on hand will simplify things. Also, it's possible that he has been searching for his birth parents already. If his DNA is on file, the mystery is solved."

It sounded so final when she said it, as if that would be the end. When it would only be the beginning.

"Any idea how long it takes to get those results? And which company do you think we should use?"

She'd done some research online that morning. "Ancestry.com has by far the biggest data base, so we might as well start there. The website says it takes six to eight weeks to get results once they've received the sample at their lab. Allowing for the time needed to ship the kit here and back, we're definitely looking at two months or more."

"And in the meantime? We just wait?"

"No. We can't pin our hopes on the DNA. To get any useful results, my brot—" She broke off, swallowed, and then started again. "My half-brother or his descendants would have had to submit samples. If we do get any matches, we'll need to determine exactly how they are related. Other than DNA that connects us to their son and my half-brother, we'd be looking for Marjorie and Clarence's grandchildren, or my nieces and nephews. We might have to wait years before we get a hit, and there's no guarantee we ever will."

"We don't have years." He scratched his chin thoughtfully. His nails rasped against his whiskers and a delicious thrill rippled down her spine. *Down, girl.* "Marjorie and Clarence are in good health, but they are in their eighties."

"Yes. Which means we should follow the paper trail."

"It was a private adoption. What kind of paper trail would there be?"

"Lawyers *always* write things down." It was a way to cover any eventualities, even the ones that couldn't be imagined. "Dad said he had a colleague handle the details. Even though it was a personal, confidential matter, he would have kept files, I guarantee you." She grinned, and her heart thumped when he grinned back. With a start, she realized she was enjoying herself. She'd always loved logic puzzles, and if she ignored the personal implications, this promised to be a fascinating journey.

She put down her half-drunk mug and swung to face him. "Here's what I think we should do. We need to get Dad and Marjorie to agree to the DNA tests so I can set up an account and order the kits. And we need to talk to them separately."

"Separately? Why?"

"Never assume a client has told you the entire truth. If they were a couple that had come to me in my professional capacity, the first thing I would do would be to question each of them on their own. While I am sure they'll agree on the main facts, they'll have different memories of that time, remember different details, have experienced different emotions."

"I get that."

She offered her next thought with trepidation.

"There's something else to consider. It's possible that one of them has already tried to find the baby and didn't want the other to know. Talking to them alone might be the only way to get them to admit that."

He dropped his feet to the floor, jackknifed upright, and met gaze squarely. "I never thought of that. Do you really think that's probable?"

"I don't know. If it were me?" She bit her lip, and then went with the truth, knowing she was dragging hurtful memories to the surface. "If I'd given away my first child—my only child—and then spent decades separated from the father, the thought would have at least crossed my mind."

She watched in fearful fascination as he slid from the couch and knelt in front of her. He didn't touch her, but gripped the arms of the chair, enclosing her. Protecting her. Her fingers twisted together in her lap as she suppressed the urge to place her hands on his shoulders.

His mouth opened, and then closed. She could see conflicting emotions chasing across his face, the need to say something, anything, but not knowing what.

"I'm sorry." Sincerity and regret rang in the simple syllables.

"Me, too." For so many things, spoken and unspoken, done and not done. "But Marjorie's baby is not Samantha, and I'm dealing with separating the two. As horrible as losing our daughter was and is, not knowing what happened to her would be worse. Marjorie and Clarence need resolution, and we can help give them that."

Aubrey said her goodbye to Phillip a few minutes later. It wasn't quite dinner time, but she was exhausted from a combination of last night's sleeplessness, exercise-induced discomfort, and emotionally draining conversation. Stopping at her favourite sushi bar, she ordered take out and took a seat at a corner table while it was prepared.

Downtown Prince George late on a Sunday afternoon was not ideal for people-watching. Pedestrians were few and far between and traffic infrequent. Yet she found the quietness of the streets restful and let her mind drift.

Now that she'd committed to helping find Marjorie and Clarence's son, she had a sense of peace. Indecision was wearing on the soul, and choosing to act was freeing, even if there was no guarantee it would end well. Phillip had promised to talk with Marjorie in the next few days, and she had assured him she would talk to Clarence soon, as well.

"Are you okay with doing that?" he had asked as she hobbled her way down the stairs to the door. "I know you and Clarence had a difficult relationship, even before all this. If it's going to be too hard for you…"

She shook her head. "Thanks, but I'll be fine. My father must be held accountable, and if he truly wants to find his son, he'll answer my questions honestly. And agree to the DNA test."

Phillip frowned. "You think he might not want to find him?"

"I'm not sure he's as invested as Marjorie is. But if he loves her the way she seems to think he does, it doesn't matter what he wants. He'll do it for her."

It was still mind-boggling to imagine Marjorie and Clarence nursing a star-crossed love all these years. No child was comfortable envisioning their parents in a romantic scenario, but for Aubrey it was almost impossible to see her father as the hero in this story.

It just goes to show, she thought ruefully, *there is someone for everyone, even those that seem most unlovable.*

Which led to a surge of guilt. Her father wasn't *unlovable.* She loved him. Her mother had loved him. It was just, on the surface, he didn't seem the type to inspire a passion that would last five decades.

Her order was called, and she rose, gratefully discarding her uncomfortable thoughts.

As had become her custom, she used the alley to access the rear of her home and parked on the packed dirt that passed as a driveway. Carefully carrying the containers of her dinner, she manoeuvred through the gap in the fence where a gate should have hung and made her way into the unsightly back yard.

Phillip's landscaping quote had been extremely reasonable, yet she'd hesitated to accept it. It would be a tacit agreement to seeing him on a regular basis, to being a part of his world, at least while the job was in progress. Not that she thought he would be doing any of the manual labour, but still—

In the end, she'd gone for it. Even before she'd decided to help with the search for her half-brother, she'd known there would be little chance of avoiding Phillip since he was determined on the quest. She figured in for a penny, in for a pound.

Demolition—for want of a better word—of the yard was slated to begin in a week or so. She wasn't in a hurry, as she hadn't yet confirmed any of the renovations to the house. In the meantime, for her own pleasure, she'd cleared a space near the steps leading to the back door, dragged out a small, rusty table she'd discovered in the basement, bought two cheap but comfortable outdoor chairs, and planted three terracotta pots with geraniums, impatiens, alyssum, and petunias. The cheery blossoms added colour and scent and made it easier to ignore the rampant weeds and scrubby grass infesting the rest of the area.

Her tiny patio was currently bathed in sunlight, so she decided to have her dinner outdoors. Placing the containers on the table, she went inside, leaving the door open to let in fresh air. She changed into denim shorts and a T-shirt, poured herself a glass of wine, and headed back outside.

She came to a sudden stop at the open door, involuntarily emitting a startled "Hey!"

A scrawny orange blur streaked off the table, where the creature had been investigating her dinner. She hustled down the steps, confirmed the containers were still intact, and then peered into the undergrowth hiding the lower part of the fence separating her yard from the neighbour's.

Two green eyes stared back at her, unblinking.

"Here, kitty, kitty, kitty." She crouched and held out her hand, rubbing her fingertips together. "Where did you come from?"

No answer.

The grass and weeds where the cat had taken refuge weren't much of a hiding place, and the bumps of its spine were visible under its matted fur. "You look hungry. Don't you have a home?"

One ear twitched. The one that didn't have a chunk taken out of it. From its looks, the cat had been on its own for a while. Her heart melted.

"If you promise to leave my dinner alone, I'll go inside and get you something." She eased to her feet. The cat watched her with suspicion but didn't move.

Worried, not for her own meal but that the cat would use her departure as an excuse to disappear, she snatched up a can of tuna, a saucer, and a can opener and rushed back outside. The bedraggled beast was still crouched in the thicket of grass.

"If that's your idea of a safe place to hide, no wonder you're having a rough time." She kept her tone low and conversational as she cranked the opener around the rim of the can, holding it over the saucer to catch the juice. "You don't seem very street savvy."

She scraped half the tuna onto the saucer and the cat's nose flared as it caught the scent. Carrying the dish, she made her way in a wide arc toward the end of the fence nearest the alley. She placed the saucer on the ground about five metres from the cat and then slowly retraced her steps.

"I'd love some company for dinner." She opened her containers and took a bite of maki. "We're both having tuna, even."

The cat watched her for a few minutes, and then cautiously rose into a loose crouch and took a slinking step. She ignored it, sipping her wine as she munched her meal. She was half done by the time the cat reached the saucer. It attacked the fish, swallowing in great gulps.

"Slow down," she warned. "You don't want to get sick."

The cat ignored her.

"I've never had a pet before." *That* got its attention. It paused in its chewing long enough to shoot her a disgusted look. "Sorry, you're not a pet. Mine or anyone else's. I didn't mean to be insulting." Appeased, it went back to its single-minded consumption.

Dealing with the cat had distracted her from the topic that had engrossed her for days. Even if she never saw it again, she was thankful for that. She went back inside to refill her wine, and then returned to the patio to watch her new acquaintance fill its stomach while enjoying the heat of the June sun on her face.

CHAPTER TWELVE

Phillip watched Aubrey enter Café Voltaire through the rear door. She paused, scanning the scattered tables, and he raised a hand to catch her attention. She gestured to the order counter, making the universal sign for *drink*. He nodded and waited for her to join him, curbing his impatience.

Several minutes later she wound her way to his table, carrying a thick white mug with something foamy in it. Her butt had barely hit the chair when he blurted, "She named him Joseph. She was allowed to hold him for a few minutes after he was born, and she named him Joseph."

Sadness and understanding softened her expression. "That's my dad's middle name. She wanted to give him something of his father, even if it was only temporary. The adoptive parents probably changed it, but at least, for a little while, he was theirs."

"Yes." Out of everything that Marjorie had said during their conversation yesterday, that small fact had made the biggest impact, sliding under his skin like a sliver. It stuck there, infected and irritating. "She cried when she told me. Just a little, but she never cries."

Aubrey patted his hand, her fingers warm from the mug and slightly rough. "The pain never goes away completely. You know that."

"So do you." He resisted the impulse to turn his hand over and clasp hers. "I just hope that digging through the past is the right thing to do."

Her eyebrows rose. "Now *you're* having second thoughts?"

"No, not really. It was just hard watching her remember those days." He sipped his tea. "How did it go with Clarence?"

Her lips pressed together. "I still get the feeling he'd rather let sleeping dogs lie, but I don't think he'll obstruct the search. He agreed to do the DNA test and gave me the name of the lawyer he asked to arrange the adoption. Duncan Truble."

"That's a good start." He flipped open the small notepad he'd brought and asked her to spell it. "According to Marjorie, Clarence never told her the lawyer's name, and she didn't ask."

"The whole process was very secretive. It was all done under the table." She wrinkled her nose. "That sounds bad, but I don't know how else to describe it. Dad didn't hire Truble. They were friends, and he handled it as a favour."

"If the affair had gotten out, it would have been a terrific scandal. Add in the fact Marjorie was pregnant"—he swirled his mug gently as he worked out what to say next—"it could have ruined her chances of getting into university, then medical school. To say nothing of your father's marriage and his career."

Her eyes flashed. "I have much less sympathy for my dad, to be bluntly honest. Not only was he the only one married—and a pious Catholic, to boot!—he was her *boss*. He held all the power, and she was the one who suffered for it."

"You might be underestimating Marjorie's role. I know she was barely nineteen at the time, but I find it hard to believe she wasn't a full and active participant."

"Do you think I *want* to believe my father took advantage of his secretary?" Her words rose above the clatter and clamour of the café and a few heads turned. She crossed her arms on the table and leaned forward, lowering her voice. "This is making me rethink everything I believe about him."

Despite her condemnation, her tone was soft and pleading, begging for reassurance. "He's a human being, Aubrey. He made mistakes. He hurt people." He decided not to point out that one of those people was his own daughter. "But Marjorie has forgiven him. She still loves him. If she can let it go, I guess we can, too."

She breathed out a soft sigh and he caught the flavour of cinnamon and coffee and the hint of fresh mint. She relaxed back in her seat. "I suppose. It just made me so mad when he told me what happened after Marjorie discovered she was pregnant."

"She told me she felt lucky in some ways. It was simple enough to tell people she was leaving Clarence's firm and the city because she'd taken a new position in Kamloops. She didn't have to make up a lie about visiting relatives, like other young women did."

"It was still a lie."

"Yes, but a better one, one that was easier for people to believe. Especially when she did go. Her parents knew the truth, of course, and after their initial shock and disappointment, she says they stood by her. Her mother spent weeks at a time in Kamloops under the guise of helping her get settled. She rented a small apartment and arranged for a doctor's care."

"And needed to lie again. She said she was a widow and used her mother's maiden name instead of her own."

He was relieved Clarence and Marjorie's stories matched so far. "It was the best she could do in the situation. It was crappy then and is unbelievable now, but it would have seemed necessary at the time."

"According to Dad, he and Marjorie agreed not to go through an adoption agency. They felt it was too risky, that the chances of someone finding out their secret would be greater through official channels. He and Duncan Truble had gone to law school together, had kept in touch after they started their own firms, Dad in

Prince George and Truble in Kamloops. He was the reason Marjorie went there instead of somewhere else. Dad couldn't be with her, but he trusted Truble to stand in his stead. He was the only person who knew the truth, that my dad was the baby's father. All their correspondence implied it was someone else. Even the birth certificate didn't include his name."

It was his turn to be shocked. "Clarence wasn't noted as the father on the birth certificate?"

She shook her head. "Dad said Marjorie listed the father as unknown. Didn't she tell you?"

"No. She never mentioned it." He'd been suppressing his protective instincts ever since learning about Joseph, even before he knew the name Marjorie had given her baby. But the glowing embers he'd been tamping down heated at this news. "Now *that* makes me angry. What was Clarence thinking? He knew how that would make her look."

"She was shielding him. And still is. I imagine that's why she didn't tell you even now."

When Samantha died, he had ached to protect Aubrey, to take away the pain and suffering that etched lines in her face. Maybe he could understand Marjorie's need to shelter Clarence. But he'd never understand how Clarence could *allow* her to do so. If taking the responsibility for Samantha's death might have helped Aubrey, he would have. He would have done *anything* to take the burden from her shoulders.

He could feel a muscle flexing in his jaw and had to force his words out through gritted teeth. "Marjorie was alone and frightened, and yet she carried all the blame. She should have demanded Clarence take his share of the responsibility. *He* should have refused to let her do it all on her own."

Aubrey sympathized wholeheartedly with Phillip's bitterness. "I agree. Really, I do. To give my father a tiny bit of credit, though, he says he argued against it. He trusted Truble and thought he should be told the whole story. But Marjorie insisted."

"According to him." His clenched expression did not bode well for his next encounter with her father.

"Yes, according to him. But before you start scattering too much blame, why don't you ask Marjorie?" Since meeting him again, he'd rarely shown as much emotion as he had today, had been the stalwart bulwark on which she'd leaned after learning about Joseph. It gave her a little thrill to think she might also help him through this turmoil.

"Oh, I will." His eyes were flat and grim. "And if she agrees with Clarence's statement, I'm going to give her a piece of my mind."

The old-fashioned phrase tickled her, and she snorted a small laugh, a welcome relief from the tense conversation.

"What?" He glared at her suspiciously.

"I'm sorry. It's nothing. You just sounded very...cantankerous. Grouchy."

"I know what cantankerous means."

She relaxed when his expression eased, the on-the-edge-of-losing-it look fading. "Why berate her about something she did almost a decade before you were born, something that can't be undone?"

"You didn't have quite the same carefree opinion of your father."

She shifted to loosen the band of guilt cinching her chest. "Maybe not. But I'm working on it.'

He scanned her face a moment or two, and then leaned back in his chair, shoulders slumping. "You're right. It doesn't change anything, since *we* know who the father is, no matter what's on the birth certificate."

She decided it was time to get off that particular subject. "Did she agree to the DNA test?"

"Yes. She's had a little experience with them in a health setting, and understands the limitations, but agrees it's a path we can't ignore."

"Great. I'll order them today."

"And we should try and track down Truble. It's probably too much to hope he's still practicing, especially if he's the same age as your dad."

She bit her lip. "I hope you don't mind, but I've already started on that."

"Of course you have, and, no, I don't mind. What did you find?"

"Dad said he didn't keep in touch with Truble after the adoption—*Joseph's* adoption." A shiver whispered over her skin when she said her half-brother's name out loud for the first time. Even if it wasn't the name he was now known by it was still a powerful connection. Shaking off the tug of blood, she continued. "He knew Truble was in Kamloops at least until the late sixties, but lost track after that. So I spoke with a former colleague at Wakim, Wing and Wright." It had felt very odd, calling her old firm as an outsider—and evoked a tiny pang of wistfulness. She'd enjoyed much of her time there, after all. Her colleague had sounded pleased to hear from her and her initial nervousness had passed quickly. "Not that every lawyer in British Columbia knows every other lawyer, but he is one of the older partners, so I thought it was possible he might recognize the name. He didn't."

"I can see how that would be a long shot." Phillip lifted one shoulder in commiseration.

"He said he'd ask around for me, but I'm not holding my breath. Then I checked the Lawyer Directory on the Law Society of British Columbia website. There's no Duncan Truble, or any person with that last name, listed."

"That would have been too easy, I guess."

"Yes." Her conviction that finding Joseph was the right thing to do was still a little fragile, and she wasn't sure if she was relieved or frustrated the search had started with a whimper. "Lastly, I did a Google search using Truble and Kamloops. I was hoping his name was still attached to a law firm even if he was no longer practicing, or that someone else with the same surname might pop up. No luck there, either."

"I assume that means our next step will be to call every firm currently operating in Kamloops and see if they've heard of him?"

She nodded. "I can't think of anything better."

"We can split that job, if you like." He pushed his empty cup to one side as if ready to tackle the task immediately. "Draw up a list and give me half."

"All right." She sipped her cappuccino and fiddled with her spoon. Even though the coffee shop was full of babble and clatter, the silence between them stretched taut.

He broke in before she could leap to her feet and flee out the door. "How are the renovations going? You're still good with my crew starting next week, right?"

She grasped the conversational branch gratefully. "Yes, that should work. If they can clear out Steve and the other overgrown areas it will make access easier for the renovation contractors. Then, while the house is being worked on, I can confirm the garden design with you, and we'll jump into the actual landscaping as soon as the worst of the exterior work is done."

"That's the plan."

Despite his agreeable tone, she flushed. He had known all that, since he was the one who'd suggested the schedule. Maybe it was time to leave, before she said anything else ridiculous. They'd met specifically to talk about the adoption search, and that conversation was over. But despite her discomfort, there was something very pleasant in sitting with an attractive man, whiling away quiet moments without purpose or agenda.

"I made a friend after I left your place on Sunday." *I guess I'm not leaving yet.*

"Oh?"

"A stray cat. He appeared in my back yard and has

hung around ever since."

Phillip shook his head, smiling. "You're feeding it, aren't you?"

She grinned self-consciously. "He was really skinny. I couldn't *not* feed the poor thing."

"He's never going to leave if you keep that up."

His tone was amused, rather than condemning, and her chest warmed at the gentle ribbing. It had been a long time since she hadn't had to weigh every word, fearful of being misquoted or misinterpreted.

"Is it a he?" he asked. "Can you tell?"

"He hasn't let me touch him, but I got a good look as he ran away. Definitely a he."

"Should I open book on how long it will take you to make him a pet?"

"Don't call him a pet. He doesn't like that."

Phillip's eyebrows rose and he chuckled. "I won't ask why you think you know that." He tilted his head. "Have you ever had a pet? I don't recall you having one as a teenager, and you and I never did."

She shrugged. "No. Not unless you count Sophie's goldfish, which I looked after for the few weeks it lived."

"Goldfish don't count. They're disposable." His gaze was affectionate and friendly and the warmth lit in Aubrey at his earlier teasing heated to an amber glow. "Maybe it's time you had one."

Despite the red cat's continued skittishness, she had hopes he was losing the worst of his fear. He was spending more time in full view, not skulking in the bushes, and the day before had relaxed enough to doze in a patch of sunshine while she'd scraped the worst of the rust off her outdoor table.

She found comfort in his undemanding company. Not that she minded being alone, which was a good thing given the amount of time she'd spent in that state. After she and Phillip divorced, she had gone to university, and then law school, and then started her career. She met Oliver when she was in her late thirties, but at the time he was only recently divorced, and it had taken him half a decade to convince her to marry. The years that followed had been good—personally happy, professionally productive—and when he'd died in the plane crash, she'd grieved him deeply and honestly thought she'd be alone for the rest of her life.

Now Phillip was back in her sphere, she had a half-brother to find, and if she wanted, she could have a pet...er...animal companion.

"Maybe." She tapped her nails on the table thoughtfully. "Maybe it is."

CHAPTER THIRTEEN

Dexter and Phillip unhooked their bikes from the chairlift and wheeled them down the unloading ramp. The view from the top of Tabor Mountain on this Saturday morning left much to be desired, as the bright June weather had broken, allowing thick, low clouds to roll in and hide the landscape. The air was damp and chill and beads of moisture condensed on the nylon sleeves of their jackets.

"I'm getting too old for this." Dexter shook one leg as if his foot was asleep. "It's going to rain later, I'm sure of it."

"Your bursitis acting up?" Phillip said with mock solicitousness as he buckled the strap of his helmet and pulled on his full-fingered gloves.

"Screw you. You're the one with a bum hip. You'll be laughing out of the other side of your mouth when you can't walk later."

Because he only spoke the truth, Phillip ignored him. "I'm not ready for the rocking chair yet. Saddle up."

Since he wasn't insane and didn't have a death wish, he led Dexter to Baby Moose, a beginner trail that would be just right as a warmup. Downhill mountain biking was a different skill set than the cross-country they usually did, and he took the big, round rollers at a controlled pace. Even so, by the time they reached the base of the mountain and lined up to ride the lift back to the top, adrenaline rushed through his veins.

"How's the mid-life crisis going?" Dexter asked casually as the chair scooped them up and carried them a few metres before stopping to allow a pair of riders behind them to load their bikes. "You seem a little less cranky."

The hill was busy, and it would be a slow, jolting journey to the top. Phillip sighed. He could avoid the question and his ex-brother-in-law wouldn't force it, but they might as well talk about something. And when he thought about it, Dr. Dexter Seymour might have some useful insight.

"I'm not as...itchy," he admitted. "Asher had an interview early this week that he thought went really well, but he hasn't heard anything definite yet, so I'm trying not to angst until I have to. And work is still work—I haven't made any decisions there, either. But at the moment I've been distracted by a mystery Marjorie sprang on me."

He recapped the last few days quickly. "Aubrey sent my half of the list of lawyers Thursday, but I didn't have time to do anything with it yesterday, so now it will have to wait until Monday, when the offices reopen. We've agreed emails are too easily ignored, so we intend to call each one."

The chair swooped and swung as it passed over a tower, the unloading ramp in sight. "How's she handling this? Learning you have a long-lost sibling can be very distressing."

"I think she's better now she's decided to do something about it. It's given her a sense of purpose."

"That can be beneficial. If she wants to talk, I can suggest a couple therapists. Or I can point her to resources that might be useful if she wants to do her own self-help."

"Thanks. I'll let her know." The chair stopped at the upper reaches of the lift and they dismounted, detached their bikes, and began another descent.

On their fourth trip, the threatening rain made its

appearance. Droplets pelted his goggles and pinged against his chest as they raced down the mountain. He stood on his pedals and allowed his bike to jolt and jump beneath him, hip aching as his body flexed in response. When they braked to a stop near the lodge, he was more than happy to agree to Dexter's suggestion they check out the comforts of the common room and have a bite to eat.

They bought overpriced hamburgers and fries and sugary soft drinks, and then found a table in a corner with a view up the mountain. It was raining in earnest now and many riders were making their way to the parking lot.

"I've been thinking about Marjorie's story." Dexter dipped a fry into ketchup. "If you do find your cousin, what are you going to do? Will Marjorie be happy knowing what happened to him and leave it at that, or does she intend on making contact?"

"She hasn't said, but why go to all this trouble and *not* try to meet?"

"Which leads to a whole host of other issues. What if he doesn't know he's adopted? How does she feel about being the catalyst for that revelation to a sixty-year-old man? If he does know, what if he has no interest in meeting his birth parents? There's a lot of potential for heartbreak in this."

"I know. Aubrey and I have talked about this a little already. But Marjorie and Clarence can make that decision when we come to it. We have to find Joseph first."

Dexter paused in mid-bite. "Joseph?"

He nodded. "It was the name she put on his birth certificate. I'm not sure if allowing the birth mother to name her child before taking it away is cruel or compassionate."

"At least she had the chance."

A bitter edge to his tone made Phillip frown. Dexter ate another fry, then shoved his still half-full plate away.

"Did Jeanette ever mention our older sister?"

Phillip froze. "No. Never. You have an older sister?"

Dexter toyed with the straw in his drink, avoiding his stare. "Ever hear of The Sixties Scoop?"

Those two words told him all he needed to know. "My god, Dex, I'm so sorry." The wide-spread and long-enacted practice of removing Indigenous children from their parents played a dark role in Canada's history, and he certainly recognized the bone-chilling name of the massive action that resulted in many of those children being stripped of their heritage when placed with Euro-Canadian families.

"Mom and Dad's first daughter was taken away before she was a week old." Dexter's quiet voice brimmed with weary anger. "She was born on the reserve, and when news of the birth reached government officials, a social worker came to visit. It was late September, and Dad and most of the men from the village were on a hunting trip. Grandmother and the aunties were with Mom the first time, but she was alone when the social worker came back the next day with two more colleagues and took my sister."

He sucked in a breath. "Damn it, Dex. I don't know what to say. Here I've been bending your ear about Joseph when you..." He trailed off, realizing there was nothing he could say.

"Our sister may be lost to us, but she is not forgotten." The smile he offered was sad but proud. "And though the circumstances are entirely different, all I see are two mothers, one white, one Indigenous, both grieving. If there's anything I can do to help, just let me know."

Saturday's rain continued through Sunday but had eased by Monday morning. Aubrey poured her second cup of coffee and tucked herself into the corner of the worn sofa in her living room, wriggling to get into the right position so the springs didn't poke her in the butt.

She lit up her tablet and tapped to the spreadsheet she'd created with the list of lawyers from Kamloops. She'd found nearly thirty firms—some that appeared to be only a single lawyer, others with multiple partners and associates. A few sounded familiar from her years at Wakim, Wing and Wright, but her network of contacts had thinned since she'd left the industry, and none of the names stood out as potential allies in her search.

She had started making cold calls on Friday, her heart pounding in her throat as she'd dialled the numbers. There was no guarantee this plan would lead them to Duncan Truble, but it was certainly a *possible* outcome. Which meant that each time she reached out, her gut churned.

After getting in touch with five firms, she had been exhausted from nervous tension, and unreasonably disappointed at her lack of success. Three had been young sole proprietors with no historical knowledge or connections and could be quickly crossed off. At the other two, the receptionists had allowed her to make appointments to call back, but not until Monday.

Between nervous anticipation and the dreary weather, it had been a long, long weekend.

She'd woken before her alarm and now had to keep occupied until such time as she could start calling again. She had just tapped over to the online house design program on which she'd whiled away several rainy hours when a knock sounded at the front door. She opened it to reveal a short, stocky young man with long dark hair under a ball cap with the *Twin Rivers* logo on it.

"Aubrey Windt?"

"Yes. You're the landscape crew." She hadn't expected them quite this early, but she should have known Phillip would run his operation efficiently.

"I'm Jackson. Carly is unloading the machine." He

jerked a thumb over his shoulder, drawing her attention past Steve to two pickup trucks parked at the curb, one towing a flat deck loaded with a small skid steer, the other attached to a large dump trailer. "We should go over the scope of work before we get started."

"Of course. I'll come around and meet you."

He nodded and traipsed down the steps. She shut the door and made her way through the house to the mudroom in the addition and out the back. The next several minutes were spent pointing out what was what and confirming her expectations. Carly, similar in build to Jackson though the ponytail sticking out of the back of her ball cap was blonde, competently backed the skid steer off the flat deck amid piercing warning beeps and a growling engine.

Jackson spoke over the roar. "I think we're good to go. You sticking around to watch?"

She shook her head. It was silly, but she didn't think she could bear witness to Steve's destruction. "No, I'll leave you to it. I'm going to grab some things and head out for the day."

He shrugged. "Whatever works for you. I've got your cell if we have any questions."

She took a couple steps toward the house, and then paused.

"Just one more thing." What she was about to ask felt a little ridiculous. The cat was smart enough to stay out of the way of an excavator. But she'd feel worse if she didn't and something happened. "Can you and Carly keep an eye out for a cat? A red cat? He's a stray that's been hanging around, and I don't want him to get hurt by accident."

She'd stood at the back door several times over the weekend, can of tuna in hand, chirruping an invitation to refuge, thinking the rain might convince him to cross her threshold, but she hadn't caught a glimpse of him. She assumed he was holed up somewhere, and hoped it was dry.

"Will do." Jackson waved to get Carly's attention, and she halted the skid steer halfway down the ramp. "I'll tell her right now. Anything else?"

"No. Thanks." She strode back to the house, leaving Steve to his fate.

CHAPTER FOURTEEN

It had been several days since Aubrey had been to her condo. Since she couldn't be at Cedar Street, she decided she might as well check on things and take advantage of the quiet there.

And it was definitely quiet. She still wasn't sure why her solitude at Cedar Street was both comforting and comfortable, while the same isolation was the exact opposite in her condo. But it would only be for a few hours. She could handle it for that long.

She settled at her dining room table with her tablet, old school notepad and pen, and cell phone, determined to get through the rest of her half of the list of lawyers that day. Taking a deep breath, she found where she'd left off on Friday, and dialled the next number on her list.

"Presley Whitman Law Firm. How may I direct your call?"

The male voice was brisk and professional. She introduced herself and slipped into the patter she'd perfected. "I am trying to find the current contact information for Duncan Truble. He began practicing law in the Kamloops area in the late 1950s."

"I'm sorry, but Mr. Truble passed away last year."

The reply came so quickly and was stated so matter-of-factly that for a moment Aubrey wasn't sure she'd heard correctly. "You knew Mr. Truble?" This was her first phone call of the day. It couldn't be that easy.

"I knew *of* him," the man clarified. "He retired many years before I came to work for Presley Whitman, but his photo still hangs in our boardroom, along with all our former partners."

"He practiced with your firm?" Her stunned shock was fading, excitement taking its place. "He was a partner there?"

"Yes. It was Presley Whitman Truble at the time. I'm sorry, Ms. Windt, but can you tell me what this is about?"

She scrambled to sound coherent, still reeling that she'd gotten a result so quickly. "Mr. Truble was a friend of my father's. He was hoping to reconnect. My father, I mean." She and Phillip had agreed not to mention the true reason for their quest until necessary. Doing so to anyone other than Truble himself could create complications, given the adoption had been handled with no formal agreement.

"I see. I'm sorry to give you news of his death, then."

It had always been a possibility, of course, so she had prepared a follow up question. "Could you put me in touch with a member of Mr. Truble's family? I'm sure my father would still like to speak with someone, perhaps a son or daughter?" She held her breath and waited for the receptionist's response.

"I believe there may be someone here who could assist you." Exhilaration washed from her head to her toes, and she clenched her fists to hold back a shout of glee. "May I have your phone number? I will speak with them and get back to you."

"Thanks very much for your time." Phillip disconnected his most recent call to a lawyer in Kamloops and leaned back with a sigh.

He'd come into the office early to get a head start the day, including making sure Jackson and Carly left on time and had all the information they needed to start demolition at Aubrey's. Then he'd closed his door and started on the list she had assigned him. He hadn't talked to her since she'd sent the names on Thursday, and he wanted to be able to give her a progress report when she did get in touch.

Not that he had any news yet. He was batting .000 after seven attempts.

He had time to make a couple more calls before it would be necessary to get back to his real work. As he reached for the phone, the screen lit up.

Asher.

He took a deep, steadying breath, then swiped to connect. "Hey, bud! How's it going?"

"I got it." Asher sounded stunned. "I got the Winnipeg sports anchor job. I start in three weeks."

His heart dropped out of his chest, and he closed his eyes. How was it possible to be so incredibly proud and yet so terribly sad at the same time? "Congratulations!" He hoped Asher wouldn't hear the dismay in his voice. It was one thing to be disappointed his son was leaving town. It was another entirely to let that same son know how much it cost his father to be happy for him.

"It's amazing. I'll be covering the NHL and all the junior hockey teams, and the city is hosting the World Figure Skating Championships next year. I'm the main sports anchor on the weekends and late night on three weekdays, while doing reporting as well. And I'm fill-in for the senior sports anchor when she isn't available." His excitement grew with every word, and Phillip tried to match his enthusiasm. This was what Asher had worked so hard for, and in many ways, it was also what Phillip and Jeanette had striven toward, too. Sons who were independent, happy, successful, and thriving.

He just wished—he cut off the thought. It was selfish to want to keep his boys close. Sure, he'd see less of Asher after the move, but he'd just have to make time to visit his son as often as his Twin Rivers duties would allow.

Finally, Asher's well-deserved elation ran down. "I haven't told anyone else yet. Not even my boss. I want to make sure it's all tied up first. So keep it a secret for now, okay?"

"Of course. Let me know when it's public. I'm proud of you, Asher. Very proud. You deserve this chance."

"Thanks, Dad. I'll call you later."

Silence rang through the room after he disconnected. Phillip stared blindly at the list Aubrey had given him, the words blurred and indistinct. Any energy he'd had for the search for Joseph had leaked out of him with Asher's news. He'd get to it tomorrow. Maybe.

A voicemail notification flashed on his phone. Dispiritedly, he started the recording.

Aubrey's voice emanated from the speaker. "Phillip. Call me. It's about Joseph."

He couldn't help a shiver of interest at her words. He tapped the screen and Aubrey answered after one ring. "What are you doing at two o'clock today?" she said without preamble.

"Nothing I can't get out of." His spine straightened and his grip on his phone tightened. "What's going on?"

"I found Duncan Truble."

Phillip pulled out the chair next to Aubrey and sat. Her phone lay on the surface in front of them. 1:58 was displayed in large numbers on its screen.

After giving him a concise precis of her conversations with the Kamloops law firm, she'd instructed him to meet her at her condo. He'd spent the next few hours rearranging his schedule, cramming in any tasks he couldn't put off, and had managed to ring the buzzer at the main entrance right on time.

The moment he had seen her at the door of her apartment, he had felt an almost overwhelming urge to tell her about Asher, despite his promise to keep the news under wraps. She could be trusted not to reveal the secret—he knew that in his bones. But he couldn't betray his son for his own comfort and clamped his lips together.

She ushered him into her apartment with an air of distraction. He looked around curiously, knowing she'd lived here for numerous years and expecting to see the stamp of her personality everywhere. But it was as soulless and tidy as a hotel room, and the chill in the air wasn't just from the air-conditioning.

Wishing they were at Cedar Street, which felt much more like a home, he dragged his focus to the matter at hand, pushing Asher and the mystery of Aubrey away. "Who's this lawyer we're going to be talking to?"

She replied without taking her gaze from the phone. "She's a partner at Presley Whitman, the law firm where Duncan Truble last worked."

"What's her connection with Truble? Other than the law firm, of course?"

Aubrey didn't reply. She was vibrating with suppressed emotion, her knee jogging under the table so quickly it made his own chair shimmy. He placed his fingers on her thigh, and she stilled.

Heat snaked from his palm to his cock like a spark running along a fuse. He unlocked his muscles, gave her a pat he hoped she'd interpret as comforting, not sexual, and returned his hand to the table. "Her connection with Truble?" Desire roughened his voice.

She shot him a glance from the corner of her eye, a faint flush on her cheeks. "I don't know. All the receptionist said was that she's willing to talk to us."

"Well, that's a start."

At exactly two o'clock, the phone rang. She snatched it up and connected the call, bringing it to her ear.

"Aubrey Windt speaking."

"Annamarie Whitman. I understand you have some questions about Duncan Truble." The words were muffled, but Phillip could make them out if he concentrated.

"Do you mind if I put you on speaker?" Aubrey's voice was calm and professional, but she was pressing the fingers of her free hand onto the table with such force the nails were bloodless. "I have Phillip Church with me. He has an interest in this, as well." At Whitman's agreement, she laid the phone on the table and switched to speaker mode. "Can you hear me, Ms. Whitman?"

"Yes. So, to confirm, I'm speaking with Aubrey Windt and Phillip Church?"

"Nice to meet you, Ms. Whitman." He couldn't take his gaze from the phone's screen, as if staring at it would coerce her to spill her secrets sooner.

Her voice was light and crisp. "I understand Clarence Windt wants to speak with the family of Duncan Truble. I knew Mr. Truble a very long time and I don't recall him ever mentioning that name."

"They lost touch many years ago, but my father is anxious to reconnect."

"I Googled you, Ms. Windt, and your father. Given both your backgrounds in law and politics, I'm sure you'll understand why I am wary to pass on private information."

"Of course. But couldn't you give whoever you know my phone number and perhaps persuade them to call me? We just want to talk." If he hadn't been able to see the lines of stress around her mouth, he would have thought this phone call meant nothing to Aubrey. How could she sound so serene when his heart was beating so hard it choked him?

"If you could perhaps explain why your father wants to reconnect..."

Her mouth opened and closed and she shot him a look of mild panic. He decided to lay their cards on the table. "My aunt and Aubrey's father conceived a child out of wedlock in 1959." For some reason, the occasion seemed to call for the old-fashioned phrasing. "The child, a boy, was born in 1960 and placed for adoption with the unofficial help of Duncan Truble. They now want to learn what happened to the child."

Whitman was silent for several decades. He clenched and unclenched his fists to relieve his growing tension.

"Why now? Why do they want to find him after sixty years?"

It was a fair question. He did his best to explain Marjorie and Clarence's circumstances clearly and succinctly.

"I see." She sounded curious and thoughtful. He began to take heart. At least she hadn't dismissed them out of hand. Yet. "You said Truble helped unofficially?"

"Yes." Aubrey breathed in through her nose. "My father needed to keep the baby a secret. I know it sounds bad, but they were only doing what they thought best at the time. Do you think you can help us?"

"What information do you think Truble's family will be able to provide?"

"We're hoping he might have left notes in a private file or diary." She shifted and her chair creaked. "Something that might lead to the adoptive family, or perhaps the organization that arranged it."

The condo was silent except for the whirring of the refrigerator motor and muted traffic noises from outside. He strangled his impatience through another lengthy pause.

"You must know the chances of something like that existing after so many years are infinitesimal." Whitman was still cautious but seemed willing to be convinced. "If it does exist, however, there's a good chance my father kept it somewhere."

His breath snagged in his throat. Aubrey stared, eyes wide. Their gazes locked. "Your *father?*" he demanded.

A sigh sounded through the speaker. "I hope you'll forgive my subterfuge, but I needed to find out what you wanted before I revealed my own connection. Duncan Truble was my father."

Aubrey tapped the screen to disconnect the call and leaned her elbows on the table. Her hips ached—whether from the chair's hard wooden back and stiffly padded seat or the tension of the last few minutes she wasn't sure.

"What are the chances she'll be able to find anything?" Phillip asked. "Unless her father was a true packrat, why would he have bothered keeping his notes for sixty years?"

"Most lawyers I know *are* packrats. We have a horror of throwing away something that we'll need someday. Especially, if we think there is a chance the issue might be resurrected or is of a sensitive nature."

"Like adoption?"

She nodded, twisting slightly in her seat to face him. "Like adoption. And even though this was a favour for a friend, I have hopes that Truble will have followed his instincts and kept a paper trail." For the first time since Phillip arrived, she focused on him. She'd been too wrapped up in what Annamarie Whitman might reveal to even offer him coffee. "I'm sorry. Did you want a drink or something? I forgot—"

"You had other things on your mind." He smiled, and the grooves at the corners of his mouth set something fluttering deep in her belly. She'd lamented to Natalie how he had lost none of his good looks during their years apart. What she hadn't confessed, and had no intention of *ever* confessing, was how she found him more attractive than ever.

"What are your plans for dinner tonight?"

His husky, low voice swept over her skin like a hot June breeze. Her thigh, where he'd touched her earlier, felt seared, branded. "Why?"

His smile widened, as if he found her caution

amusing. "Well, we both have to eat. I thought it might be nice to do that together. We might even talk about something other than Joseph and Marjorie and Clarence."

Sun slanted in the window, bouncing off the shiny surface of the table and glaring into her face. That's what caused the sudden moisture in her eyes, not this overwhelming craving for solace, for companionship, for connection. She shouldn't read too much into his simple dinner invitation.

An invitation she yearned to accept yet feared.

He waited for her answer, shoulders relaxed, slumped slightly in his chair. She, on the other hand, was so tightly coiled she thought she might launch from her seat. She had no intention of examining why she felt that way. "What else do we have to talk about?"

"Old times? The last thirty years?" He stretched out his arm and the fabric of his shirt tightened across his chest. His fingertips bumped over the knuckles of her hand as it rested on the table. It was the barest whisper of a touch, yet she felt it in her toes.

"I don't—" She couldn't finish the sentence, not sure what she had intended to say, too confused by the conflicting emotions roiling through her to articulate them.

"It's just dinner, Aubrey, not an indecent proposal." The teasing smile lingered on his lips, but impatience edged his tone.

It was ridiculous to feel this churned up, and Aubrey *hated* feeling ridiculous. So why on earth would she commit to spending more time with the man that created that feeling? Opening her mouth to make a polite refusal, she heard herself say, "What time and where?"

CHAPTER FIFTEEN

Aubrey drove from her condo to Cedar Street on automatic pilot, her thoughts preoccupied with Annamarie Whitman's revelation, Phillip's unexpected invitation, and her brain's insubordination.

What else did you call it when you intended to say one thing and something else entirely popped out?

She hadn't been able to retract her acceptance without looking foolish, so was stuck with the mutinous decision made by her subconscious. As her wardrobe at Cedar Street was limited to jeans and T-shirts, she'd ransacked the closet in her condo for something appropriate to wear. Unable to commit to one outfit and feeling the insistent tug of home, she'd grabbed handfuls of loaded hangers and draped the clothing haphazardly on the back seat. The bag of shoes she'd filled to overflowing bulged on the floor behind her.

Turning into the alley, she drove slowly past her neighbours' back yards, most hidden by neat fences, pulled into her parking space, and blinked at the open vista before her.

She could see through the gap between her house on the left and the fence on the right straight to Cedar Street. All the scrubby bushes and dried thickets of grass and weeds along the foundation were gone, as were the boards that had long ago separated the back yard from the alley.

Unloading the car could wait. She needed to see what else Jackson and Carly had accomplished.

She picked her way over the pattern of tire treads snaking everywhere. If there *had* been a lawn to demolish, the skid steer would have done a thorough job. The ground around the house was now a treacherous mess, but it was the start of something new, and excitement dawned like a summer's sun inside her. Resisting the urge to look over her shoulder, she traversed a ridge of soil, the ghostly remains of Steve's existence. The Twin Rivers trucks and trailers were gone, as was the concrete path that had led to the front door. Standing in the approximate place it used to join the sidewalk, she spun slowly to face the house, anticipation and anxiety warring in her chest.

Now it could no longer hide behind Steve's bulk, the house appeared even more forlorn and unloved. The peeling paint and scaly shingles drew her eye and while the bottle dash stucco still clinging to the walls sparkled in the afternoon sun, it only emphasized the decades between the house's past and its present.

Needing a wider view, she jogged across the street. Without its camouflage, her house was like the rotten tooth in a mouthful of shiny white caps. The homes on either side had been updated within recent memory with modern siding and wide-framed windows. They boasted neatly mown lawns and colourful flowerbeds. Now that she could *see* her house, she could also see how much work was needed to bring it up to par.

A smile spread across her face. She couldn't wait to get started, her fingertips itching with ideas.

But first, she had to get through tonight's dinner with Phillip.

Trudging back through the torn-up yard, she went to unlock the rear door in preparation for hauling in the wardrobe she'd brought. Near the wooden steps, a darting movement caught her eye.

"Red Cat?" She hunkered down on her haunches and peered under the stairs.

The addition did not include a basement, as she'd

discovered while exploring on her first day. The house inspector had assured her the foundation on which it rested was sturdy enough to last many more years, though the plywood that had been used to hide the gap between the earth and the floor was in the same state of disrepair as the rest of the house. Behind one of those splintered panels, she saw a flash of red.

"Hey, buddy." She spoke soothingly, coaxingly. "Is this where you've been hanging out?"

A pink nose and glittering eyes peeped out from the shadowy depths.

"Well, I'm glad all the noise didn't scare you away." She'd half-expected never to see Red Cat again, almost certain the commotion would frighten him off. The depth of her relief surprised her. "Just let me get my car unloaded and I'll bring out your supper."

Phillip knew he tended to show up unreasonably early when he eagerly anticipated an event.

Said knowledge didn't seem to be helpful in *changing* that tendency, however. Which was why he was killing time playing a word game on his phone while parked outside the restaurant twenty minutes before he was supposed to meet Aubrey.

He wasn't sure what impulse had caused him to extend his dinner invitation. It might have had something to do with Asher's news and the shock of finding Truble. It might also have had something to do with the fact that, ever since Aubrey had come back into his life, the sense of restless unhappiness that dogged him had lessened. As he'd told Dexter, he assumed it had more to do with the quest they were on than a deeper change in his psyche. But he'd take what he could get.

Looking up from his screen as he waited for the commercial between levels to end, he looked in his rear-view mirror and saw her car pull into one of the angled parking stalls on the other side of the street.

Apparently, he wasn't the only one arriving anxiously early.

Lights flashed and died as she put the sedan in park and killed the engine. He waited, but she didn't get out. Other vehicles passed between them, flashing across his mirror like minnows in a bowl and occasionally obscuring his view entirely as they waited for the lights to change at the end of the block.

Minutes ticked by and she remained stubbornly inside her vehicle. A large panel van concealed her entirely for several seconds, and when it finally moved, he was astonished to see the rear lights on her car were activated and she was backing out of the slot. He twisted in his seat and stared through the rear window of his pickup. As she paused to switch to drive, he caught a glimpse of her face, pale and set. Then she was gone.

What the hell?

He dropped into his seat and picked up his phone. There was still five minutes before their reservation. Had she forgotten something and intended to return? Or was it what it looked like—a frantic escape?

He was still wondering what to do when she pulled back into the still empty slot behind him. She'd only been gone long enough to drive around the block.

Now thoroughly confused, he leaped out of his truck and dodged across the street, threading between vehicles. He yanked on the driver's side door handle, but the vehicle was still running with the safety locks engaged. He'd caught her attention, though, and she looked up at him through the window.

Doing his best *not* to look crazy, he smiled, wiggling his fingers to indicate she should open the door. She did, and he backed up far enough to let her emerge.

"Good evening." With dismay he noted she once again had the shiny, shellacked look of Aubrey the politician. Then she adjusted the light scarf at her throat, and he heard the scratch of roughened skin on silk. He studied her and realized the veneer was cracking already. Her eyes were wary, her teeth worrying her bottom lip. He relaxed. His Aubrey was in there somewhere.

Her gaze flickered as if searching the line of vehicles parked behind him. "Have you been here long?"

"A few minutes." He waited, but she said nothing about her earlier arrival and departure. "Shall we go in?"

She straightened her shoulders and lifted her chin. "Of course. Lead the way."

As she still looked as if she might take fright and bolt at any moment, he clasped her hand, which felt chilled despite the summer sunshine. She followed him across the street and into the restaurant.

The subdued clatter of silverware and conversation filled the silent space between them. The hostess directed them to a table on the second level that overlooked the huge wood-burning pizza oven below. The atmosphere was casual and charming but not romantic, and he wished he'd suggested somewhere a little more intimate. Next time, maybe.

Arrested by the realization he was already planning a next time, he barely heard the server as he announced the day's specials. When he asked if they'd like to see a wine list, though, he roused himself. "Would you like to share a bottle?"

She hesitated, and then nodded. "Why not? I prefer white, if that's okay."

"Of course."

The server rattled off a list of choices. She asked several questions that sounded knowledgeable to his untutored ear. When she raised an eyebrow as if asking for his opinion, he waved her on. "You choose. It sounds like you know what you're doing."

The server faded away and another silence descended over them. Her face was placid as she looked everywhere but at him, though she fingered the napkin-wrapped bundle of silverware before her, ticking it back and forth like a metronome.

He'd felt so comfortable in her presence this afternoon. Why did it seem so awkward now? Searching for something to break the ice, he settled on, "How do you know so much about wine?"

"Oliver." A small smile curled the corners of her mouth. "He loved all things wine, including talking about it, and I couldn't help but learn."

He wondered if she ever smiled like that when she thought of him. He doubted it. Jealousy burned with green fire in his gut. "I've never offered my condolences. It was a shock to the whole community when he died in that plane crash."

"Thank you." Her lids lowered, concealing her thoughts.

"Do you miss him?" Her lids lifted at that, eyes wide with hurt, and he immediately wished the words back. "I mean, of course you miss him. He was your husband. I wasn't implying—"

She raised a hand, and he stopped babbling. "He's been gone four years now. I do miss him, but it's an easier ache. You know how it is."

He did. He hadn't lost a spouse—though divorce had its own grief cycle—but he had been old enough when his parents had drowned to understand the enormity. And then there was Samantha.

The server returned with the wine and poured a tiny amount into Aubrey's glass. He had always thought this ritual rather pointless—what kind of jerk would send back an already open bottle?—but she sniffed and sipped and savoured with a serious expression before nodding her approval. The server filled their glasses, took their orders, and vanished again.

She swallowed more wine and licked her lips as she placed the glass precisely back in place. "I hope it doesn't take too long for Annamarie to get back to us."

He didn't intend to talk about the search for Joseph

tonight. Tonight, he wanted to get to know Aubrey again. The more time he spent with her, the more he realized he was doing her an injustice with his constant internalized comparisons to the young woman she'd been. *He* wasn't the same man he'd been when they were married, so why should he expect *her* to be unchanged? Besides, he found this Aubrey intriguing. She had layers and depths and hidden secrets. He wanted to unwrap her.

For now, though, he'd follow her lead.

"What's your best guess? Could we hear tomorrow?"

"I have no idea. I can understand why she wants to take some time to absorb what we told her. Even though there was no attorney-client privilege between her father and mine, as a lawyer herself she'll want to consider the nuances before she goes any further."

It was easy to segue from that to a more personal topic. "Will you go back to practicing law, now that you're not in political office?" A thought struck him. "Or do you intend to run again in the next election?"

"No!" It was more exclamation than answer and he raised his eyebrows. Avoiding his gaze, she continued in a more moderate tone. "No more politics for me. I was honoured to serve, but one term was enough."

"So, back to the law, then?"

"I don't know. For now, I'm focusing on the house, taking some time for myself."

During the years between the dissolution of their marriage and reconnecting last month, he hadn't exactly *followed* her life and career, but he hadn't been able to avoid it entirely, either. The law firm she'd worked for was well known in Prince George, and while not the one that represented him or his business, he'd had some connections that did, and her name had come up occasionally. Then she'd married Oliver and, though not in the spotlight herself, he kept track of politics enough to be aware of her husband's career. Of course, the last few years she'd been very visible as a Member of the Legislative Assembly.

Nowhere in there was he aware she'd ever *taken time for herself.*

"Good for you. It sounds like the right time to re-evaluate things. I envy you."

He meant it sincerely but her brows vee'd with suspicion. "You do?"

He shrugged, and it was his turn to avoid eye contact. "I've been feeling at loose ends recently. My business is doing well, my boys are grown." He still didn't have the all-clear from Asher so couldn't mention that news yet. "It might be time for a new challenge. I just have no idea what."

He risked a glance across the table. She regarded him with a thoughtful expression, her head tilted to one side.

"Have you considered—" Her reply was cut off by a muted ringtone. She twisted in her seat and reached inside the leather purse hanging from the chair ear. "I'm sorry, I should have turned that off. Let me just—"

She turned back to him, phone in hand, her eyes wide. "It's Annamarie."

CHAPTER SIXTEEN

Aubrey had intended to ignore whoever was on the phone. Despite her initial misgivings about dinner with Phillip—to the extent she'd even changed her mind after arriving at the restaurant and driven away, before browbeating herself into returning—she'd begun to relax and enjoy herself. Learning that he also felt dissatisfied with his life had tweaked her interest, and she would have liked to explore that with him. Maybe he'd understand her own restlessness better than she'd thought he would.

"Aren't you going to answer it?"

His voice broke into her scattered thoughts, and she jolted. "Of course." She swiped to connect the call. "Aubrey speaking."

"I hope you don't mind me calling this late in the evening."

"Of course not. I am available at any time for this." She was pricklingly aware of Phillip studying her face, as if trying to read Annamarie's words in her expression.

"I thought of a few more questions I'd like to ask."

Sweat beaded her palm, and she gripped her phone tighter. "Of course. What would you like to know?"

"Has your father reviewed the information regarding reunions on the Government of British Columbia website? And has he requested a copy of the birth certificate, which would reveal any name changes?"

"Yes, he has." She had covered those topics with her father during their private conversation. Despite his age, he wasn't a Luddite, and as a lawyer was comfortable dealing with bureaucratic red tape. "He's waiting to hear back, but there is a complication. My father asked for an out of province adoption. If your father did as requested, the government won't have the information we need. We might have to reach out to every province in Canada. We were hoping your father would be able to narrow down the search."

Warmth enveloped her free hand where it lay on the table as Phillip twined his fingers with hers. She offered a weak smile and gripped tightly.

Annamarie said, "You do understand my father is not responsible for anything that may have happened *after* the adoption was completed."

"This isn't a search for revenge." She might not completely understand her father's motives, but she knew it wasn't that. "It's a search for closure. No matter what happened to their son, knowing is better than not. Neither my father nor Marjorie is looking to blame anyone for what may or may not have happened in the last sixty years."

A burst of laughter from a nearby table masked what Annamarie said next. "I'm sorry, I didn't get that."

"You've answered the questions I had for now," Annamarie said. "Why don't we talk again tomorrow?" They arranged a time for the following afternoon.

With regret, Aubrey slipped her hand out of Phillip's enveloping hold in order to disconnect the call.

"That didn't look like good news." He leaned back in his seat.

"It wasn't exactly *bad* news. Annamarie still hasn't decided what she's going to do."

"But she's still considering it?"

"I think so. She asked if we've tried the usual channels through the government." She met his inquiring gaze. "Maybe she just wants to be assured we've done what we can before she lets us see her father's private records."

"Do you think that means she *found* the notes? It's all moot if she can't lay her hands on them, after all."

"That's an excellent point. I'll talk with my dad, get all the details of what he's done so far and any updates there might be. Then I'll impress upon Annamarie the urgency to our search, try and pump up a little sympathy for an elderly couple finally getting their happy ending but still distraught over this missing part of their lives."

"That's the spirit." His grin warmed her chest, and a blush heated her cheeks. "What kind of law did you do? Were you ever in a courtroom, battling it out with opposing counsel?"

She laughed. The gloom that had settled over her at the disappointing news quickly dissipated with his astute comments and unquestioning support. "No. I'm a solicitor not a barrister."

"Come again?"

"In Canada, lawyers can call themselves both barristers and solicitors, but they usually focus on one or the other. The difference lies in what they do."

He made an encouraging gesture. "And that would be..."

It was a common question, and she'd long ago perfected an answer. "The easiest way to explain it is that solicitors help clients make deals and avoid problems, while barristers help clients after problems have occurred."

"So, you were the problem-preventing type of lawyer?"

"Yes. I did lots of contract work—boring, practical stuff. No *Perry Mason* or *L.A. Law* dramatics for me."

The server appeared with their meals, and Phillip led the talk into more general areas. She listened to tales of his sons when they were small, answered questions about her stepdaughter, and filled him in on her attempts to befriend Red Cat.

"Are you going to name him?" He sipped the last of his wine.

"I tried, but nothing seemed to fit. I think he's stuck with Red Cat for good." She crossed her silverware on her plate and leaned back in her chair. "That was delicious."

"You looked like you were hungry."

"It must be all the outdoor work I've been doing. I've been eating like a horse since I bought Cedar Street."

He tilted his head and regarded her thoughtfully, his brown eyes warm. "You look better than when I first saw you."

"I do? What do you mean?" Flustered, she voiced the first thought that popped into her head, and instantly regretted it. "No, don't answer that. It sounds like I'm fishing for compliments."

He ignored her plea. "When I saw you on TV on election night, I thought you looked ill. Tired, thin, stretched out. And then the day we met at Riverbend"— he quirked one side of his mouth as if rethinking what he was going to say, and then went on—"you looked shiny and brittle and ready to crack."

She gaped, disconcerted that he'd thought about her enough—*cared* about her enough—to worry about her appearance. Because that was what she heard in his voice—thought, care, worry. "I don't know what to say."

"There's nothing to say. I'm just glad you're looking better. More relaxed, happier, healthier overall."

Made speechless by this declaration, she remained silent while he paid the bill—they'd argued about that earlier and she'd conceded defeat before his stubborn insistence—and they made their way out of the restaurant. On the sidewalk, she paused.

"Thank you for a lovely meal." She didn't mean just the food, or the fact it had been his treat. She hoped he understood what she didn't say.

"You're welcome." He stopped a polite arm's length

away

It wasn't near enough. She longed to step closer, to feel the heat of his skin, smell his subtle cologne. "I should be going."

The sun, low in the sky and invisible behind the nearby buildings, still cast enough light to glint off the short, salt-and-pepper stubble bristling on his chin. It gilded his silver hair, and she curled her fingers against the urge to thread them through the strands.

"You'll let me know what happens with Annamarie tomorrow?"

She nodded, watching his lips form the words as a mouse might watch a cobra. Wary and mesmerized, yet longing. "Goodnight, Phillip."

"Goodnight, Aubrey." Neither of them moved. Traffic was scarce and pedestrians random.

Before she could chicken out, she stepped forward, lifted slightly on tiptoe and kissed his cheek. His whiskers tickled her lips and his scent—warm, masculine, enticing—filled her nostrils. His hand gripped her elbow briefly as if steadying her, but he released her as soon as she pulled back.

"We're not the same people we used to be." He spoke as if continuing an earlier conversation. She had no problem catching up with his thoughts.

"No, we're not. We're more sensible. Possibly wiser. Definitely older."

"I don't feel older when I'm with you. I feel very much the way I did when we were together."

She wasn't sure that was a good thing. Her memories of those years were turbulent and passionate and wild, and she didn't have the strength to handle those sorts of emotions again.

"At first, I missed the old Aubrey, but I'm enjoying getting to know the new one." He brushed the backs of his fingers on her cheek, watching the movement of his own hand, his brown eyes unfocused. She shivered.

This time, it was he who kissed her, his lips pressing

against the corner of her mouth. Before she could give into the craving to turn her head so she could take his mouth in a true caress, he backed away.

"Goodnight." He shoved his hands in the pockets of his trousers. "I'll wait until you're in your car."

Uncertain whether her wobbly knees would hold up, she crossed the street with careful steps. Sinking into the driver's seat with relief, she started the engine with deliberate movements, shifted into reverse, and backed out of the slot. He stood where she had left him. She gave a small wave, which he returned, and then she drove away.

Marjorie had always been an early riser, so Phillip didn't worry about calling her before he left for work the next morning.

Aubrey had said she would talk with Clarence about the steps he'd already taken, and while he trusted her to follow up, he *didn't* trust Clarence to the same extent. It was still difficult for him to wrap his brain around the concept that Marjorie had cherished an unrequited love for such a hard, unyielding man for so long. Whether she wanted—or needed—his protection, she was going to get it. And his first step would be to make sure she was completely in the loop on the search for Joseph, including whatever Clarence was telling Aubrey.

Instead of her familiar brisk, no-nonsense tone, though, her voice was pale and weak when she answered.

"Marjorie? Is everything all right?" He'd dialled her number while collecting his keys and coffee mug and now paused halfway down the stairs on his way to the garage.

"I'm fine." Her reply was a faint echo of her usual spirit. There was something else odd about her speech—it was muffled and indistinct. "I didn't sleep well, is all. My back is bothering me a bit."

Just the fact she'd mentioned *any* discomfort was a worry. She rarely complained.

"Do you need anything? I can stop by before work." He was usually in the office by eight, but he could easily make an exception. Resuming his descent, he mentally rearranged his schedule while opening the door connecting the ground-level hall to the garage and striding to his pickup.

"I'm just going to lie here for a while. I'm sure it will get better soon."

Lie here? It dawned on him what was wrong with her voice. She didn't have her dentures in. "I thought you would have been up hours ago. Are you still in bed?"

"Where else would I be with a sore back?"

"It must be bad, then." Apprehension had sharpened his tone. He softened it. "Stop being so stubborn. What do you need? I can be there in ten minutes."

A long sigh eased through the speaker. "I have never lied to you, not from the day your parents died, and I won't start now." She added in a warning tone, "Don't make me regret that."

The hairs on his forearms rose in alarm. "What the hell is going on?"

"Don't get all dramatic. It's not a big deal. I might have fallen getting out of bed this morning. Maybe it would be best if you did come over."

CHAPTER SEVENTEEN

Phillip switched to hands-free in his truck and stayed connected with Marjorie on his way to Riverbend. He drove quickly but cautiously, and his initial panic eased as he extracted more details.

"I'm a doctor," she said testily in answer to his repeated questions. "I did not hit my head, I have not broken a hip, I am not seriously injured. It happened about half an hour before you called, and I was able to get back up and return to bed all by myself. But I'm hungry and I want my coffee and I am smart enough to know I shouldn't attempt getting up yet."

"Okay, I'm just about there." He swung into the parking lot. "Don't do anything. I'll only be a couple more minutes."

She must have reached the end of her patience as all that greeted his final words was the silence of a disconnected call. After backing with less care than usual into a stall, he hustled to the building, grateful that he'd convinced her to provide him with a fob for the exterior doors and a key to her apartment. He'd imagined an event much like this when he'd badgered his way past her objections. Until now, he'd respected her privacy by always waiting to be allowed in, but this morning he had no qualms as he unlocked her door.

"Marjorie?" He headed straight to the bedroom.

"Stop sounding as if the Grim Reaper is hovering over me." His anxiety eased further at her irritated tone. *That* sounded more like her.

She was lying on top of the rumpled blankets, her navy-blue housecoat draped crookedly over her in an attempt to cover her nightgown-clad body, her cell phone clutched in her hand. Thank goodness she always kept it near, so she'd been able to answer his call, though he wished her pride had let her use it to ask for help sooner. He lowered himself gingerly to the mattress. "I'm sorry, but you scared me."

"Bah." She waved his concern away, her free hand flapping and then stopping abruptly as a spasm scrunched her features. Without her dentures, her face looked shrunken, collapsed.

"All right." He repressed asking yet again if she was okay. "What do you need first?"

"To go to the bathroom." She glared at the ceiling, her lips pressed together. "But I do *not* want you to help me do that. For now, bring me my teeth and a couple of the pain relievers you'll find in the medicine chest."

He did as instructed. She slid in her dentures and immediately looked more like herself. Then she dry-swallowed the capsules and folded her hands on her belly. "We'll let those kick in before I attempt the washroom. Give me twenty minutes or so. In the meantime, you can make the coffee."

He lifted off the housecoat, tugged the blankets out from under, and tucked them neatly around her. "Call me if you need me."

She lay with her eyes closed and a determined expression on her face, as if she could will the pain away. A dip of her chin was all that indicated she'd heard him.

As he waited for the coffee to perk, a firm knock sounded at the door. There was no reaction from her room, and he guessed the pain killers had kicked in and were letting her get some rest.

The knocked sounded again, this time a little louder.

Not wanting her to be disturbed, he opened the door

to discover Clarence standing in the hall.

The colour drained from the older man's cheeks. "What are you doing here? Marjorie was supposed to meet me in the library."

"She's okay." He made soothing motions with his hand. "She had a fall, but she's resting now."

If anything, Clarence's gaunt face paled further. "She fell?"

"Why don't you come in?" He stepped back, sympathy swelling at his obvious distress. "No need to have this conversation out here."

Clarence's cane tapped lightly on the hardwood floor as he entered the apartment. "Marjorie's never late, so when she didn't arrive, I thought I'd better come up and see. Did she phone you for help?"

He wondered if Clarence's feelings were hurt because Marjorie hadn't reached out to him. "Actually, I just happened to call her. I could tell something wasn't right, but I had to drag it out of her." He recapped what he knew, after which Clarence peeked into the bedroom before returning to his post near the kitchen counter.

"She appears to be sleeping now, but we shouldn't let her do so too long, just in case she does have a concussion."

"Yes." Clarence gave no sign he intended to leave the apartment. Again, sympathy tugged. "Would you like a coffee?" He wasn't halfway through the question before the old man nodded. He settled in Marjorie's chair, which gave him a view into the bedroom.

Phillip filled two mugs, handed one to Clarence, and took a seat on the sofa.

After that, silence fell between them.

He tried to think of any other time when they had been alone together and couldn't. He hadn't been the type of father-in-law to invite confidences from his daughter's husband—especially a husband he despised for accidentally impregnating that daughter.

Now he knew about Joseph's birth, Phillip

wondered how that had coloured Clarence's reaction to Aubrey's news. He would never forget the fury in his face the day they had told her parents she was going to have a baby. He'd been prepared for their disappointment—few parents of their generation would have been *happy* to learn their unmarried daughter was pregnant—but the violence of Clarence's reaction had been shocking. His ice-cold tone, his refusal to listen to Aubrey's pleas that they were in love, his rejection of Phillip's assurances he could support her. Alice Windt hadn't been much better, her expression sorrowful, the few sentences she uttered echoing her husband's opinions.

It had only made Phillip more determined to save Aubrey from such condemnation.

Becoming a father at nineteen hadn't been in his plans. He had loved Aubrey, though, and had looked forward to marrying her, regardless of the reason. He'd had to put aside his intention to go to university, but he'd only applied because it was the thing to do, not because he'd had any specific goal in mind. With an inward wince, he could see how that might have looked to a man as driven and career oriented as Clarence.

"You must think I'm a hypocrite."

Clarence's voice jolted him out of his reverie. "I'm sorry?"

"You must think I'm a hypocrite, now you know about the son I had with Marjorie. My response when Aubrey told us she was pregnant, I mean."

It seemed he hadn't been the only one reflecting on past years.

"Not a hypocrite." He paused and reconsidered that statement. "At least, not exactly. But I would have thought that experience would make you more...understanding."

"Understanding." Clarence almost snorted the word. "I knew from bitter experience how an unplanned baby could tear lives apart. I didn't want that for my daughter, and yet, there you were. Both of you, naïve and hopeful and foolish, too young to realize you were not mature enough to deal with such an event."

Phillip clenched his teeth to keep back the sharp retort that first came to mind. He was right in some ways. He and Aubrey *hadn't* been prepared for what life had in store for them. If they had been older, maybe they would have handled Samantha's death differently.

But none of that mattered now. "You don't want to find Joseph, do you?"

The older man closed his eyes briefly and he felt a tiny twinge of remorse. Clarence was almost ninety years old, after all. He deserved respect for that if nothing else.

"No, I don't." He ruined his decisive reply with a sigh. "And yes, I do. I share Marjorie's wish to know what happened to the boy, to assure ourselves we did the right thing giving him up. But I worry what we'll find will make things worse, not better."

"Don't you think knowing the truth, regardless of what it is, is better than living with uncertainty?"

Clarence met his gaze directly. "We've lived with uncertainty for six decades. I doubt I have another decade left to live. Why should we risk change now?"

He had never heard Clarence speak so openly of his own feelings. If he wasn't careful, he might grow to like the crotchety old man. "Well, none of this matters if we can't find him." It was rather backhanded solace, but it was all he could offer.

The rustle of bedclothes reached them. "Phillip?" Marjorie's drowsy voice drifted from the other room. "Are you still there?"

Before he could answer, Clarence replied. "I'm here, too, dear." He pushed to his feet, using the arm of the chair and his cane for leverage. "May I come in?"

"Of course you may." He heard her pleasure. "Did I miss our appointment? I'm so sorry."

By the time she finished speaking, Clarence was in

her room and settling on the side of her bed.

He watched the elderly couple for a moment. Their hands entwined, gripping tightly. Clarence leaned over and kissed Marjorie's forehead, and the gesture eased a knot of worry he had carried with him since the elderly couple had announced their engagement.

Aubrey was surprised at how well she slept Monday night. She'd thought she'd be kept awake with thoughts of Annamarie's disappointing news and Phillip's tender, tantalizing kiss, but instead had fallen into slumber, waking ready for the day at seven-thirty as usual.

To prepare for her conversation with Annamarie that afternoon, she needed to confirm the steps her father had taken to find Joseph, but that could wait until later in the morning. After taking a shower and eating a bagel, she brought her coffee into the living room and settled with her laptop. It was time to get quotes for the house renovations. Seeing the dramatic changes the rough yard work had wrought had fired up her desire to get moving on the next stage.

During their dinner, Phillip had offered a few suggestions, and she'd made a list of those businesses on her phone. She called that up now and began her research. In less than an hour she'd chosen her top three and arranged appointments with each to come to Cedar Street the following week to discuss her requirements.

That done, she couldn't put off calling her father any longer.

She smiled wryly. Her subconscious obviously knew she'd prioritized calling construction companies over her father for a reason other than the early hour.

She dialled his cell phone and waited for him to answer, mentally running through her list of questions. After three rings, she suspected she would get his voicemail.

"Hello." His gruff response came as she'd been formulating what message to leave.

"Morning, Dad. Did I catch you at a bad time? I can call back."

"I'm with Marjorie. She had a fall this morning."

Her breath caught. "Oh, no! Is she okay?"

"She seems to be fine, but I'll stay with her to make sure." True to his nature, Clarence sounded angry rather than concerned, but she was coming to understand he hid his softer feelings behind a wall of ill humour.

At least, that was what she *hoped* he was doing.

"Does she need anything? I can stop by if you want. Does Phillip know?" It was good that Clarence was there, but with his bad hip his help would be limited. It might be best if someone else checked in as well.

His reply alleviated her concerns. "He just left. He says he's coming back later today. I don't think he trusts us to take care of ourselves." His tone held a hint of disgust, as if he were insulted. Which he probably was, she pondered, given his dislike of Phillip and belief in his own capabilities.

"He's a good nephew." She didn't think twice about planting herself firmly on Phillip's side. "This relationship between you and Marjorie is new to him, remember. He just wants to make sure she's okay."

Her father's harrumph travelled easily over the connection. "Why did you call?"

She had to think for a moment. "Oh, right. I had some questions about Joseph. But it can wait if you need to get back to Marjorie."

"I've just settled her in her chair. I have a few minutes."

"Okay, then." She paused, and then dove in. "We found Duncan Truble's daughter."

CHAPTER EIGHTEEN

If Aubrey thought to please Clarence with this news, his dismissive answer disabused her. "Yes, Phillip mentioned that this morning. I didn't think it would be too difficult."

She heard a second voice in the background but couldn't discern the words. "Is that Marjorie?"

"Yes. She wants me to put you on speaker phone."

"If she feels up to it, that's a good idea. She should hear this, too, but I don't want to bother her if she isn't well."

A moment later, she heard "Hello, dear," come clearly over the connection.

"How are you?" It was a relief to hear her sound much as normal. "What happened?"

"I had a tiny dizzy spell this morning getting out of bed. I am fine now, despite what the men in my life might have told you." Her voice was vigorous and more than a tad frustrated.

Aubrey smiled. "I'm glad you're okay. Back to Phillip, then. What else did he tell you?"

Clarence answered. "That Duncan's daughter is still deciding whether to let us see any notes he made, if she finds them."

"Yes. We think she has—found them, I mean. Or at least has a good idea where they might be. Otherwise, why wouldn't she just say there is no way she can help?"

"That makes some sense," he said grudgingly.

"She is also concerned about the adoptive family's

149

rights. She asked if you'd started the request for reunion process on the government website, and if you'd applied for a copy of the birth certificate."

"I told you we have."

Marjorie's voice overrode his testy reply. "It shouldn't upset you that she is being cautious. It's only proper. You must be patient."

Aubrey was more inclined to believe his reaction was at the implication his word had been doubted, not impatience. She said soothingly, "I told her that you did. But if she doesn't ask the questions, she doesn't get the answers. I have another phone call scheduled with her this afternoon. I'll provide your reassurances and hopefully we'll be able to move on."

"I should phone her myself." Clarence sounded determined, even a little belligerent.

The last thing she wanted was to have him put Annamarie's back up. "Let me talk with her first. I'll let you know how that goes and then we can decide next steps."

Aubrey's conversation with Annamarie did not go as expected. In fact, the other woman threw two curveballs her way.

The first was a request to speak to Clarence directly, echoing his desire to speak with her.

"I know you've told me he wants closure," she said, "but I'd like to hear that from him. And to be honest, I want to confirm his story about knowing my father. I'm having trouble believing he would have agreed to arrange an adoption through back door channels. It feels out of character."

"I can understand that. But I don't want my father to give you the wrong impression." She paused, searching for the right words. "He seems to have...misgivings...about this search and might sound as if he's putting up roadblocks. I truly believe he wants answers, though."

"It's only natural to have conflicting feelings about a situation like this. I'd be surprised if he didn't, to be honest."

Annamarie's concession relieved the worst of her worries, and she set up a time for the two to meet over the phone.

Then she tossed Aubrey her second curveball. "If all goes as I expect with your father, I think it would be best if he came to Kamloops to review the documents."

"You've found them?" She stared blindly out her living room window. With Steve gone, daylight flooded through the wide bay, warming the scarred hardwood floors to a golden hue. Her heart lurched with excitement. "You found your father's notes?"

"Yes. But I don't want to let them out of my possession. I'd rather they stay here, and you come to see them."

"My father doesn't travel well, as he has a bad hip. And Marjorie had a fall just this morning. Nothing major, we hope, but I don't know when she'll feel up to a six-hour drive." Flights were a possibility, but the ones that connected the two cities were awkward and expensive.

"If they would rather you came in their place, I have no problem with that."

"All right." Through the window, Red Cat came into view, stalking over the rutted tracks the skid steer had made on what would someday be her lawn. "If we were to get everything organized in the next day or two, could we come down the end of this week?"

"I can make that work."

Phillip had left Clarence in charge with a lighter heart than he'd expected. Despite the older man's continued gruffness, he treated Marjorie with gentleness and respect—and just the amount of firmness needed to get that stubborn lady to take it easy for at least one day.

He still intended to convince her to see a doctor sooner rather than later. The light-headedness that she blamed for her fall had to be caused by something, and he wouldn't let her ignore it. But that argument could wait for a couple of days. In the meantime, he'd keep a closer eye on her.

When he finally made it into the Twin Rivers office, he wasn't sure whether to be pleased or chagrined that no one seemed to have missed him. It was a good thing the place continued to run smoothly without his presence, given the unexpected amounts of time he'd taken off recently. Dexter was right—he should be proud that his company was doing so well, that his boys had grown up to be independent men. And he was.

But he was also rather thrilled that Marjorie had asked him to help find Joseph. It was nice to be needed. Maybe that was the root of his restlessness—he wanted to feel necessary again.

Just before three o'clock, he was wrapping up one last task with the intent of leaving early and heading back to Marjorie's when his cell rang, indicating a call from Aubrey. He couldn't stop—didn't *want* to stop—the smile that curved his lips. With all the unexpected events of the day, he hadn't spent much time thinking of their kisses, though the memory had tickled just under the surface of his skin. He'd been surprised that she'd made the first move, and though her kiss had been no more than a chaste peck on the cheek, his body had reacted as if she'd wrapped her naked form around him. And he hadn't been the only one physically affected. Her eyes had dilated when he'd told her he liked the new Aubrey, and she hadn't retreated when he given her his own soft kiss. He loved how dazed she'd looked after such an innocent exchange and wondered what she'd be like if he ever focused on seducing her.

That was a thought...

His phone rang again, and he snatched it up.

"Am I interrupting something?" Her voice curled out of the speaker and into his belly. "I talked with Clarence and Marjorie, so I know your day has been a bit of a mess. If you don't have time right now..."

"No, I'm good. You heard about Marjorie's fall, then?" It hadn't crossed his mind to let her know what had happened. He'd have to remember to do so in future. After all, Marjorie would soon be her stepmother. That fact hadn't quite sunk in.

"Yes. She said she was dizzy. Do you think she has low blood pressure, or maybe low blood sugar? It was first thing in the morning."

"Both are possible. I plan to browbeat her into seeing a doctor soon. She doesn't have a GP since she just moved back to town, but I think I can convince mine to take her on."

"That's good. I have a feeling doctors make the worst patients. You may have to nag her to make sure she goes."

"Oh, I will." It felt right to be talking about Marjorie with Aubrey. She brought a calm sense of logic to what had been—he could now admit—his own slightly panicked reaction. Though Marjorie would never be a burden and caring for her was a privilege, having someone else to share his concern sparked a warm glow in his chest.

"If you're sure I'm not interrupting anything, I wanted to tell you about my discussion with Annamarie."

He didn't smack his forehead but felt like he should. "I'd forgotten all about that. How did it go?"

"Let me bring you up to speed." She filled him in on her conversation with her father and Marjorie as well as with the lawyer in Kamloops. "I've arranged for Dad and Annamarie to talk tomorrow morning. If all goes well, I'm thinking of driving to Kamloops on Thursday. I don't want to give her time to change her mind. If I leave early enough, I can be there by lunchtime."

"Let me know what happens and I'll come with you."

"That's not necessary. I'm fine driving on my own."

"That's not the point. This is my family, too. I want to be there." In fact, his urge to study the information himself was surprisingly strong.

"If I do go Thursday, you'll have to miss more work. There's really no need for you to come. I'll tell you everything that happens, I promise."

She wasn't worried about being alone with him, was she? If their kisses had rocked her as much as they had him, maybe she was concerned what enforced proximity might do. Well, he for one was ready to explore that thought further.

"Aubrey, I'm coming with you. What's the point of being the boss if I can't rearrange things to suit myself?" Given the reaction today, he wasn't sure anyone would even notice he was missing. Carla had barely blinked when he appeared so late, despite no warning of a change in his plans.

"We can talk more tomorrow." Her tone told him she wasn't convinced, but he didn't care. He was coming along no matter what and would drive his own vehicle in convoy if she really put up a fuss. Not that he envisioned being forced to such an extreme measure, but you never knew.

CHAPTER NINETEEN

Aubrey had forgotten how much she enjoyed road trips. She'd always liked driving—the powerful engine at her command, the swoop and swerve of well-cambered curves, the scenery sliding by in an ever-changing panorama.

During her marriage to Oliver, she'd taken on the main driving duties. He preferred to be a passenger, as it freed him up to answer any phone calls or emails he might get, especially on longer journeys. While Sophia was growing up, most of her chauffeuring had fallen to Aubrey as well, but she'd never minded. It had given her one-on-one time with her stepdaughter.

She slid a quick glance to the person now in the passenger seat.

Phillip wore well-fitted jeans and a short-sleeved shirt in an ocean blue that emphasized his deep brown eyes and silver hair. After an initial exchange of greetings when she'd picked him up thirty minutes before, there'd been no conversation. He seemed content to let her concentrate on driving and, while the silence had felt constrained at first, she had slowly relaxed.

As they neared Stone Creek the highway split, and she followed the other southbound traffic down toward the Fraser River. The muddy waters flowed smooth and wide on their right, while a precipitous cliff held up by huge cement blocks flashed by on their left, before they climbed back up and rejoined the northbound lanes.

"We're meeting Annamarie at six o'clock?" Phillip's question revealed at least one of the thoughts that had kept him silent so far.

"Yes. It was the soonest I could arrange."

Annamarie had called almost immediately after her conversation with Clarence. Though she still sounded cautious, she confirmed her offer to share her father's notes. Not wanting to give her a chance to change her mind, Aubrey had pushed for a meeting the next day, but she had balked at the rush. In the end, they'd settled on Friday evening.

The drive to Kamloops usually took less than six hours, but she hadn't wanted to risk being late, and Phillip had agreed, so they'd left Prince George at eight o'clock that morning.

He'd been unshakeable in his decision to go with her, and despite her early objections, she was glad he'd insisted. Though he didn't appear to be insulted by her first refusals, she felt she owed him an explanation.

"I didn't mean to sound ungrateful when I said you needn't come on this trip." She kept her eyes on the road but sensed his gaze swing in her direction. "I just didn't want to take advantage of your good nature. I don't need the company, and I would have been fine meeting Annamarie on my own." He snorted and she hastened to reassure him. "I *am* glad you came, honest."

"It's not that I don't trust you."

She widened her eyes and shot him a quick look. "Of course not. You know me better than that."

"I do. And I'm glad *you* know *me* that well, too."

"I do." The faint echo of their wedding vows shivered over her skin.

As if he'd felt the same phantom memory, he said, "You know what's odd? I feel like I know you better now than I did when we were married. It doesn't matter that we hadn't spoken for thirty years before I met you at Riverbend, or that it's only been a month since then.

Maybe it's the crucible we've been thrown in, with Joseph and Marjorie and Clarence. It has heightened my awareness of you." His gaze traced her profile, and she gripped the steering wheel, searching for an anchor in the swirl of emotions his words evoked. "And I like what I'm seeing."

Phillip watched Aubrey's knuckles whiten and hoped he hadn't pushed too fast or too far. In the two days since they'd scheduled the trip to Kamloops, he'd seesawed back and forth on whether to test the attraction she'd revealed after their dinner. Thoughts of her consumed him at the oddest times, powerful enough to distract him from Asher's pending departure, which was now common knowledge.

He was ready to see what might happen next with his elusive ex-wife and waited, impatience simmering, for her to respond. She licked her lips, drawing his gaze to their shiny pinkness. She wore makeup today—discreet eyeshadow, a natural-looking blush, and a hint of plum on her mouth. Since she'd moved into the Cedar Street house, he'd seen her most often with an unpainted face. He couldn't decide which way he liked her best. Good thing he didn't have to choose and could simply appreciate her as she was.

"Phillip..." She trailed off, and his heart sank. Before he could form a reply, she continued. "Is it weird that I like what I'm seeing, too? We've been divorced for three decades. What do we think could happen between us?"

The bubble of hope that filled his chest was out of all proportion to her cautious statement, but he didn't care. She sounded open to the possibility of...something. He wasn't yet ready to give it a name.

"The past shaped us and I will never forget that time with you." How could he? It had made him the man he was today. "But we're both in a new place now, and if those two new people want to spend time with each other, what's wrong with that?"

She rolled her shoulders and slowed to match the speed of the battered pickup truck ahead of them. "Nothing's *wrong*." She still sounded hesitant. "But if it didn't work the first time, why try again?"

"I'm not the young, naïve boy I was then. And the woman I'm getting to know is not the same woman, either." Though she did give guarded glimpses of the teenage girl he'd fallen in love with at unexpected moments. "When we first reconnected, it was hard to get past what we'd put each other through. But it was a long time ago and memories become distorted. All I know for sure is that my pain and grief has softened, eased."

"But will never be forgotten." The pickup in front of them slowed further as they came to a long uphill climb, but she seemed content to follow while other vehicles barrelled by in the passing lane. "At the time, I didn't know how I could go on breathing."

Was she talking about losing Samantha or their divorce? Maybe it didn't matter. The two events were so entangled it was impossible to separate them.

There was one question he'd wanted to ask for decades, and if he was serious about a second chance with Aubrey, perhaps he shouldn't let it fester any longer. He watched her, searching for a reaction.

"When you left me, you told me it was because you didn't love me anymore. Was that the truth?" Already distraught over Samantha's death, hearing her say those words had flayed the remaining flesh from his bones.

She froze, her expression blank, her hands clamped to the wheel. With a jerk, she pulled the car to the shoulder of the road, gravel crunching under the wheels as she braked to a sudden halt. An angry honk blared as a transport truck swooped by from behind. She didn't seem to notice as she twisted in her seat to face him.

"Aubrey!" His heart raced from her precipitous

action.

"Of course it wasn't the truth!" Angry red patched flushed her cheeks and her eyes stared with dagger-like intensity. "And you should have known! You should have told me I was a liar and fought for me. But you didn't. You just let me go without a word."

"That's not true! I begged you to stay."

"You didn't, not once. Don't you think I'd remember if you had?"

He cast his thoughts back, searching for the memory. For years it had been vividly easy to recall— Aubrey standing straight and cold before him, saying she no longer loved him, that she was going home to her parents, that she wanted a divorce. Even now he could still see *her*—but where had the scene happened? Which room in their tiny home? Or had it been at Clarence's, where she had fled mere weeks after Samantha's death?

"I'm sure I did." But had he? Or had he only pleaded with her in his own mind, too proud and broken to speak the words aloud?

She shook her head wearily, the fury already fading from her face. "I waited for you. You never came."

He would never forget her shriek of horror and grief when she'd discovered Samantha that morning. Moments before they'd been cuddled together in bed, thankful for their first full night's sleep since her birth only two months before. Then Aubrey had tiptoed out of the room and into the nursery, and their life had shattered. The following hours and days were a jumbled puzzle—tiny vignettes standing out stark and clear, other memories a swirling mass of images distorted like reflections in a funhouse mirror.

"Why did you go back to your parents?" The cocoon of the car interior felt fragile, as if any sudden noise might shatter it. He spoke quietly. "Why did you leave in the first place?"

"I don't know." Her gaze dropped to the fingers she

was twisting in her lap. Then those fingers stilled, and he saw her draw her courage around her. "No, that's not true. I went because I couldn't bear to be around you anymore."

A prickling sensation crawled from his belly up his chest and neck to his cheeks. "What?"

"I needed you so much, and yet you acted as if I wasn't there. Instead of drawing us together, Samantha's death pushed us apart." He opened his mouth—to say what, he wasn't sure—but she stopped him with a raised hand. "I know, that's incredibly unfair and insensitive. You needed *me*, I'm sure. But I couldn't see past my own pain to yours. When my father said it would be best to start fresh, that I was young and had time to build a new life—" She quirked her lips in a sad moue, leaving the rest of the sentence unfinished.

"He never accepted me, did he?" It was an old bitterness, but one he couldn't forget. "The only reason your parents even tolerated our marriage was because you were pregnant. And the minute there was no reason for us to stay together, he schemed to take you away."

"They were wrong." She reached out and gripped his hand, her fingers warm and comforting. "I truly believe they thought they were doing what was best for me. I *have* to believe that, or I'd never be able to speak to my father again. But they didn't give you enough credit. And neither did I. I'm sorry for that, sorrier than you could ever know."

He studied their clasped hands. His skin was a darker tone than hers, his fingers longer, but they fit together well. He traced her knuckles with his fingertips. She wore no rings, and the skin on the back of her hand was ridged with veins, dusted with an age spot or two. He wondered what she'd do if he kissed those signs of a life lived. "None of us come out looking too good, do we?"

"It was a terrible time. Maybe if we'd been together longer, our marriage could have survived it. But it didn't, and we moved on. It's no use looking back. Our lives are what we make of them. Moving forward is all we can do."

He gave in. Lifting her hand in both of his, he kissed each knuckle. She watched him, wide-eyed, her hand loose and relaxed.

"I love you, Aubrey." He didn't know what those three words meant for the future, but he hoped she understood he meant them for the past, as well.

"You're a good man, Phillip." She squeezed his fingers. "I love you, too."

CHAPTER TWENTY

Aubrey didn't know for certain Phillip shared the same sense of freedom and relief she did after their cathartic conversation, but she suspected it. During the remaining hours of their drive and through the late lunch they had upon arriving in Kamloops, she perceived a lightness about him that was reflected in her own heart.

Maybe closure was more than just a word. Maybe it was this aura of peace and tranquility—a feeling she hadn't missed until it returned.

Even when he told her about Asher taking a new job in Winnipeg and his worries about losing touch with his son, there had been something in his tone and posture that made her wonder if simply being able to talk to her about it made the change easier to bear.

She was under no misapprehension regarding their relationship, no matter how much his touch seared her heart and soul, heated her breasts and womb. Their exchange of *I love yous* hadn't been the beginning of a new scene in their lives, but the conclusion to a long, unfinished chapter. It had been time to turn the page.

Even after checking into their hotel, there was still more than two hours before their appointment with Annamarie. As neither of them was familiar with the city, they'd used the navigation system in her car to find McArthur Island and had burned off their restlessness by walking the three-kilometre trail.

Now it was quarter to six, and they were parked in

the large lot behind the glass and concrete tower that housed Annamarie's office. Though she had made it perfectly clear the documents she was prepared to share were not official, she had preferred to meet with them here.

Aubrey swallowed the last gulp of water in her bottle and screwed on the plastic cap.

"Ready?" Phillip lifted an eyebrow.

She drew in a deep breath, let it out slowly, and nodded. "Let's do this."

Side by side, they walked to the rear entrance they'd been directed to use. No one waited in the foyer, visible through the wall of glass.

She tried the door, rattling it to no avail. "What if she's changed her mind?" She tried to keep the panic from her voice. It wouldn't be the end of the world if she had. But it would be a major setback, and Clarence and Marjorie would be so disappointed.

"It's not even six yet." Phillip sounded calm, but he kept glancing obsessively at his watch. "Give her a minute."

Reminding herself she was a professional woman with years of experience in stressful situations, both in the law and politics, she made a determined effort to relax her shoulders and jaw. The longer she was out of those worlds, though, the harder it was to erect the facade she'd lived behind for so many years. She felt like a snake who had shed its skin—itchy and defenseless and exposed.

Her breath caught when the elevator doors on the far side of the foyer opened. The woman who stepped out appeared about sixty years old, was short with a full figure, straight dark hair cut to her chin, and dark eyes. She strode toward them with firm, business-like steps, neat and sedate in a navy pinstriped skirt suit, white blouse, and low black pumps. Aubrey suddenly second-guessed her own casual outfit of capri pants and loose, sleeveless top. She had dressed to appear accommodating and friendly, not aggressive or lawyerly, but now wondered if Annamarie would think she didn't care enough to wear professional attire. Also, the day had been hot and sunny and she'd worked up a light sweat during their walk. She'd been so eager to get to the meeting, though, that she'd shrugged off Phillip's suggestion they make a quick return to their hotel first.

A decision she now regretted. She really wasn't thinking clearly these days.

Annamarie pushed the door open. "Aubrey Windt and Phillip Church?" Without waiting for their reply, she gestured them in. "I'm Annamarie Whitman."

The exchange of pleasantries that followed had Aubrey suppressing a slightly hysterical giggle. She couldn't explain the sense of unreality that cloaked her. None of this felt as if it was really happening—not Annamarie's handshake, the ride in the elevator to the seventh floor, the walk down the hall to a corner office.

Thank god Phillip was there. He'd answered Annamarie's impersonal questions about their drive, the weather, where they were staying, and by the time they were all seated in club chairs around a low table she had managed to regain her equilibrium.

They politely refused Annamarie's offer of water, tea, or coffee. The other woman gave a small smile. "I imagine you're eager to see the file."

"We are very grateful for your cooperation." Aubrey breathed carefully around the pain in her sternum, a familiar symptom of anxiety. "It will mean so much to Phillip's aunt and my father."

"The situation is a little unorthodox. It has incited several vigorous discussions around the office." A sharp gleam in Annamarie's eyes seemed to indicate there was nothing she liked better than *vigorous discussions*.

"You spoke about this with your colleagues?" She was taken aback. This was a personal issue, not professional.

"In a general sense only," Annamarie replied. "It

poses a pretty puzzle, but in the end we all agreed attorney-client privilege wouldn't apply, because of the lack of a formal contract."

She couldn't wait any longer. "Can we see it now?" Her fingers curled into claws on her thighs as she struggled to stuff her impatience back into its cage.

Phillip wished there was a couch in the office, so he could sit closer to Aubrey. As it was, they were separated by an arm's length with a narrow glass table between their chairs. The distance did nothing to lessen his awareness of her nervous tension—she was visibly vibrating—and he wished he could take her hand, attempt to calm her with his touch.

To be honest, he could use some comforting himself. He was doing his best to provide steadfast, staunch support, but his gut was twisting wildly now they were so close to discovering more about Joseph. He breathed in deeply through his nose and concentrated on Annamarie.

"As far as I know," she said, "this was the only adoption my father was involved in, private or otherwise. In Canada it is not necessary for a lawyer to be retained as adoptions are processed either through public agencies or private organizations licensed by the government. And while my father was doing this for a friend, I was certain he would have kept records." She smiled, a twinkle lightening her so far sober expression. "When he and my mother downsized from the house I grew up in, we discovered boxes and boxes of memorabilia from our school days, his school days, my mother's life before they married—anything and everything."

He envisioned a warehouse full of banker's boxes stretching into the distance, rather like the final scene in *Raiders of the Lost Ark*. "And the notes were in one of those?"

"Yes." Annamarie shifted in her seat, crossing her ankles. "We discarded most of them, of course. We had to—there simply wasn't room where they were moving. It was tough on Dad. The more we decluttered, the more upset he grew. I think he felt we were throwing his life away. When we came upon a small shoebox, he grew even more agitated. He insisted it be saved, but that I was under no circumstances to look inside. He was in such a state, I agreed. I took it home and tucked it onto the top shelf of a closet and promptly forgot all about it. Until I talked to you."

She rose, moving to the wide, black desk set at an angle in the corner of the office. For the first time, he took a comprehensive look around. The room was a good size and would have been spacious if it hadn't been crammed with file cabinets and tilting stacks of cardboard boxes. Her desk was piled with buff-coloured files stuffed within an inch of their lives, bursting with enough sheets of paper to thrill a pulp baron's pocketbook.

From behind one of those teetering stacks, she lifted a rectangular blue and red box. She returned to her seat, and Aubrey slid forward on her chair, her hands lifting then dropping back to her lap, as if resisting an urge to snatch the box away. His fingers itched with fellow feeling.

"Is that it?" she whispered.

In answer, Annamarie held it out. For a moment, she simply stared at it, and then took it with trembling hands.

Aubrey placed the box on her lap and smoothed her hands over it. On the lid were the words *Gold Bond X-15 Jet Moulded Shoes for Boys*, along with the illustration of a fighter plane trailing a swoosh of red and gold. Given it was sixty years old it was in excellent shape. Unexpectedly, tears blurred her vision. She blinked to hold them back.

"I should warn you," Annamarie said gently. "I've looked inside, to make sure it was what I suspected. I'm not sure it contains anything helpful."

"It doesn't matter. It will be more than we know now." She hooked her fingertips under the lid and paused yet again.

"Go on, Aubrey." She raised her gaze from the box on her knees to Phillip's face. His eyes were warm, his expression wry yet understanding. "We already suspected this wouldn't be the end of the search. Let's find out what we have to deal with next."

CHAPTER TWENTY-ONE

The box was half empty. Lying on top of a scanty pile of yellowed sheets was an unaddressed envelope. With reverent hands, Aubrey lifted it out and removed a typewritten letter. The paper was thin and fragile, and she unfolded it cautiously.

"It's from my father to Duncan Truble." The faded, old-fashioned type made their quest seem *real* in a way it hadn't felt before. It was physical proof of Joseph's existence. "He's asking if he'd be willing to handle a private matter." She scanned the contents, coming to an abrupt halt at the letters just below the signature. In the traditional custom of a formal business letter, the person who typed the correspondence had included her initials in lower case after the uppercase *CJW*.

She raised her gaze and met Phillip's. Tears filled her eyes, and her view melted, blurring his features. "Marjorie typed it. She typed the letter asking someone to give away her baby."

He held out his hand, palm up, and she laid the page on it gently, almost reluctant to let it go. Annamarie rose, disappeared for a moment, and returned with a carton of tissues which she placed on the table between them. With a grateful smile, Aubrey wiped her eyes before turning her attention back to the box.

After reading each enclosure, she passed it to Phillip. When she handed him the final page, she replaced the lid on the now empty box, rested her hands on top, and waited for him to finish. Annamarie continued to sit quietly, showing no signs of impatience.

With a gesture of finality, Phillip added the last page to the pile he'd collected at his elbow and looked at Aubrey. "The priest?"

She nodded. "It's the only lead I can see."

Annamarie released a long breath. "Me, too."

He unerringly drew a thin sheaf of paperclipped sheets out of the tidy pile. Aubrey realized he'd left them askew for that purpose. When she'd read them, her impulse had been to grab her phone and start a Google search. Instead, she'd forced herself to go through the rest of the documents calmly, scouring them for more details. Nothing else had been revealed, and now she was chomping at the bit to move on.

He tapped the pages and turned to Annamarie. "These are carbon copies of two letters your father sent to Father Murray Athol at an address in Regina, Saskatchewan. In the first, he explains that he is arranging the adoption of an as-yet-unborn child. The birth father's preference is that the child be placed with a Roman Catholic family outside British Columbia. Mr. Truble appears to have attended boarding school with this priest—he includes a couple of anecdotes at the start of his letter—and explains that Athol came to mind. Truble hoped his old friend might know a family looking to adopt. In the second, he thanks Father Murray for his reply—though there is no copy of that letter—and says he will be in touch with further details once the baby is born."

Aubrey couldn't stay silent any longer. "Had you heard of Father Murray before this, Annamarie?"

She shook her head. "No. I knew my father was born and raised in Saskatchewan, of course, so that makes sense. And he was deeply involved in our local parish throughout his life, too, so the Catholic connection is also logical."

It also explained Clarence's choice of lawyer. But none of that got them any closer to finding Father Murray.

Phillip smoothed the topmost page with a gentle hand. "The letters include the full name and address for this priest, so it should be reasonably straightforward to find him."

"Maybe." Annamarie's brows drew together. "It is what's *not* in the file that concerns me. If correspondence that revealed who adopted the child ever existed, I am certain my father would have kept it. Since it's not with the rest of the letters, my gut tells me Father Murray didn't come through. So, in effect, all you've learned is the name and sixty-year-old location of a man who more than likely had nothing to do with the adoption."

"For now, he's all we've got. We have to follow up, no matter how hopeless it looks." Aubrey dug her phone out of her purse and unlocked the screen. "First things first." She typed the name into her search bar.

The good news about the all-encompassing knowledge base that was the internet was that you learned bad news quickly. "Nothing." She tried not to be disheartened. "That would have been too easy, right?"

"Had you already done that?" Her head snapped up at Phillip's question. It hadn't occurred to her that Annamarie might have done some investigating herself.

The other woman shook her head. "No. I was curious, I have to admit, but the decisions on what to do next are completely up to your families."

A silence filled the room. Aubrey didn't know about the others, but she wasn't sure what she was feeling. Confusion about the potentially missing information? Excitement due to a new lead? Trepidation over where it might take them?

All of the above?

Something that had been niggling in her

subconscious took form. "Does it seem odd there is no copy of the birth certificate? Wouldn't your father have kept that with his records?"

"If he was ever in possession of it, I assume he would have sent the original with the baby. He could have taken a photograph if he wanted a copy, I suppose. But this is all I found."

"I see." Aubrey straightened her shoulders, opened the shoebox, and began putting the papers back inside. "I don't suppose you'd let us take this."

"I'd prefer to keep the originals." Annamarie rose and stepped to her desk. "Not for any reason other than the usual lawyerly reluctance to let any records out of our hands. But here." She opened a drawer, removed a bright green folder, and handed it to Aubrey. "I made copies of everything. I wish you luck."

Together they walked to the elevator. As they waited for the car to arrive, a question burbled to the surface of Aubrey's mind. "In his final letter to Father Murray—the last in the file, anyway—Mr. Truble says he will be in touch after the baby is born. Why wouldn't he have kept the letter that mentions the birth? Do you think it was lost somehow?"

"It must have been." The door slid open, and Phillip stretched out an arm to keep it that way. "Two of the few facts we have are that a baby was born, and that he was adopted."

Aubrey stared, thunderstruck. "What if we're wrong about that?"

He frowned. "We know Marjorie had a baby. Why else would we be looking for him?"

"What if the baby was never adopted?" At her side, Annamarie twitched, as if she'd realized where Aubrey was going. She swallowed, and then said the terrifying words. "What if the baby died before his new family could take him?"

"I still think Truble would have made a note in his file." Phillip knew he was being stubborn, but he couldn't let the subject go. "If you expect him to have documents regarding an adoption, shouldn't you also expect him to have documents regarding a death?"

He and Aubrey were sitting side-by-side in low chairs in a corner of the dimly lit lounge located off the hotel lobby. Two martinis sat untouched on the knee-high table in front of them. Shellshocked by her horrifying theory, he'd suggested a drink before dinner.

Maybe the respite would give his appetite a chance to return. The thought that Marjorie's baby might have been dead all this time had soured his gut.

"You're right." She rubbed her temple in a vulnerable gesture. "But it's a trail we have to follow."

"How? How do we follow it?"

"In British Columbia, death records older than twenty years are available online."

He pulled out his phone. "Let's look right now."

She gripped his wrist. "Please, Phillip. Can't it wait? I don't think I can take anymore drama today."

He'd only heard her end of her conversation with Clarence after they'd left Annamarie's office, but he'd seen how it taxed her. While she had said her father had been unusually understanding about their lack of progress, he still sensed she was carrying a heavy burden of guilt, one he wished he could take from her shoulders.

In the shadowy room, her skin looked smooth and youthful, but when he looked closer, he could see the dark circles under her eyes, the pinched corners of her mouth. "It has been a long one, hasn't it?"

"Yes." She released his wrist, and he tucked his phone back in his pocket. "I don't mean to be an ostrich, but for now I just want to relax, enjoy the music"—she nodded at the piano near the bar where a woman in sequins was softly playing something that sounded vaguely familiar—"and have a drink."

"All right." After all, what difference would a few more hours make? He leaned forward and lifted both their glasses, handing Aubrey's to her and lifting his in a wordless toast. She mirrored his motion. He took a sip, and the bitter burn of excellent gin seared his sinuses.

For awhile they simply sat, savoured, and listened. Her attention appeared to be on the pianist's performance, but occasionally he caught a faraway look in her eyes. He didn't call her on it. Her dictate had been not to *talk* about Joseph. Neither of them could avoid *thinking* about him.

She finished her martini as he crunched his final olive. "Ready for dinner?" She nodded. He offered his hand and together they left the lounge and crossed the lobby to the restaurant. It was a high-ceilinged, echoing space, with multiple large television screens mutely displaying sports scores and baseball games and professional poker. Servers threaded through the crowded tables carrying trays of drinks, and raucous feminine laughter screeched out from what looked like a bachelorette party at the back of the room.

As they waited for the host to acknowledge them, she touched his arm.

"I don't think I'm in the mood to handle Friday night at a place like this. What would you say to ordering takeout and eating in my room?"

"I'd say that's an excellent idea." He snagged two menus from a stack on a nearby sideboard and handed her one. When the host arrived, they gave their orders and were told their meals would be ready in fifteen minutes.

"Why don't you head up?" In the harsher light of the restaurant her cheeks took on a blueish tint that made her appear wan and ill. "I'll wait for the food."

"Would you?" She smiled, a faint spark of animation. "That would be great. Thanks."

"No problem. See you in a few minutes."

CHAPTER TWENTY-TWO

Phillip knocked on Aubrey's hotel room door using his elbow, a large paper bag with twine handles gripped in one hand and a tray with drinks in the other. There was something satisfying about bringing a woman food. Perhaps it was a vestigial instinct from humanity's earliest days. He grinned at a mental picture of himself armed with a spear chasing down some ancient form of deer while she crouched near a flickering fire.

After a short delay, Aubrey opened the door. "Sorry about that. I thought I had time for a quick shower while I waited."

That explained the damp warmth of her skin and the scent of mint dancing lightly over the heavier aromas of hamburgers and fries.

His smile didn't falter, but he felt it tighten. She had pulled her hair up into a loose knot on the crown of her head and changed from the pants and blouse she'd been wearing into a long dress made of a soft, clingy material. It drifted over her body, and though she was covered from neck to toes with only her arms bare, he was more aware of her breasts and hips than he had been all day.

He cleared his throat. "No problem."

She reached for the drink tray as she sniffed with appreciation. "That smells wonderful. Come on in. I cleared a space on the desk." She glanced over her shoulder. A darkened tendril of hair clung to her neck and a taut tendon emphasized the line from jaw to collarbone.

He wanted to lick that line. Slowly. With great care and attention.

Gathering his wits, he walked by—careful not to brush against her—and placed the bag where she'd indicated. "I wasn't sure if you wanted ketchup with your fries, so I had them throw in some packets." He distributed the containers.

"Mayonnaise?" She peered into the now empty bag with a hopeful expression.

The single word tweaked his memory. "No, I'm sorry. I'd forgotten that's what you like." She was the only person he knew who did—a custom she'd learned from her Dutch grandmother.

"And I'd forgotten you eat your fries plain." She spoke cheerfully but absently, absorbed in opening the waxed cardboard container that held her hamburger. "Ketchup's fine."

Her shower must have refreshed her spirits. She'd lost the fatigued, crushed aura that had been wrapped around her since leaving Annamarie's office. Her revived energy made his own blood rush through his veins.

Or maybe that was desire.

She'd dragged the room's single upholstered chair from its corner and placed it at the end of the long, low credenza that served as TV stand, dresser, and desk space. Stepping onto the seat cushion with her bare feet, she lowered herself into it, curling up rather like a cat with her knees tucked in. He pulled the hard plastic chair from under the desk and sat.

His burger was delicious, but he was greatly distracted by the alluring sounds Aubrey made, the way she licked a droplet of sauce from her fingers, the precise placement of each fry between her white, strong teeth.

She leaned back, wiping her hands on a napkin, and sighed. "God, I needed that. I was starving."

He looked down to realize he'd finished his meal as

well. He barely remembered chewing. "I'm glad you enjoyed it."

"I did." She tossed the napkin into the delivery bag and reached for her drink, tucking the straw between her lips. He turned his attention to clearing the trash from the desk, but he couldn't stop seeing her pink mouth puckered, her cheeks drawing in as she drank.

"Thank you for coming with me."

He met her gaze. She looked shamefaced, though he wasn't sure why. "You're welcome. We're both in this, you know. You don't have to deal with it alone."

"I know. And it is...nicer...to have the company." She paused, twisting the paper cup between her fingers, and then continued. "No matter how this all turns out, even if we don't find Joseph, I'm glad you and I have reconnected. I'm glad we can be friends again."

He supposed he was glad about that, too. But he had a sinking feeling being *friends* wasn't all he wanted from her.

If only he had some hint that she might feel the same way.

Phillip didn't look at her. Tying the handles of the bag together seemed to require all his attention. Aubrey wondered if she'd gone too far. He couldn't be angry that she wanted to be friends, could he? That was a pretty innocuous wish.

"Only if you want to, I mean." The hamburger she'd eaten congealed in her stomach, the meal solidifying with nerves. "I'll understand if, once this is over, you'd rather we didn't see each other. Except with Marjorie and Clarence getting married, I don't suppose we'll be able to avoid it completely."

He lifted his chin and gave her a level look. "What exactly have I done that suggests I want to stop seeing you any time soon?"

"Nothing!" Oh, god, now she'd offended him.

"You're much too polite."

His eyes narrowed. "Polite? You think I'm only doing this to be polite?"

She spread her hands, bewildered. "It's not an insult. Why are you upset?" Where had she gone wrong? She'd only been trying to give him an out, explain to him—and remind herself—that this new connection between them was temporary.

He jerked to his feet, dropped the trash bag, and kicked it under the desk with suppressed violence. "You sit there, looking like *that*, and tell me we should be *friends*?" His pointing finger slashed up and down as if dissecting her.

Her hand flew to the messy knot on the top of her head. "I know I'm a little untidy right now, but what does—"

He leaned over, one hand on the desk, one hand on the arm of the chair, his face lowered to hers. "You look like dessert." His brown eyes flared with amber coals. "Sweet and luscious and delectable."

Her mouth dried. Sweat sprang up on her palms. She swallowed, hard, and could think of absolutely nothing to say.

"I could never feel anything as bland as *friendship* for you." His conversational tone was at odds with his looming stance. His arms caged her, his gaze trapped her, but she had no urge to break free. She sat rooted in her seat, curled like a seed in its shell, mesmerized by his voice. "Not thirty years ago, not now. That's one thing that hasn't changed, for me at least. We can't erase the past. But that doesn't mean we're doomed to repeat it."

"What do you mean?" She'd meant to sound firm, confident, but the words came out in a hesitant whisper.

He answered with questions of his own. "Is that really all you want, Aubrey? To be my friend?"

Her heart pounded high in her chest, choking her. Her breasts and belly buzzed with tingling heat. His scent dizzied her, warm and potent and male. She wrapped her arms around her bent legs, rocking slightly.

"I don't know if I can be anything more."

He leaned in closer as she spoke. Her eyes closed briefly, her senses overwhelmed. "Why not?" It was a challenge, a dare.

"No reason." Her pulse scurried like a mouse on snow, fast and frantic. "And too many reasons."

Surprisingly, he nodded as if agreeing to this befuddled sentence. "If, when we met a few weeks ago, that had been the first time...if there was nothing between us but the thoughts and actions and feelings of the present...would you still deny what's happening right now?"

How many times had she wished she'd never fallen in love with him? How many times had she wished the heartbreak and grief they'd shared, the same heartbreak and grief that had torn them apart, had never happened? Only to feel searing guilt that those same wishes would have erased Samantha's too short appearance in this world?

"That's not a fair question. It's impossible to answer." Her eyes traced the lines bracketing the corners of his mouth, the grooves dug into his cheeks—proof of just how many years had slipped away. "You said it yourself. We can't erase the past."

"But we can use it to nourish the future." He knelt, tucking in close to her chair, so close his chest brushed her crossed arms where they clasped her knees. "The roots of things often live on, dormant and waiting, even when the plant appears withered, is given up for dead. All that's needed to bring it back to life is a little attention, a little care."

She knew he was talking about their marriage, their relationship—but he could have been talking about her soul. For years she'd felt like a dried husk, blown in random directions by whatever wind was strongest. He was telling her it wasn't too late to find fertile soil and start to grow again.

Could he be right?

Releasing from the closed, compact ball she'd formed, she laid her palm on his cheek. The scruff of his whiskers rasped her skin, ruffled along her nerves. She stroked the curve of his jaw, tracing his bottom lip with one fingertip. His eyes grew diamond-bright, and she shuddered when his tongue flicked out to taste her touch. She laid her other hand on his chest, shyly pleased to discover the frantic thump of his heart.

Still, uncertainty frayed the edges of her desire. "What happens if—"

"No." He tilted his head, resting his cheek in her palm. "No *what ifs*. Answer me this. Do you want me? Tonight, right now?" He asked the questions confidently, as if he had no doubt of her answer, but his eyes watched her warily. She took heart at this sign of vulnerability.

"Yes." Her heart swooped into freefall. His hands lay on the cushion of her chair, and she lowered her feet, feeling the stiffness of her joints and ruing the aches and pains of age. Spreading her knees just the tiniest bit allowed her to feel his fists like heated embers on either side of her thighs. "But—"

"No." He was stern. "If you have any doubts at all, tell me now and I'll go to my own room. If you want me to stay, you have to promise me one thing."

"What?"

"That you won't regret it in the morning. That you won't feel guilty or ashamed or any other emotion that might taint something so lovely as desire."

He was right. Desire *was* lovely, and even more beautiful when felt for someone so honest and trustworthy and genuine. He didn't deserve to be the subject of her insecurities.

She spoke slowly so he would know she meant every word. "I promise you. I will not regret tonight. No matter what happens."

"And what's going to happen, Aubrey?" He leaned closer, their breath mingling, the heat of their bodies entwining. "Am I going back to my room?"

"No," she said.

And kissed him.

CHAPTER TWENTY-THREE

Phillip tasted a hint of hesitancy in Aubrey's kiss and set about making her forget her worries with single-minded determination.

Without taking his lips from hers, he gripped the legs of her chair and twisted so she faced him directly. She clutched his shoulders for balance, gasping, and he let his tongue dance into her mouth to play with hers. The press of her fingertips eased, and she tilted her head to better accept his caress. Still on his knees, he shuffled forward, settling himself firmly between her legs and winding his arms around her waist.

She wriggled in his embrace, and he felt the tug of fabric between them. He eased his hips back a fraction—his bad hip already twinging a warning that he couldn't remain kneeling much longer—and she dragged the long skirt of her dress out from between them. Freed from the confining material, her calves hooked around his thighs, her ankles fitting perfectly into the bend of his knees.

His palms slid from the small of her back, slipping under the bunched fabric to find the bare skin of her thighs. Mouths still locked, his groan mingled with her whimper. The muscles under his hands jumped and twitched and when he circled his thumbs she almost rocketed from the chair.

God, she was so responsive. His cock, already hard and aching behind the confining fly of his jeans, stiffened further.

"I want to lie with you." Her lips skimmed his jaw as she spoke. "I want to feel you from head to toe."

"I'm okay with that. More than okay." He released her, hitching to his feet with a wince he hoped she didn't notice, and held out his hand. She placed hers in it and rose with smooth grace, her skirt falling to hide the curvy length of her legs. Drawing her with him, he took two short steps backward and sat on the foot of the bed.

Still standing, she released his hand, crossed her arms low at her hips, and in one swift move—a move that roared defiance and trust and confidence—pulled her dress over her head and tossed it to the floor.

Lust, already fierce and intense, grew volcanic.

She wore white cotton panties with purple violets. Her mismatched bra was a dull beige with thick fabric cups and wide straps, worn for comfort, not titillation. The sun-gilded skin of her arms and neck and lower legs contrasted with the milky paleness of her belly and thighs.

He couldn't stop looking at her, savouring every inch, wanting to touch, unsure where to start.

She shifted restlessly and he dragged his gaze to her face. Her glow of passion had faded, and his stomach cramped, certain she was one wrong word, one misstep, away from bolting. She'd taken his silence as disapproval, when it was a symptom of his stunned amazement that she stood here, before him, perfect in her imperfect beauty.

He raised his hands slowly, placed them on her hips. A tremor ran through her, but she held her position. With gentle touches, he urged her to turn, never relinquishing contact, his palms sliding over her skin until she faced away from him. Sweeping his fingers up her softly ridged spine, he undid the clasp of her bra and slipped it from her shoulders, letting it drop. Still wordless, he lowered her to his lap, nudging her legs so they spread over his.

She hissed, obviously noting the bulge under her

bottom, and he rolled his hips to make sure she'd have no doubt of his arousal. Dropping his chin to her shoulder, he nuzzled behind her ear, where the minty scent he'd noticed earlier lingered. He breathed in deeply and let the air trickle lightly from his lips, making the hairs that had escaped from her loose bun dance and sway.

Her head fell back to lay in the crook of his neck. The move lifted her breasts. They stretched in a gentle slope, and when he cupped them from below, his arms encircling her, they filled his palms perfectly.

Aubrey raised her arms over their heads and gripped his skull, bringing her breasts even higher. Her nipples hardened and he hadn't even touched them yet. The sight from this angle—the same angle Aubrey could see—was so erotic he had to close his eyes a moment, seeking control. She wriggled on his lap, demanding, urging, and the pressure in his groin grew, a painful intensity he welcomed.

Using his thumbs and forefingers, he pinched her swollen nipples, the barest touch. She jolted and the odour of her arousal deepened. It was a uniquely female scent—musky and fertile—and he repeated the caress. Her breathing sharpened into pants, her spine stiffened, and her hips jerked. He kept up the pulsing rhythm, her wordless sighs and mewls guiding him how hard, how fast. Her clasp on his skull tightened, her fingers twining in his hair and tugging with no care for his comfort, and she arched her back, bowing her neck over his shoulder. The tendon he'd wanted to nibble was there—right *there*—so he did.

Her hips launched off his lap, leveraged by her feet twined around his calves. The rush of her orgasm dampened his thighs. Her ecstasy was silent, but no less powerful for that. Her body racked and juddered and he wrapped his arms around her torso, supporting her. When the last tremors faded, she softened, limp and supple in his embrace once more.

I think I needed that, Aubrey thought hazily through the lingering sparks and explosions. She felt boneless yet powerful, satiated yet aroused.

Phillip held her, stroking her right arm from shoulder to fingertips in a lazy caress. She had collapsed against his chest and the firmness of his erection pressed tantalizingly against her backside.

She didn't like to talk while having sex, having decided long ago actions were more compelling than words. She slid off his lap, and without turning around wiggled out of her drenched panties, bending at the waist as she stepped out of them. A pained groan assured her he wasn't missing the show.

Straightening, she turned and allowed a small, satisfied smile to curve her lips at his glazed expression. She might have been hesitant at first, but no more. She was going to wring every second of enjoyment out of this night—and had already made a fair start. Now it was his turn.

She unfastened the top button on his shirt. He reached for the next one himself, but she gently slapped his hands away. Taking the hint, he laid his palms flat on the mattress. His gaze was tactile, a trail of heat on her face, her neck, her breasts, but he remained passive as she concentrated on each individual button, taking her time, letting her own arousal rebuild. She tugged the fabric out of his waistband to undo the last button, making sure her knuckles bumped and rubbed the bulge in his groin as she did so.

"Aubrey." Her name was barely a breath on his lips.

Slipping the shirt from his shoulders, she tossed it behind her. The strength and form of his chest and belly gave evidence he was an active man, but not one who spent hours at the gym. A small scar, faded almost to nothingness, crossed one pectoral. His body, like her own, showed signs of a life lived. It was beautiful in its maturity, in its unapologetic existence.

With one hand against his shoulder, she impelled him to lie on the bed and turned her attention to the fly of his jeans. With delicate care she unhooked the button, lifted the tab of the zipper, and slowly lowered it. His breathing remained deep and even but, when she slipped her hand inside to free his cock, his hands crushed the bedcovers, and he sucked in a sharp gasp.

Crouching at his feet, she removed his shoes and socks, and then reached up to hook her fing,ers in the waistband of his jeans. He lifted his hips and between them they worked the denim down until she could pull it free.

Her leisurely, deliberate undressing didn't only affect him. When she rose to her feet and surveyed him spread out before her, his cheeks flushed, eyes glittering, she felt the heavy swell of desire rise in her womb, her breasts.

A memory from the past floated to the surface. She'd shed tears on their wedding night—four months pregnant and distraught at her parent's continued disapproval, she hadn't been able to hold back her fear. Phillip, defiant and certain their love for each other would conquer all, had caressed and soothed her.

She pushed it away. They'd made their peace with the past, and tonight had nothing to do with the future.

There was only now.

She gestured him to move up the bed, and he scooted back using his elbows and heels, never taking his gaze off her. She followed on her hands and knees and straddled him. Taking his hot, heavy length in her grasp, she pumped it slowly, letting her fingers slide up and down with silken movements.

"Aubrey." His eyes closed, his jaw tightened, and he let her know with tiny motions and sounds exactly what she was doing to him, for him.

When he grew more urgent, when she recognized the signs he was reaching his tipping point, she rose on her knees, guided him to her entrance, and welcomed him in. His hands gripped her hips, adjusting her, and she flattened her palms on his chest, leaning forward.

They found a rhythm, advancing and retreating, and she realized she'd closed her eyes to better focus on the wonderful sensations of being filled again and again. Even when he rolled her over and pushed her knees up, changing the angle, increasing the tempo, she kept them closed. A kaleidoscope of colours danced on the inside of her eyelids, pulsing reds and oranges to match the heat growing in her belly.

His thrusts grew shorter, more frantic, less coordinated, and the randomness did nothing to weaken her own enjoyment. She clutched around him, heat flooding from her womb once more, and he grunted long and low. A moment later, he pushed against her once more, holding hard as he shuddered, as she wrapped her legs around him to keep him tight, and then lowered himself onto her with a care that brought tears to her eyes.

"Aubrey." His murmur branded her soul.

She had promised not to feel ashamed of the passion they had shared. And she didn't. But once her senses stopped reeling, she did come to an abrupt realization. "We didn't use a condom."

Phillip was stretched on his side next to her, one arm casually draped over her stomach, his head pillowed on his other elbow. He stiffened.

"Not that I can get pregnant. I had an IUD inserted when I was forty-five." Oliver had agreed to try for a child during the first two years of their marriage. But when that deadline came and went, she'd reluctantly accepted the gaping hole in her life would never be filled. As much as she loved Sophie, the yearning for another child of her body had never left her. "We should still have used one."

"You're right." She turned her head, her hair, long since fallen from its loose bun, rustling on the pillow. The skin around Phillip's eyes was creased with chagrin. "I haven't slept with anyone since Jeanette and I divorced. But I should have thought to protect you."

"I'm not blaming you. I'm responsible for my own actions. And it is as much to protect you as me. Though I haven't been with anyone since Oliver died." In fact, she'd almost forgotten the IUD was there.

"Neither of us should have anything to worry about then."

"No." It was only the truth. So why did she feel as if she was lying? "We should have nothing to worry about."

CHAPTER TWENTY-FOUR

The next morning began with yet another lie—if it was possible to lie to yourself. Aubrey thought it might be rather like playing solitaire chess. You knew you were thinking what you were thinking, but somehow managed to ignore it.

She was thinking she was disappointed to wake up alone, and the lie she told herself was that she wasn't.

Phillip hadn't rushed away last night. In fact, after their conversation about condoms, they'd risen from the bed, washed, dressed, and then settled in to search for Joseph Clarence Windt in the online death registry.

It had seemed a safe, if slightly morbid, topic that would ease them from the intensity of their lovemaking back into a quest she now saw as less volatile than the relationship growing between them.

Thankfully, they'd found no record, though they'd been careful to search various versions of the name and dates. He had then kissed her briefly on the corner of her mouth, wished her a goodnight, and retreated to his own room.

The sex they'd shared hadn't changed anything between them, she assured herself as she packed the few items she'd brought and prepared to leave the room. Like their conversation in the car and their exchange of *I love yous*, this had been the conclusion of a stage between them, not the start of a new one. No matter that he had wooed her with the idea of nourishing the withered roots of her soul, she couldn't trust this tentative connection. Beginnings were scary, middles terrifying. Endings, however, she had plenty of practice with.

Phillip wasn't sure what he'd expected when he met Aubrey outside her hotel room Saturday morning. After the experience they'd shared, would she be shy and self-conscious? Cold and distant? Painfully cheerful?

It turned out to be none of the above. She replied to his greeting with a casual friendliness that was neither overdone nor unnatural. He was the one that bumbled his good morning, swamped by memories of the night before and struck by the force of his longing to repeat it. His mental confusion manifested in physical ways, as he didn't seem to know where his arms and legs ended. He banged into the still-opening door of the elevator they rode to the lobby and smashed his knuckles when he placed his bag in the trunk of her sedan. They picked up coffee and muffins from Tim Horton's for an on-the-go breakfast, and though he scattered muffin crumbs everywhere, at least he didn't spill hot liquid on his lap.

Aubrey gave no indication she noticed his fumbles and stutters. He hoped she wasn't just being polite. He prided himself on his composure and revealing—even unintentionally—how shaky he'd been since their encounter last night would be a blow to his self-esteem.

Only an hour into their drive, when they were well on the highway heading north to Prince George, did he finally relax into some semblance of normalcy and leave the fractured emotions of the morning behind. "So, when are you taking the file to Clarence?"

"I managed to put him off until Monday." Her mouth lifted in a sly smile. "The DNA kits are supposed to arrive then, so I'm using it as bait."

"Still worried he might balk at providing a sample?"

"Not really, but I'm taking no chances. Also, I want to spend a day alone in my garden, in my house. I know we were only gone one night but it feels so much longer.

I miss it."

She didn't emphasize the word *alone,* but it echoed in his mind like a mournful bell. He'd been wondering how soon he could get her back in bed. She didn't seem to be having similar thoughts.

The rest of the journey passed in silence other than desultory comments about rest breaks and coffee stops. She left him at his condo with a wave and smile. He waited until she'd made the turn onto the street before unlocking his door and heading up the stairs and dropping into his favourite chair, the black leather one she had used the only time she'd been inside.

He swivelled the seat, surveying the space with new eyes. When he and Jeanette had agreed to divorce, they'd remained living together in the house where they'd raised their boys while they sorted out the details. Looking back on those months, he felt a sorrow he hadn't experienced at the time. Then, he'd been happy they'd been able to stay friends, that the decision to dissolve their marriage hadn't fomented bitterness and anger. Now, he realized how pathetic that was. Had their marriage been so pale and insignificant that its death had caused barely a ripple in their lives?

Was that complacency another reason for the restlessness he'd been feeling? Could it be that his recent desires to shake things up, to welcome upheaval and disruption, were signs he was no longer content to live a life of half-measures?

Good enough *wasn't* good enough anymore.

He wanted it all. And though he wasn't one-hundred percent sure what *all* was, he knew one thing. It included Aubrey.

He just had to ensure whatever *she* wanted included *him.*

Aubrey left Phillip at his door with a sigh of relief. She didn't think he'd noticed her turmoil, but the struggle to keep up the facade had exhausted her.

She pulled into the parking space behind her house with a welcome sense of homecoming, which was further heightened when, as she took her first step into the yard, a red streak shot out from behind the stairs leading to the back door.

"Hey, Red Cat. Did you miss me?" He circled her feet, an action he'd never done before, meowing in a demanding screech. "Careful, I'm going to trip on you. I bet you missed your dinner more than me, didn't you?"

She unlocked the door and placed her overnight bag on the closed lid of the ancient washer just inside. As had become her habit in her crusade to befriend the feral feline, she left the exterior door open while she went to the kitchen to get his dinner. Glopping the disgusting mess into his bowl, she turned to take it outside.

And froze.

Red Cat crouched, half in and half out of the opening leading from the hall to the kitchen. His tattered ear flicked and pink nose twitched, hungry yet suspicious.

Slowly she lowered to her knees and placed the bowl on the floor. Even more carefully, she slid it toward him. His back arched, eyes narrowing to slits. She stopped and drew her hand away, leaving the bowl where it was. Making no sudden movements, she settled on her butt and scooted in reverse until her back met a cabinet door. She would have liked to give him more space, but it was as far as she could go, and he was blocking the only exit.

Sitting tailor fashion, she waited.

As if he had no interest in her or the food, Red Cat sank into a relaxed posture, his front paws tucked under his chest. His gaze flitted around the room, landing on her only briefly, but coming back time and again to the bowl.

She felt a strange affinity with the scrawny beast. She, too, knew what it was to long for something yet be too scared to do what was necessary to achieve it.

Her bent knees protested but she sensed any movement would send him dashing out the door.

"Come on, sweetie." His tail lashed back and forth, belying his comfortable pose. "You know you want it."

Was this what people saw in her—this wariness? She scoffed at her own thoughts. It wasn't *people* she cared about, it was Phillip. Did he see the guardedness forcing her choices, and if so, why did he seem determined to break through?

Red Cat rose abruptly and, as if he had done it a thousand times before, strode straight to the bowl and began eating. She held her breath. He swallowed in great gulping mouthfuls and remained standing, tail and ears twitching with nerves. It took him barely a minute to finish the food. He looked right at her, licked his lips, and then without further ado strolled out of the kitchen and disappeared in the direction of the back door.

She groaned to her feet, her knees protesting audibly, picked up the bowl, and peered around the corner. Red Cat sat in a pool of sunshine just inside the door, washing his face. A low, rumbling purr resonated through the air.

Monday morning, the ringing of her doorbell interrupted Aubrey's first coffee of the day. When she opened the front door, the parcel delivery man was already on the sidewalk. At her feet, a package rested against the doorstep.

The DNA kits.

She picked it up and retreated to the kitchen, where she regarded the package with as much suspicion as Red Cat continued to eye his meals. The day before he hadn't been willing to come into the kitchen—she assumed his hunger wasn't as sharp as it had been the day of her return from Kamloops—but had condescended to come a few steps into the utility room. Today she would try to lure him a few inches farther. She still intended to capture him so he could be neutered but was unwilling to break the fragile truce so soon. She'd give him a few more days to grow accustomed to entering the house.

Thinking of Red Cat was only useful as a distraction in the short term. Taking a deep breath, she cut open the package and lifted out the three DNA kits. Opening one, she carefully read the instructions. It seemed too straightforward for something that could cause such dramatic repercussions.

She dialled her father's number. He answered with his usual gruff bark.

"The DNA kits have been delivered." She stacked the three boxes precisely on top of each other, then unstacked them. "When would you like me to bring them and the file from Duncan Truble to you?"

"As soon as is convenient." His tone was only slightly sarcastic. Despite the fact she'd told him everything they had and hadn't discovered, he'd been quite put out when she refused to rush him the file the minute she arrived home. Given those circumstances, his response this morning bordered on friendly.

"I'll be there at ten o'clock. Should I buzz your apartment or Marjorie's?"

"Marjorie's. We'll meet there."

She'd been about to ask him to tell Marjorie not to bother with coffee or treats, since they weren't allowed to eat for thirty minutes before giving their saliva samples, but he rang off before she could say anything further.

With a sigh, she went to get dressed for the day. She had a feeling she was going to need all the armour a well made-up face and designer clothes could give.

CHAPTER TWENTY-FIVE

Phillip wasn't sure how to decipher Aubrey's expression when she walked into Marjorie's apartment and saw him. "Oh." Confusion, acceptance, and relief layered one over the other, with a final icing of surprise. "I didn't realize you'd be here. Shouldn't you be at work?"

"Maybe, but Marjorie called half an hour ago to let me know you were coming, so I skipped out." Even though his staff didn't seem to mind if he escaped for an hour here or there, even took a last-minute day off like he had Friday, he needed to decide about his future commitment soon. It wasn't fair to keep flitting in and out like he had been the last few weeks.

Marjorie, enthroned in her upholstered chair, smoothed her palms on the arms. He knew she was nervous but doing her best to conceal it. "This feels a momentous occasion, and something we should do together, as a family. Also, I wanted to talk to you both about the wedding."

The furrows in Aubrey's brow deepened. "I'm sorry, Marjorie. I would have offered help sooner if I'd realized you were already making plans."

"Of course we are making plans." Clarence was blunt as usual. "We want to be married right away, as we've waited long enough. We are more than capable of arranging the details ourselves, though, and have done so."

The older man had been ensconced in his chair,

looking very much at home, when Phillip had arrived. The sight grated on his nerves, but he'd have to get used to it, he supposed. He didn't think he'd ever get used to the way Clarence spoke to Aubrey, though. He couldn't believe she put up with it. Had done so all her life.

Even now, she ignored his rudeness. "Of course, Dad."

"Did you bring the file with you?" He held out his hand demandingly.

She pulled the green folder from the canvas bag slung over her shoulder. "There's nothing in here I didn't tell you over the phone. I've copied the information I need, so I'll leave it with you to study in your own time." She directed her next words to Marjorie. "If everything is set for the wedding, what did you want to discuss?"

The older woman glared at her fiancé. "The nuts and bolts are all arranged, as your father says. But I would love your input—and Phillip's, too—on some of the finer details. Like flowers and the cake and such."

Since he'd had little to do with those areas for either of his marriages, he didn't think he'd be much use, but it was sweet she wanted to include him.

"I'd be more than happy to offer suggestions and ideas." Aubrey's smile was sincere. "How does this sound? The first step to collecting the DNA is to clean our mouths, and then we can't eat or drink anything for thirty minutes. I brushed at home, but why don't you and Clarence take care of that and then we can talk while we wait?"

With a disgruntled grumble, Clarence departed to his own apartment. More cheerfully, yet with a nervous air, Marjorie disappeared into her bathroom.

It wouldn't take her long to return, so Phillip dove right in, keeping his voice low. "I'd like to see you tonight. We could do dinner, or I could come by your place. Or you could come to mine if you'd rather."

He'd prepared a much more urbane invitation this

morning in front of his mirror, but the words had vanished from his mind.

A faint blush coloured her cheekbones. "I don't know if that's a good idea."

"Do not say Friday was a mistake. You promised you wouldn't regret it." He certainly didn't.

"I don't. But that doesn't mean we should repeat it."

"I'm not a one-night stand kind of guy, Aubrey. You knew that before we slept together." He'd do whatever it took to convince her.

She shot a worried glance at the closed bathroom door. The sound of water rushing from a faucet began and the pinched corners of her mouth eased. "I'm not that kind of woman, either. But where exactly do you see this going between us? Been there, done that, remember?"

He thought she was going for offhand, but her final words sounded more wistful than nonchalant. That gave him heart.

"We don't have to jump back into bed." His pulse kicked in his throat. Being patient might be harder now he knew their shared attraction burned as brightly as it had all those years ago. "We could just—"

The bathroom door opened, and Marjorie emerged. Aubrey made a chopping gesture with her hand, and he took the hint. He was no more ready for Marjorie to find out about their relationship than she was.

At least not until he'd figured out what to call the connection they were building.

Aubrey didn't want to know how Phillip had planned to end his sentence. She was rather insulted he had agreed so easily to put sex aside—and the fact she was affronted was more than a little alarming. She wanted him to want to have sex with her, but at the same time was frightened that being intimate again would only complicate matters further.

If only she could figure out what *she* wanted—no sex and a placid friendship, or more sex and be damned to the tangled emotions that entailed?

Clarence returned shortly after Marjorie interrupted their murmured conversation, and the next half hour was spent on the much less distressing topic of the wedding. Though even that had its pitfalls.

Marjorie had agreed to a Catholic ceremony, though neither she nor Phillip practiced the faith they'd been baptized into. Aubrey had long suspected that had been one of the reasons her parents had disliked Phillip on sight, and she had to bite her tongue to avoid making a snide comment on her father's hypocrisy. How could he have held that against the man Aubrey loved when he himself was in love with a woman with the same beliefs—or non-beliefs, as it were?

"The diocese insists all engaged couples participate in a Marriage Preparation Weekend." Clarence's disgust was plain. "Given our stage of life, this was a ridiculous requirement."

A giggle gurgled in Aubrey's chest at the image of Marjorie and Clarence sitting in a room full of twenty-somethings discussing sex, birth control and child-rearing. Phillip, next to her on the sofa, offered an expression of bland interest, though his throat flexed with repeated swallows as if he, too, was suppressing laughter.

"Clarence convinced the pastor to modify the course and present it to us privately." Marjorie smiled at him with approval. "We'll be done our meetings in mid-July, so we've reserved the first Wednesday in August."

"A Wednesday? And just over a month away?" Aubrey scrambled to reorganize her thoughts now she was aware of the short timeline.

"We are not having an elaborate celebration," Clarence said. "All that is strictly necessary are ourselves, two witnesses, and the celebrant."

"We've talked about this." Marjorie had steel in her

voice. "While I don't need hundreds of guests and an expensive party, I refuse to be married with no fanfare at all. I want to show people how proud I am that you will be my husband—though when you act like this I have to wonder."

Aubrey goggled at her father's abashed expression. Phillip's fortunately timed cough allowed him to cover his face with his hand.

"Speaking of witnesses," Marjorie continued serenely, now she'd put her fiancé in his place, "we would like to ask you to stand up for us. Phillip?"

"Of course I will." He rose to kiss her cheek then sat down again.

Aubrey met her father's stare. His grim mouth softened, and he dipped his chin briefly. Her throat constricted. "I'd be honoured." It hadn't crossed her mind he'd want her in this role.

"Invitations will be going out soon, but will you tell the twins the date?" A shadow flickered in Marjorie's eyes. "I don't suppose Asher will be able to join us now. He'll only be at his new job a couple of weeks."

"I'll ask him, but I don't imagine it will work." Aubrey remembered her heartache when Sophie moved to Toronto and suspected Phillip was equally distraught, but he hid it with his usual composure. "I'm sure he'll be very disappointed."

Marjorie straightened her shoulders. "Well, we can't expect him to put off this wonderful opportunity for a couple of old fogies like us." She turned to Aubrey. "You will let Sophie know? We realize a Wednesday event might make it impossible for her to come on such short notice, but that's the day we've chosen." The smile she offered Clarence implied forgiveness of his earlier unromantic notions and hinted at a secret understanding. Aubrey's throat tightened at this wordless sign of affection. "The ceremony will be at the church at 2pm, followed by a small reception here in the activities room."

Though a definite improvement on her father's plans, it still sounded rather drab.

"Marjorie? Is this what you want?" Phillip leaned his elbows on his knees and looked past Clarence to his aunt. "You've never been married before. Wouldn't you prefer something more"—he waggled his hands—"well, just more?"

A fleeting expression of yearning crossed her face, but she answered firmly. "As long as my closest family and friends are with me, it will be wonderful. There's no need for anything extravagant."

Screw that, Aubrey thought. Marjorie had the right to experience all the special treatment a bride deserved. Plans began percolating as the discussion turned to the topics of flowers, cake, and decorations.

Clarence looked disapproving but made no disparaging comments, and when the thirty minutes was up filled his tube with saliva without complaint. She still had trouble thinking of her father as *in love*, but he appeared willing to make compromises for Marjorie, which boded well.

Phillip said his goodbyes when she did. Together they made their way to the parking lot.

Wanting to forestall a continuation of any personal conversations, she patted the canvas bag where she'd placed the samples. "Well, I should get these shipped off. It will be weeks before we get any results, so the sooner I send them the sooner we'll hear back."

He kept pace with her. "I was thinking about our next steps, while we wait. There can't be that many Catholic dioceses in Saskatchewan. We should call them and see if we can track down Father Murray Athol."

"That's an idea." And one she should have thought of herself. "I have appointments with contractors this afternoon and tomorrow, but I'll get on that as soon as I can." She stopped next to her car and searched in her bag for her keys.

"Or I can do it. I was the first to agree to this search, but you seem to be doing all the heavy lifting."

"Sure, that's fine. You go ahead." The door handle was hot to her touch, the late morning sun beaming down out of a cloudless sky. Escape was imminent.

"About tonight. What do you say?"

He stood between the vehicles, half a car length away. One step and an outstretched arm and she could touch him. The urge to do so was fierce—which was why she couldn't let herself give in.

"Not tonight." Then she cursed, knowing she'd left the door open instead of slamming it shut.

"I'm not giving up, you know." He didn't move, yet the force of his presence wrapped around her like a weighted blanket. "You accused me of letting you go the first time. I won't make the same mistake twice."

"But what if I *want* you to let me go?" She didn't bother to hide her desperation.

He shook his head. "I won't do your dirty work for you. If you want me to go, you have to tell me in no uncertain terms." She stared at him, wordless, and he gave a sharp nod. "Okay then. Ball's in your court. You know I want to be with you, and not just because we're working on finding Joseph together or will soon be step-relatives of some sort. When you're ready to see me for *me*, let me know."

He strode away, leaving her clinging to her door handle, as well as the last shreds of her will power.

CHAPTER TWENTY-SIX

The next days should have passed with excruciating slowness as Phillip waited for Aubrey to call. Instead, they flew by so quickly he didn't have the time to start his search for Father Murray Athol.

His erratic attendance at the office had finally caught up with him. There were still several duties that only he could handle, and while his staff didn't appear to miss him when he was gone, their power was limited in certain areas.

As he tidied up what had been left unfinished and jumpstarted new projects, he paid close attention to which tasks made him happy and which chores he had to grin and bear. The days he spent mostly at his desk made him jumpy and irritable, but when he had a chance to leave the office and get his hands dirty, he went home satisfied in a job well done.

When he'd started Twin Rivers, he'd had to do it all—the paperwork, the client calls, the manual labour. Over the years, as was only natural, he'd become cocooned in spreadsheets and schedules and sales figures.

It was time for a metamorphosis. Or maybe less of a reinvention than a getting back to basics.

Thursday being July 1, Twin Rivers was closed for the Canada Day holiday. Aubrey still hadn't called, and with his sons busy with friends and Dexter off on an extended weekend camping with his family, Phillip was at loose ends. Deciding he might as well get work done, he headed into the office.

It should have been easier to concentrate without the usual interruptions—most of which were necessary but all of which were disruptive. Today, however, he was unable to focus despite the quiet, substituting one task for another task without finishing any.

Giving up in disgust, he launched his landscape design software and opened Aubrey's project.

She was never far from his thoughts, no matter how busy he was. It was pointless to brood on why she hadn't called yet. At least working on the design for her currently deconstructed yard would be productive.

He reviewed the notes he'd made and remembered the visceral feeling of inspiration he experienced the day he done the walkaround. His body twitched, eager to bring his vision to life, but first things first. He needed a plan.

He was noodling with the landscape software, playing with layouts and options, when his phone vibrated with an incoming call.

"Finally." Seeing Aubrey's name on the screen flooded him with relief and soothed the prickly sensation that had annoyed him all week. He hadn't realized how stubborn she could be. Their night together had been amazing. How could she ignore that, pretend that it never happened?

He connected the call, leaned back in his chair, and swivelled to look out the window behind him. "How are you doing?"

"I'm well, thank you." Her tone was brisk and unapologetic. "I have a favour to ask."

That didn't sound promising. She was supposed to call because she wanted to be with him, not because she had a job that needed doing. "Yes?"

"I want you to throw my father a bachelor party."

If he'd been drinking his spit-take would have been of epic proportions. He bolted upright in his seat, the chair rocking wildly. "You want me to *what*?"

"I'm throwing Marjorie a bridal shower next Friday. It seems only fitting you welcome Dad into your family with something equally appropriate the same night."

His mouth opened and closed like a fish gasping for water. "Clarence doesn't even *like* me." And that was an understatement. "Why on earth would he want me to throw him a party?"

"He doesn't know I'm asking. It would be a surprise, like Marjorie's shower. So don't tell her about it."

Well, the request had certainly surprised him. He hoped Clarence wouldn't have a heart attack when he found out what was going on.

"Who would I invite? What would we do?" He sounded pathetic and helpless. Reeling, he scrambled to organize his thoughts.

"I'm not talking strippers and Jell-O shots." Aubrey's tone was dry. "Marjorie sent me the guest list yesterday. It's less than thirty people, including family. Two are colleagues of Dad's. I'll send you their names and numbers. You could invite Zach and Asher, too."

Mentally, he reviewed his calendar. Asher started his new job a week from Wednesday, and was planning to leave the Sunday before, so he'd still be in town. Phillip had talked with Jeanette—who was devastated her son was leaving but doing her best to hide it—and they'd planned a goodbye party for the Saturday.

His Friday was open. Unfortunately.

"I suppose I could make that work." Not because of Clarence, though. Because of Aubrey and Marjorie.

"Have dinner at a nice restaurant, share a glass or two of scotch, have him home by ten." It sounded easy when Aubrey said it, but it would be anything but, he was sure. Hours of conversation would need to be filled. Maybe having a couple old friends around would take the edge off Clarence's tongue and he wouldn't flay Phillip the whole evening.

"What do I get in return?" Waiting for her to admit she wanted a relationship with him hadn't gone as planned. But she'd called him, and he wasn't going to let her slip away now.

"I'm hosting Marjorie. That's the trade off."

"Nope, not good enough. She likes you, and you like her. Clarence can barely stand to be in the same room with me."

"Then this will be an excellent opportunity to start mending fences, won't it?"

"What are you doing tomorrow evening?"

"Tomorrow? Noth—" He could practically hear the brakes in her brain screeching as she cut herself off. "Actually, I'm busy."

"Nice try. Let's go on a picnic."

"A picnic?" She sounded as shocked as if he'd invited her to dance naked in the moonlight.

Now *there* was an image...

"You said you don't regret having sex. Now prove it. Come on a picnic with me."

Her silence went on so long he woke up his phone screen to make sure the timer was still moving and they hadn't been disconnected. Had he pushed too hard? His heart thudded with mournful beats.

"All right." She was more resigned than welcoming, but he'd take what he could get. "Pick me up at seven."

Aubrey knew Phillip had basically blackmailed her but couldn't work up any outrage.

Instead, she spent most of her time in slightly breathless anticipation.

Restraining herself from calling after he'd left her outside Riverbend on Monday had been exhausting. Despite her uncertainty at what was happening between them, her fear of how badly it could all go wrong, she had to admit she *wanted* to take the chance he'd offered.

In fact, if she were completely honest, she'd used the idea of a bachelor party for her father as a face-saving excuse to get in touch. Thank goodness he'd suggested the picnic, otherwise she might have had to eat humble pie and extend an invitation of her own.

Though the first weekend of July in northern British Columbia was often cool and rainy, today was proving the exception to the rule. The sky was a clear, uncluttered blue that look solid enough to touch, and a gentle breeze softened the heated air. Phillip hadn't told her where they were going, but he'd instructed her to wear decent walking shoes and casual clothes. She'd spent far too long wavering between a sporty dress or shorts and a T-shirt. She'd compromised on a knee-length canvas skirt, sleeveless light green blouse, and a pair of well-worn running shoes.

Now she waited, perched on the front stoop. Red Cat, who grew friendlier each day but still declined to be pet or eat in the kitchen, was curled two steps below, lying couchant like a scrawny and battered heraldic lion, his eyes narrowed drowsily against the sun's glare.

Phillip's white pickup pulled to a smooth stop at her curb. Red Cat widened his eyes and regarded it balefully for a moment before slinking off the step and whisking around the corner of the house.

She plucked her brimmed straw hat from beside her and went to meet him on the sidewalk, belly quivering with anticipation.

"It sure looks different without Steve." He made a sweeping gesture toward the house.

"I kind of miss him." She wasn't sure if she was irritated he hadn't commented on her appearance after all the angst it had caused her or relieved to begin the evening with a neutral subject. "It made the front yard cozy. I know I said I wasn't going to replace him, but I think I've changed my mind."

"Funny you should say so." He opened the passenger door and gestured her in. "When you called yesterday, I was working on your landscape design. I was thinking the same thing. Caragana is hardy, easy to keep under control, and traditional in this neighbourhood. It would suit nicely."

She stepped onto the running board and into the cab. His hand cupped her elbow lightly in unnecessary support, his touch sending a flush of heat along her nerves.

"Where are we going?" she asked once he was behind the steering wheel and navigating them away from Cedar Street. "Or is it still a secret?"

"It was never a secret." His grin made her insides melt like a mushy schoolgirl's. "I just hadn't decided yet. Have you been to the Cranbrook Greenway Trails before?"

"A few times, but years ago. Before I was elected."

He nodded. "It's one of my favourite areas for biking. There's a lookout with a table and a view about a twenty-minute walk from the parking lot. I thought we'd go there."

Fifteen minutes later they were on the wide, well-maintained path leading into a forest of large birch trees and leafy bushes. He slung a compact backpack onto his shoulders, and after a few steps, took her hand. Startled, she tried to tug away, but he only gripped tighter.

"Please?" His mouth curled up at the corners, but his eyes were serious. She had an uneasy feeling this was a small challenge, and didn't want to fail. "Just for a little while?"

It would be ridiculous to make an issue out of it. After all, he'd touched almost every inch of her body last week. She squeezed his fingers in agreement.

Their steps matched easily, feet thumping softly on the peaty trail, hands swinging between them. A wooden, rail-less bridge crossed a meager creek, and an easy incline led them around gentle corners until another, longer bridge spanning a swampy patch came into view. Before they crossed it, he let go of her hand and led her onto a secondary trail. She followed, furtively enjoying an unimpeded view of his butt in his lightweight grey hiking shorts, the bunch and stretch of his calf muscles.

Birch gave way to a forest dense with evergreens not much taller than Aubrey, offspring of the enormous Douglas firs towering straight as telephone poles overhead. Distant traffic sounds filtered through the hushed air. Playful puffs of wind set the needles rattling, and the staccato rat-a-tat-tat of a woodpecker echoed. A mound of pinecone scales on a stump the size of a small table gave evidence of a squirrel's banquet.

The trail dipped and wound and climbed and spiraled, a cakewalk compared to the scramble up Mount Pope. She was content to follow along in silence, and he didn't appear to need the distraction of conversation, either. Occasionally he would look over his shoulder as if reassuring himself she was still there, smiling when he caught her eye.

She was rather disappointed when they reached a picnic table high on a bluff overlooking a pair of shallow ponds ringed with rushes and reeds. "Are we here already? I was enjoying our walk."

"We can take a longer route back if you like. There are dozens of trails." He shrugged the backpack off his shoulders and placed it on the table. The wood was rough and splintered, rotten in spots and carved with initials and symbols, the red paint that had once covered it peeling and flaking. "Are you hungry?"

"I am, but you know, I think I just want to appreciate the view for a bit." She walked to the edge, the steep slope falling away from her toes to the marshy border of the water below. "You're not in a hurry to get back, are you?"

CHAPTER TWENTY-SEVEN

Aubrey stood with her back to Phillip, framed by the trees arching overhead, bowing branches forming a window through which the linked ponds below could be seen. The scarf tied around the crown of her floppy hat fluttered, tangling with the long strands of her blonde and silver hair. She rarely wore it loose, but she had today, and the breeze teased it, set it sparkling in the sunlight. Her hands rested on her hips, arms akimbo, defining the slim muscles of her biceps and forearms. Below her skirt, the curving line of her calves led to strong ankles.

He swallowed, remembered she'd asked him something, and replayed her last few words in his head. "No. No, I'm not in a hurry. Take your time." He caught a glimpse of her profile as she turned her head left and right, and then moved two steps to sit on a fallen tree that formed a natural curb at the edge of the lookout. Propping her elbows on her bent knees, she rested her chin on her palms.

And then sat there, looking out over the tiger's-eye waters below.

He lowered himself to the table's bench seat, his knees unaccountably wobbly. He wasn't sure he'd ever seen her so at peace. She was most often in motion—if not physically active, then exercising her fierce intelligence. To watch her simply *being* was a revelation.

A revelation that exposed his own feelings.

He loved her. He wanted her—in sickness and in health, for richer and for poorer. In anger and sorrow, serenity and joy.

It wasn't the same love he'd felt as a teenager. It couldn't be. He wasn't the same man he'd been then. His new feelings weren't better or purer or stronger. They were simply *right* for where he was in his life right now.

After all, she wasn't the woman she'd been then, either. At seventeen, he'd had no doubts about her love for him. At fifty-three, he had nothing *but* doubts.

Staggered at the direction his thoughts had taken, he sought refuge in routine. Dragging his backpack onto the bench beside him, he unzipped the largest pocket and pulled out the cooler bag he'd stored there. From that bag, he removed a bottle of white wine and two insulated stemless wineglasses and set about pouring. The mindless actions helped settle his turbulent thoughts, and by the time he handed her one of the glasses he was able to smile with relative calm.

"What service." Her fingers brushed his as she accepted his offering, the brief touch an electric shock that raised goosebumps on the back of his neck.

"You're welcome." Desire roughened his voice, and he sipped his own wine to clear it. "I didn't want to insult your palate, since you're an expert, so I went with the same one we had at dinner that night at the restaurant."

"I'm not that fussy, but I'm impressed you remembered." She took a swallow, and he wished she was tasting him, not the wine.

He sat next to her—not too close, yet not so far as to draw comment. It was vital he continued to treat her as she expected, without any hint of the epiphany that had just rocked his psyche.

"I know there are more awe-inspiring vistas,

grander panoramas. But right now, right here"—she waved her hand at the view before them—"this is the most beautiful place in the world."

"I know what you mean." He wasn't looking at the ponds, however. Her expression was soft, relaxed, dreamy. All he'd done was bring her here, but pride filled his chest at her admiration, as if he were responsible for the scene before them.

"It's only missing a moose." She grinned and her delight sparkled through him like a firework. "Doesn't it look exactly like that sort of a swamp?"

"I've often thought so myself."

She sipped her wine and for several minutes they sat shoulder to shoulder and did nothing but look and listen.

"We should probably eat." He was reluctant to break the spell, but the sun was dipping lower in the sky. "It will be daylight for a while yet, but it gets dark quickly under these trees."

"What did you bring?" She followed him to the picnic table and peered over his shoulder. She was so close his elbow brushed her breast, but she didn't seem to notice. He, on the other hand, felt his cock rise and decisively turned his mind to less arousing thoughts.

"The best sandwiches on Earth." From his pack, he pulled out crinkly bundles and paper envelopes. "Plus, artisan potato chips and to-die-for dill pickles."

"That's quite the buildup." She rounded the table and sat on the bench with a view to the pond, gingerly shifting on the splintery wood as she swung her feet underneath.

"You won't be disappointed. Trust me. Here, this one's yours." He handed her a hefty sandwich wrapped in brown paper marked with *no tomatoes* in felt marker.

She stared at the notation and then up at him. "You remembered I don't like tomatoes?"

"Am I wrong?" Their talk of mayonnaise on fries

had ignited a series of memories about Aubrey and food. He knew she wasn't too picky, having eaten with her enough in recent weeks, but he honestly couldn't remember seeing her eat any. "Would you rather have mine? There are tomatoes on it."

"No, you're right. I was just surprised." She unwrapped the sandwich and regarded the towering stack with appreciation. "This *does* look like the best sandwich on Earth."

He had chosen thick sliced rye bread, lettuce, sprouts, avocado, red onion, two different kinds of cheeses, and a mix of deli meats. Generous smears of butter, mayonnaise, and spicy mustard oozed from the edges. "Wait until you taste it." Deeming it safer to keep his distance, he straddled the bench across from her and sat at a right angle to the table before unwrapping his own meal.

Her throaty murmurs of delight as she munched her way through her sandwich had his cock twitching. They reminded him of her subdued but joyous reactions when they'd made love. Distracted, he took a large bite of his pickle and choked as the sharp kick of vinegar burned his sinuses.

He needed to convince her back into his bed. And soon.

Phillip seemed preoccupied on the hike back to the parking lot. Not that he was rude or inattentive—it was more an air of deep thought that made him absentminded. He remained quiet on the drive home, and worry niggled at Aubrey. He'd been so adamant they spend time together, ever since their night in Kamloops. Now it felt like he'd taken a step back.

Just when she'd decided to take a step forward.

By the time he pulled up in front of her house, she knew she couldn't let him leave while this uncertainty ate away at her. She unclicked her seatbelt and twisted slightly to face him. "Penny for them?"

He blinked. "What?"

"You look like you have something on your mind."

His expression heated, sharpened, and then relaxed. "It's nothing."

Unwilling to let it go, she probed again. "Was it something I said?"

"Of course not. I was just—" He broke off, a muscle in his jaw clenching.

She reached over and brushed her fingers over the knuckles of his hand where it grasped the steering wheel. "I'm really glad we went out tonight."

"You are?" He slid her a glance out of the corner of his eye. His diffidence eased her worry. He'd seemed so confident before. This show of vulnerability gave her courage.

"I am." She swept her fingers up his bare arm, revelling in the sensation of sleek muscles under warm skin, to his nape. She toyed with the short hairs there. The rhythm of the rise and fall of his chest sped up. "Even though you blackmailed me into it."

He turned, forehead creased. "Yeah, about that—"

She smiled, infusing it with as much warmth and humour as she could. "I know why you did it. If you hadn't, I'd probably still be avoiding you."

"Why?" His hands dropped from the steering wheel and fisted on his thighs. "Why have you been avoiding me?"

Dusk was falling, and the light in one of her neighbour's porches flickered on. "Do you want to come in? We can talk more comfortably there."

After a slight hesitation, he nodded and turned off the ignition. She led him around the house to the back door. In the shadows under the stairs, she caught the gleam of a green eye and the flash of a long tail as Red Cat vanished into his bolt hole.

Inside, they removed their shoes. She took Phillip's hand and ushered him down the short hall to her bedroom.

"I thought we were going to talk." He balked in the doorway, planting his feet. "*Just* talk."

She released him, stepped to the chair in the corner draped with previously worn but still clean clothes, and unfastened the top button of her blouse. "I've been avoiding you because I'm chicken." She chose the childish word on purpose and was relieved when his tense features softened in a small grin. Her hands moved to the next button. "You make me want things I haven't wanted in a long time."

His eyes locked on her fingers. "And is that a bad thing?"

"No." The third button gave way, and the fabric gaped. The window on the far side of her bed was open and an evening breeze wafted in, cooling her heated cheeks, the valley between her breasts. "But it is scary. I needed some time to get used to it."

His gaze dragged up her chest, along her neck, over her face. The embers kindled in her during the evening flared and ignited. "Are you used to it now?" His voice was a hoarse growl.

The last button came undone. She rolled her shoulders, and the blouse slipped into her hands. She tossed it on the chair. "Yes."

"Why?" He didn't move from his post at the door. "Why tonight?"

She undid the snap and zipper of her skirt and let it drop to the floor. She felt slightly ridiculous standing before him in bra, panties, and ankle socks, but didn't let her determination waver. "I told my father after I lost the election that I was tired of doing what other people wanted. It was time to do what *I* wanted for a change. Which means I had to make sure I wanted to have sex with you for the right reasons."

A flicker of amusement lightened his intense expression. "You didn't want it to be pity sex? Pity for me, I mean?"

"Something like that." It was easier to agree to that explanation than admit she'd been craving his touch and had finally succumbed. She crooked her finger at him. "Now come here."

CHAPTER TWENTY-EIGHT

Still, Phillip hesitated. He'd been intent on getting into bed with Aubrey for days now, and the desire had only increased during their picnic. But now that he was here, in her bedroom, and the possibility was a probability—he paused.

Her outstretched hand trembled, and then dropped to her side. "Phillip?"

He couldn't let her glow of confidence fade yet needed confirmation that her change of heart meant something more than scratching an itch. He approached her slowly, stopping bare inches away. Her gaze lifted to his, confusion lurking in the depths of her eyes.

"I very much want to make love with you. But it's only fair to tell you that it doesn't end there. Not for me." He had no intention of revealing his recently rediscovered love, but he needed to make sure she knew this wasn't a fling for him. "I told you before I'm not a one-night stand kind of guy, and I meant it."

"I know. That's the other reason I've been avoiding you." She focused on the middle button of his collared T-shirt, touching it with one fingertip as she laid her other palm flat on his chest. He felt branded by the simple touch. "I needed to be sure I was ready to explore something more than a casual relationship." She peeped up at him. "And I am."

The details of what that relationship might encompass could be worked out later. For now, he was swept away by an overwhelming sense of relief and rightness. Aubrey might not be *his*—not yet anyway—but she seemed willing to try. That was all he could ask.

His hands on her hips, he drew her against his body. She nestled against him, her head on his shoulder, her arms cradled between them. The renewed emotions he'd recognized only hours ago swamped him. Even though he wasn't ready to tell her what he felt, he could show her.

Disengaging gently, he knelt and hooked his fingers in the sock on her left foot. She rested her hand on his head and lifted her leg. He removed the sock, and then repeated the actions with her right foot. Playfully, he traced one finger along her instep.

She gasped and jerked. "That tickles." Her fingers tightened in his hair in warning. He looked up, grinning, but released her. Trailing his hand up her leg, from ankle to knee to outer thigh, he watched her face, her expression changing from laughter to passion. He swiftly stripped her panties off, mesmerized by the bounty he revealed, inhaling her scent, and couldn't resist a quick nuzzle, a teasing appetizer of what he planned to savour soon. The firm muscles of her thighs trembled, and he gave her one more nipping kiss before leaning away.

Still on his knees he reached up behind her back and unhooked her bra. With a little encouragement it fell away from her breasts, the straps slipping down her arms. Only when she was completely naked did he rise to his feet, excruciatingly aware of his erection tightening the crotch of his shorts.

She stood, arms hanging loosely at her sides, chin lifted. Her nipples had pebbled into points and her breathing was quick and rapid. Cupping her cheeks in his palms, he kissed her.

Though their bodies remained separate, he felt surrounded by her burning desire. As their lips and tongues played and teased, his skin flushed with lust and love, fiery goosebumps rippling on his chest and thighs. Escaping the inferno for an instant, he stripped as quickly as he could, staggering slightly as he kicked aside his shorts and briefs. She tore back the bedcovers and moments later they were entangled on the cool sheets, pressed so tightly together he wasn't sure where he ended and she began.

Even through the haze of her passion, Aubrey sensed something different about Phillip's lovemaking. It was both more desperate and more tender, more demanding and more giving. As his lips explored every inch of her body, his hands molded and caressed her, she fell deeper and deeper—into what, she wasn't sure. She only knew she revelled in it.

He refused to let her take any initiative. Whenever she reached for him, he gently removed her hands, pressing them into the mattress.

"Tonight's for you," he murmured against the skin of her stomach. "All for you."

He made his way lower, and when he breathed deliberately on the aching, pulsing flesh between her legs she grabbed frantically for the metal rails of the headboard, desperate for any anchor in the maelstrom brewing in her belly. With slow, purposeful licks, he brought her to a lava-like boil. Her hips thrust upward, and he gripped her, holding her still. The sweet incarceration elevated her desire, and she detonated, her sense of self shattering into pinwheels and prisms.

Before she could collect the scattered bits of her soul, he slid up her body, his mouth claiming her as his cock filled her. Still gasping from her orgasm, she wrapped her arms and legs around him and held on, letting him use her body for his own pleasure, powerful in her vulnerability, fierce in her openness.

When he collapsed upon her, panting and shuddering, she held him gently, soothing him with sweeping caresses up and down his spine, tiny kisses along the strong arc of his shoulder. Too soon, he raised himself and she clung like a limpet, dragging him down. "Not yet," she whispered into his neck. "Not yet."

After a second's hesitation, he relaxed, sliding slightly to the side, but still sheltering her, still covering her, and she closed her eyes, luxuriating in being held, being cherished.

And wondered if the awkwardness she had felt between them the last time they'd had sex would return.

"I can hear you thinking." His raspy voice was muffled against her hair. "Stop it."

"Sorry." Her voice came out low and hoarse, her lungs compressed by his weight. She didn't want him to move, but with a sigh he rolled onto his back, keeping her tucked against his side.

"What is it now?" He sounded indulgent rather than irritated and she took heart.

The greying hairs on his chest were springy and soft under her palm. "That's what I'm wondering. What now?"

He paused on an inhale and then slowly let out a breath. "That wasn't exactly what I meant, but I get it. What do you want to happen now?"

It should have felt odd to have this conversation naked and sticky from sex. But her room was dark, lit only by the subdued glow of a streetlamp outside the window, and the gloom made her feel safe, protected.

Or maybe that was his warm body snugged against hers.

"Does this mean we're back together?" she asked in a burst of bravery, "and if so, how together is *together?*"

"Who knows better than us that life isn't made of absolutes?" His right arm was under her neck, his fingers tracing small circles on the rounded joint of her shoulder. "For now, though, I say together means we're exclusive to each other. That we explore what we have at a pace that suits both of us. That we're honest and straightforward and don't play games."

"Just see what happens, you mean? Take it a day at a time, without any specific plans?"

"Exactly."

It wasn't the way she had lived her life—at least, not until she'd lost the election. But it certainly suited the mindset she'd been practicing since then. "I think I can do that."

His body seemed to sink deeper into the mattress, as if some tension that had been holding him slightly above the surface had released. "Okay then."

They lay quietly. Not having any plans was all well and good, she thought, but there were some decisions that had to be made sooner rather than later. For example—

"Would you like to stay the night?" It was easier to extend the invitation from behind closed eyelids, with his scent and heat surrounding her. If they'd been face-to-face, she didn't know if she'd have had the daring. "Only if you want to, of course."

In a sudden movement he rose over her and her eyes flared open. "I would love to stay." In his face she saw all she'd feared and hoped—joy, lust, and a shining tenderness that choked her. "I hope you aren't planning on getting much rest, though."

Phillip drifted out of sleep with a vague feeling of disorientation. It took a moment or two to remember where he was and recall the events of the night before.

He opened his eyes. Aubrey lay on her side, her hands cupped under her chin. Strands of hair draped over her face and fluttered with the soft, even exhalations of her breath. The open window at her back flooded the room with daylight, though a quick glance at the clock on her bedside table said it was well before six. Dawn came early in July.

If he'd thought sex with Aubrey had been amazing

the first two times, the next time blew him out of the water. She seemed to throw all caution to the winds, bringing an intensity to their joining that left him gasping. It was as if she'd made a commitment to not only take each day as it came, but to squeeze every ounce of enjoyment from every instant.

The thought made him uneasy. Watching her now, lax in slumber, he wondered if she'd taken his words as a challenge, not a promise. He wanted her to accept him—not instill a fervour that couldn't be maintained and might burn itself out before he had a chance to prove his love.

This Aubrey didn't do things by halves, he was discovering. She was either all in, or all out.

He'd just have to show he didn't need a bonfire. A single, steady candle flame could burn brighter and last longer.

CHAPTER TWENTY-NINE

Determined not to let Aubrey reconsider the decision she'd made in the intimacy of her bed, Phillip set about reinforcing their relationship the moment she woke on Saturday.

Unable to sleep after his dawn awakening, he slipped out of bed, gathered his clothing, and headed to the bathroom. It was a tiny, cramped space with stained but clean fixtures, and had to be near the top of her list of renovations. The house had plenty of charm and character, but desperately needed modernization. She'd mentioned appointments with contractors—he'd have to ask how that had gone.

After showering, he sniff-tested yesterday's clothes, was relieved they would do for a few more hours, and then made his way to the kitchen. By the time Aubrey joined him, wrapped in a silky pale-yellow robe with her hair still in disarray, he was on his second cup of coffee and had their weekend planned. She made a few objections, but they were half-hearted and weak, and in the end, she'd acceded to his ideas with a smile and a kiss.

Now it was Monday morning, and he could look back with satisfaction on the last two days. From when she'd come into the kitchen to his kiss goodbye last night, they'd spent every moment together, other than the hour he'd raced home to get a change of clothes and his overnight items. They'd worked in the yard, reviewed her renovation plans, gone for long walks, tried to lure Red Cat into the house, and watched the sunset from her makeshift patio while sipping wine.

And made love, of course. He couldn't get enough of her, wasn't sure he ever would.

He wasn't completely certain she was fully on board with their new rapport. Sometimes she seemed as wary as the stray cat she'd adopted. But he wasn't done courting her, and he could be patient.

In the meantime, there was a bachelor party to plan—god, he must really love her if she'd managed to coerce him into doing *that* for Clarence—and Joseph to find.

The topic had come up over the weekend, of course. On the DNA front, they could only wait until the results came back. "And even then," she had said repeatedly, "if Joseph hasn't done his own testing, there will be no matches to find." Which left Father Murray Athol as their best lead.

In his office at Twin Rivers, he Google-searched between taking care of necessary business tasks. A street view of the address in Regina where Truble had sent his letters only showed a strip mall surrounded by other strip malls, but one result led him to the Archdiocese of Regina website. He poked around there and discovered a directory of diocesan priests.

He clicked through, his heart rate accelerating. It couldn't be that easy, could it?

It wasn't. No Father Murray Athol was included, though recently retired and deceased priests were listed.

Finding the directory gave him hope, though. Perhaps the other Roman Catholic dioceses serving Saskatchewan had the same sort of listing.

And that's exactly where he found him, on a PDF downloaded from the Diocese of Prince Albert website. Under his name, the word *retired*.

Aubrey's house felt very empty on Monday morning. She told herself she couldn't grow accustomed to Phillip's presence. While she'd thoroughly enjoyed the weekend they'd spent together—more than she'd expected to, in fact—it wouldn't do to get used to it. The future was nebulous, unpredictable, and thinking about it might make her wish for something—more.

And wishes were dangerous things.

Shaking off her wistfulness, she tossed a load of laundry in the ancient washing machine, tidied the kitchen, and then stood staring into space. She was caught in the doldrums of renovations, waiting for the contractors to get back to her with quotes, and with Phillip's help she'd done the last of the clearing and cleaning the house had needed. Now all she could do was wait.

She couldn't even think of anything to do in the search for Joseph. The DNA kits had been sent off, and Phillip had insisted he be responsible for Father Murray. She had wanted to spend time on the internet over the weekend, but he had distracted her with kisses and cajoled her into a Joseph-free weekend. She hadn't put up much of a fight.

He had promised to start that search this morning, and was coming over tonight for dinner, though he had agreed to call immediately if he discovered anything exciting. For now, she would have to leave it with him.

Which left the surprise bridal shower she was planning for Marjorie. She set up in the kitchen with her laptop, a pad of paper, a pen, and a fresh cup of coffee.

She had asked for a copy of the wedding guest list under the guise of ensuring her father wasn't snubbing anyone—a prospect his loving fiancée had agreed was entirely possible. From that list she had determined that Marjorie, who had spent the last twenty-plus years away from Prince George, had invited only one female friend to the wedding, and that friend was in

Vancouver.

Knowing it was a long shot, Aubrey called her, but her suspicions had been correct. The woman was delighted to be attending the wedding but couldn't manage two trips to Prince George in the short timeframe. She promised to send a gift and asked her to give Marjorie her best wishes.

Now she had to figure out how to throw a party with no guests. It wasn't like she had friends of her own she could appeal to. She and Oliver had had an active social life, but she'd lost touch with most of those couples, many of whom had been Oliver's friends, not hers. And the only people she'd met since leaving politics were the members of the Silverberry Book Club. As much as she liked them, she didn't think they'd come to the bridal shower of a woman they didn't even know.

She paused in the mindless doodling disfiguring the blank page in front of her.

Why not? It couldn't hurt to ask. They weren't exactly strangers to thinking outside the box.

She picked up her phone to call Natalie. It rang underneath her hand, making her heart jump in fright. The name on the screen did nothing to slow her galloping pulse.

"Hello, Phillip." Her palms went damp, and she squirmed—just a little—in her chair. She felt like a schoolgirl getting a call from her first crush. Of course, he had been her first crush, but that was a long time ago.

"I found him." His tone was justifiably triumphant.

"Already? How?" She collapsed against the back of the chair, only to jerk upright when the edge of the cracked vinyl poked her spine.

"He's listed as retired on the Diocese of Prince Albert website."

"But we Googled him. Nothing came up."

"It was in a PDF I had to download to view, so maybe that's why. There was no contact information, so I called the diocesan administration office, but I had to leave a message. I promised I'd let you know when I found out anything, so here I am." When he spoke next, he sounded low and intimate in her ear. "Besides, I wanted to hear your voice."

She couldn't tell if the fluttering in her throat was caused by the excitement of his discovery or the tenderness with which he uttered the last sentence. He was at work and she should probably let him go, but she didn't want the conversation to end. She'd missed his voice, too, and if she wasn't as brave as he was, she could at least make sure he knew she was looking forward to seeing him again. "I'm glad you're coming over. Cooking for myself was getting a little old. I'm planning something special."

"Our meals this weekend weren't special?"

She laughed. "I think we can do better than tuna casserole and spaghetti with jarred sauce."

"Hey, I made the tuna casserole! I'll have you know it's my sons' favourite."

His mock affront widened her smile. "It was delicious, don't get me wrong. I just have something a little fancier planned for tonight."

"Should I bring dessert?"

"No, that's all right." She let a soupçon of wickedness seep into her voice. "I'll take care of dessert, don't you worry."

His pained groan sent her into a gale of giggles. She disconnected the call, more buoyant and carefree than she'd been in years. Still snickering quietly, she scrolled through her contacts and tapped Natalie's name.

Her friend answered after only one ring. "Aubrey, how are you?"

"I'm good, thank you." How wonderful to give the stock response to the usual question—and be telling the truth. "Very good, in fact."

Natalie's unseen smile warmed her answer. "I'm glad. Any particular reason?"

"Just life." She hugged the thought of Phillip tighter.

She didn't want to share him, not quite yet. "I have big plans for this little house of mine, we think we're getting closer to finding my half-brother, and my dad and Marjorie have picked a wedding date. That's why I'm calling."

"What can I do?"

That was so much like Natalie—an offer to help before she even knew what was needed. Her heart swelled as she let herself revel in the knowledge she had at least one friend truly worthy of the title. "Not just you, actually. I was hoping the Silverberry Book Club was up for a party."

CHAPTER THIRTY

Phillip arrived at Aubrey's just after five-thirty Monday afternoon. As much as he was in a hurry to see her, he took a few moments to sit and contemplate.

For some reason, tonight felt like a step into unknown territory. Maybe it was coming right from work that made it feel as if he were coming *home*—no longer a visitor, but someone who belonged there. Through the window of his pickup, he could see the house, the signs of neglect and abuse not yet erased by loving care and attention. It had the air of a Victorian orphan who had had a bath and was dressed in clean hand-me-downs but still needed a haircut and shoes that fit. The renovations she had planned would restore it to an understated elegance that completely suited the neighbourhood and honoured the era in which it had been built.

He hoped he'd be there to see it happen.

Picking up the bouquet of flowers lying on the seat, he exited the truck and headed around the side of the house. Morning rain showers had given way to a beautiful, blue-sky afternoon, and the door was propped open. On the threshold, half in and half out, Red Cat lay curled in a headless, legless ball, sunshine sparking like embers off his now sleek coat. The moment he placed a foot on the lowest tread the creature exploded into an arched-back, spitting fury, dove off the stoop, and disappeared under the building.

"Still working on your trust issues, I see." He hoped

227

the animal wasn't channelling Aubrey's current mood. Without ceremony, he stepped into the house, and then hesitated. Just because *he* felt at home didn't mean she would welcome him with the same attitude. Reaching back, he knocked on the door frame and called her name.

"In the kitchen," she called back. "Come on in."

He followed the scent of garlic and rosemary and other tangy aromas into the house. She was using the table as a workspace—the kitchen had a definite lack of countertop—and deftly mincing something green. She wore a thin dress in a mellow orange with a scooped neck, no sleeves, and a skirt that swirled just above her knees. It came to him that she'd lost the hard, brittle shell so noticeable during their first few encounters. She looked soft and approachable and warm.

She certainly heated his blood.

"You brought flowers." Her expression bloomed brighter than the blossoms in the bouquet. "You didn't have to do that."

"I know." He held out the cellophane wrapped package and she took it, stretching to give him a quick peck on the cheek. Before she could back away, he snaked an arm around her waist and pressed his lips to hers. Her mouth opened eagerly, the kiss flaring from welcome to passion in an instant. He lifted his head reluctantly, his lips clinging, unwilling to let go.

"That's some hello." Her voice was husky, her eyes blurry and unfocused. "You're setting the bar high tonight."

"I think we can rise to the challenge." He nudged her with his hips so she didn't miss the innuendo, and she laughed. She was doing that more often—laughing, that was. He couldn't help a swell of pride at the thought he made her happy.

She patted his chest, brows lowered with mock sternness. "Dinner first. Then dessert." He allowed her to slip out of his arms. She opened the cupboard above the fridge and removed a large glass jar that looked like it might once have held pickles. "I don't have any vases here, but this will do for now. I found it in the basement and thought it might come in handy."

Willing to accept her decree, he crossed his arms and leaned against the wall. "What is for dinner? It smells great."

She moved to the sink and unwrapped the flowers. Her swift, economical movements were a joy to watch. "Rosemary chicken breasts, lemon potatoes, and Greek salad, along with homemade pita bread and tzatziki. Do you mind starting the barbeque?"

"Of course not." He went to the patio and lit the grill. Unlike the rest of Aubrey's appliances, it was brand new, as she'd discarded the rusted-out beast left with the house, certain it was a safety hazard.

Back in the kitchen, she tossed him a quick smile of thanks over her shoulder as she snipped off a flower stem. "We have time for a glass of wine or a beer before we eat. You know where it is."

"What would you like?" He opened the fridge and took out the bottle of white wine he found there.

"I'll have some of that. Thanks."

His sense of homecoming deepening, he poured their drinks as she hummed tunelessly while arranging the flowers in their pickle jar vase. The low thrum of sexual attraction gave the everyday actions an added intensity, like the pilot light on a gas stove waiting in readiness, needing only one spark to set it aflame. He was old enough to appreciate delayed gratification— and young enough to be tempted to damn it all and entice her to the bedroom then and there.

His older self won, and with inwardly directed amusement he took a chair at the table. "So, the diocese called me back."

Her head whipped around. "Journalists call that burying the lede. When you didn't say anything right away, I figured there was no news yet. I didn't want to bring it up and spoil the evening."

"You distracted me." He waved his glass in her direction, waggling his eyebrows like a cartoon villain, and watched in fascination as a blush crept up her neck to her cheeks.

"Well, you're not distracted now." She poked the last stem into the arrangement. "What did they say?"

"I spoke with the Bishop's assistant. He confirmed Reverend Murray Athol was a parish priest in the Diocese of Prince Albert for his entire career." He frowned. "Do priests have careers?"

She waved off this detour, her hands full of flower debris. "I know what you mean. Do they know where he was in 1960? Is he still alive? And if so, can we talk to him?" She tossed the cut stems in the compost bucket under her sink, then joined him at the table.

"Yes, yes, and it's complicated. At the time Truble wrote Athol, he was posted to Nipawin, a small community in northern Saskatchewan. Over the decades, he spent time in other towns throughout the northern half of the province before retiring ten years ago. He lives in a retirement home run by the Catholic church in Prince Albert now."

It was her turn to frown. "He never worked in Regina? But that's where Truble wrote to him. Are you sure this is the right man?"

"According to diocesan records, the address Duncan Truble used was for Athol's parents. That house no longer exists." He told her about his Google Street View search. "I think Truble used a private address because he didn't want his inquiry to go through any even remotely official channels."

"Given my father's wish for secrecy, that makes sense." A bell chimed, and she opened the oven door. Heat and the scent of citrus filled the tiny kitchen. She poked at the potatoes baking in a glass dish, shut the door, and picked up another dish covered in cling film. "I'm going to put the chicken on the barbeque. Will you bring my wine?"

As she placed the meat on the grill, he continued his story. "When I heard he was still alive, I was thrilled. Until the assistant told me about Father Murray's condition." She gave him a quick, questioning look. "He has dementia. And it's quite advanced."

"That's terrible. And I don't mean that selfishly. I'm sorry for him." She closed the lid of the barbeque and took a seat. "It seems especially unfair to destroy any enjoyment a person might get in the final years of their life by stealing their memories."

She looked so troubled he couldn't resist brushing his fingers on her soft cheek, offering what comfort he could. Her skin was warm and slightly damp, perhaps from the heat of the barbeque. She leaned into his touch, and then straightened with an air of determination.

"Did you tell the assistant why we wanted to get in touch with Father Murray?"

"No. I wanted to talk to you first. If the adoption was conducted in strict confidence between Truble and Athol, the diocese wouldn't know anything about it. Do you think we should tell them? Or do we talk to Father Murray first?"

"Are we allowed to?"

"I don't see why not. We could ask for a video conference. I'm sure an aide at the retirement home could set that up. If we don't learn anything, we're no further behind. As I understand it, long-term memories aren't always affected by dementia. Maybe Father Murray will still be able to help."

"It's worth a shot." She sipped from her wineglass, the sun's rays turning the pale liquid golden. "Have you told Marjorie yet?"

"No. I thought I'd wait until we know if we can talk to Father Murray. Do you think we should tell her and Clarence now?"

She shook her head. "It's fine. We can update them

later." Her expression grew thoughtful. "I wonder if my father knew about Father Murray."

"Why would you think that? All we've learned indicates Clarence wanted to be one step removed from the adoption."

"Because of the documents that *aren't* in Truble's records. It might not have been an official client file, but he was a lawyer. It would have been second nature to keep every piece of correspondence. The fact there are no letters concluding his conversation with Father Murray has always seemed rather suspicious to me. I wondered if my father had anything to do with that."

"You think Clarence was paranoid enough about exposure that he asked Truble to get rid of evidence?"

She shrugged. "Maybe. And maybe I'm overthinking it." She rose, lifted the lid of the barbeque, and used long-handled tongs to turn the chicken breasts.

"Would it really have been such a scandal if the affair had been discovered?"

"It was a different time." Out of nowhere, she asked, "Do you know how judges are appointed in British Columbia?"

"I haven't really thought about it."

"You apply. There's a long list of criteria, but if you think you meet those standards, you put your name in the hat. The Judicial Council considers your application, which must include numerous references willing to speak to your professional qualifications, temperament, ability, and community standing. Knowing my dad, he intended to become a judge the moment he passed the bar. The fact he'd had an extramarital affair that resulted in a child would have been a big black mark against him. It could have ruined all his plans." She closed the lid with a bang. "I have no trouble imagining him doing all he could to conceal it."

CHAPTER THIRTY-ONE

Aubrey placed the laptop on the kitchen counter in Marjorie's apartment and opened the video chat application. The camera powered up and she studied the shot.

"You need to scooch closer to the table." She pointed at her father. "I can't see you on the screen."

Looking grim and grumpy—what else was new?—Clarence did as she asked. Marjorie, on the opposite side, moved in closer as well, her hands clasped on the shiny wooden surface, her expression apprehensive.

"Do you think he'll remember anything?" It was a variation of the same question Marjorie had asked many times in the twenty-four hours or so since the meeting with Father Murray had been arranged.

"I don't know." Phillip showed no signs of impatience. "We'll find out soon, I guess."

He sat where she had directed him, at the far end of the table. She would take the chair next to him once the call had come through.

She studied her father surreptitiously. He sat, stiff and stern as usual, but he wasn't fooling her. Not anymore. It had taken her more than fifty years, but she was finally catching on to her father's tells, and his inability to maintain eye contact revealed his agitation as loudly as an air raid siren.

The evening before, they had gone together to let Marjorie and Clarence know the latest news. She'd watched Clarence when Phillip announced they'd found

Father Murray Athol. A more casual observer might not have caught the tiny tightening of his lips, the faint flicker of his eyelids, the subtle leeching of colour from his cheeks, but she had.

It was no use confronting him about any prior knowledge of the priest. Clarence had read the file, too, so could guess where the investigation was headed, and would have had time to prepare a defence. But the knowledge Father Murray had been found definitely came as a shock, no matter how he tried to hide it.

"I can't believe I'm so nervous." Marjorie's calm, authoritative manner was nowhere in evidence. "I made life and death decisions throughout my career without being this anxious."

"That's why we asked Phillip and Aubrey to do the search." Clarence's tone was gruff, but he patted his fiancée's linked hands in a comforting—though astounding—gesture. "I didn't want you worrying like this all the time." In return, Marjorie gripped him tightly, the soft look in her eyes loving and warm.

Phillip's eyebrows arched and he met Aubrey's gaze with a look that mingled appreciation, surprise, and affection. She smiled back. Despite the tragedies that had dogged her love life, she found it easier and easier to believe in happy endings the more time she spent with him.

After all, if her autocratic, austere father could find happiness, *anyone* could.

The rattling ring of the video call jolted her out of her romantic reverie, and she fumbled to answer it, her finger trembling on the touch pad. "Hello? Can you hear me?"

"Yes, we can." The voice came from off camera, the screen showing nothing but blocks of colour that might have been a ceiling and a wall. "Just give me a moment."

A second or two later, the jostling video settled down to reveal two men—one elderly, the other perhaps in his thirties. They sat in what appeared to be a lounge, a large wooden crucifix on the wall behind them.

"Is this Aubrey Windt?" The younger man's dark-framed glasses, perched on a prominent nose, reflected light from what she assumed was a window.

"Yes." She adjusted the angle of the laptop and then took her place. "You've spoken with Phillip Church. This is Marjorie Strahl and my father Clarence Windt."

"Pleased to meet you. I am Tony, one of Father Murray's care aides." He turned to the man at his side. "Father, these people have some questions for you."

Father Murray Athol had a round, jowly face, thinning pale hair, and faded blue eyes. He was neatly dressed in a collared shirt and sweater vest. He smiled genially, his gaze aimed over the video screen.

"What kind of questions?" His voice rumbled with a low resonance that must have given his sermons the determined ring of authority.

"About someone you knew years ago. Just do your best, okay? It's all right not to remember." Tony directed the last sentence to the camera, as if warning those gathered in Marjorie's apartment, and then nodded. Phillip took up the conversation.

"How are you doing today, Father?"

"Very well, thank you. I had porridge for breakfast." The priest's smile widened. "I like porridge."

"That's good to hear. It sounds like they are treating you well."

"Oh, they do, they do." He turned to look at Tony. "Do you live here, too?"

"No. I'm one of the staff." Tony's voice was gentle.

"Father Murray." Phillip leaned forward on his elbows, as if that could bring him closer. "Do you remember a man named Duncan Truble? We think you went to boarding school with him when you were boys."

The priest turned back toward the screen, though still didn't make eye contact. Aubrey wasn't certain he was fully aware of the audience watching him. A small wrinkle appeared between his guileless eyes. "Duncan?

I went to school with someone named Duncan?" The upward lilt on the last word made her heart sink.

"When you were teenagers." Phillip's voice betrayed none of the tension Aubrey could feel in the tight muscles of his arm where it brushed against her. "We have a copy of a letter Duncan sent you in 1960. In it he mentions a prank the two of you pulled. You put a goat in the principal's office and were punished for it by having to clean the barn for a week."

Father Murray's face lit up. "It made a terrible mess. Ate papers right off his desk, knocked over his coat stand, and trod on his clothing. We were in terrible trouble."

Her heart stuttered and she held back a relieved sigh. Logically, she knew they'd found the right man, but this confirmation was more than welcome.

Phillip's voice was gentle and encouraging. "Duncan Truble wrote you regarding a baby available for adoption. He asked if you knew of a family that might be willing to take the child."

"Priests don't get involved in adoptions." Father Murray said the words mechanically, as if he had learned them by rote.

Phillip leaned even farther forward, urgency vibrating off him. "This was a favour for a friend. He was looking for a Catholic home for this baby and wondered if you had any suggestions."

"I don't remember." His eyes narrowed and he slid a sideways look at Tony with a cunning expression that sat oddly on his benevolent face.

Phillip persevered. "We know Duncan told you to keep the request a secret. But that was because he was asked to. By these people." He motioned at Clarence and Marjorie. "These are the baby's parents. They don't want it to be a secret anymore. They want to find their son. Can you help us?"

"I promised not to tell." Father Murray's shoulders hunched, and he dipped his head.

Marjorie gave a tiny whimper. Clarence stared, unblinking, at the computer screen. In the retirement home in Prince Albert, Tony put his hand on Father Murray's arm.

"These people are looking for their son, Father. You could reunite a family."

He shook his head vigorously. "I'm not allowed to tell." Suddenly his face cleared, as if he'd had a revelation. "It was a confession. You can't ask me about what I heard in the confessional."

"It was a letter." Desperation coloured Phillip's voice. Aubrey could feel their chance slipping away. "Duncan didn't confess to you. He wrote you a letter."

Father Murray's lips pressed together. "I was told under sacramental seal. I can't say anything. I won't break my vow."

Aubrey rested her hand on Phillip's shoulder for a brief moment, and then went to turn off the laptop. He appreciated her show of support, but it did nothing to alleviate the bitter taste in his mouth.

"I think we could all use some tea." Marjorie rose slowly, back bowed by an invisible weight. "I'll put the kettle on."

"I'm so sorry." He'd wanted so badly to make this happen. She had asked for so little over the years. "I am sure he remembers something. But once he mentioned the confessional..."

"You were never going to get past that." Surprisingly, it was Clarence who offered up this comfort. "Even a court of law cannot compel a priest to break the seal of the confessional. You could see it on his face when he decided to use that defence. And once he'd thought of it, it became the truth, in his mind."

"What do we do now?" Aubrey resumed her seat. Under the table she laid her hand consolingly on his thigh, but his attention was on Marjorie's dull, muted movements as she prepared the tea.

Damn it. Damn it. *Damn it.*

"Baptismal records." Clarence again. He eyed the older man, leery of this new spirit of cooperation, but allowed a tiny flare of hope reignite.

"In Nipawin?" Aubrey nodded thoughtfully. "If we agree that Father Murray knows something, it seems the best place to start, since that was his parish at the time."

"I wanted to have the baby baptized at birth." The words ground out of Clarence as if simply speaking them caused physical pain. "But I trusted the new family Duncan found would arrange their own ceremony. Receiving that sacrament twice is a sin, and it was important he be baptized using the name they chose."

A heavy silence fell. Phillip, though nominally a Catholic, didn't understand the theology behind Clarence's statement. That didn't mean he couldn't have sympathy for what had obviously been a traumatic decision.

The kettle shrieked, breaking the pall cast by Clarence's words. Marjorie snapped off the element and poured the boiling water into the prepared tea pot. "We did what we thought was best at the time. There's no shame in that. That's all anyone can do."

For a few minutes, the conversation was suspended while she handed out the tea and placed a dish of buttery shortbread cookies in the middle of the table.

"Either Phillip or I will call the church tomorrow." Aubrey took a cookie but only twisted it in her fingers. "I don't know how difficult it will be to find records from 1960, but I'm sure it is possible. Remind me again—what was Joseph's birthday?"

Clarence and Marjorie shared a conspiratorial look. "August 4," Marjorie said softly.

Aubrey stiffened. "Your wedding day."

His chest constricted. He couldn't believe neither he

nor Aubrey had made the connection. They knew Joseph's birthday, of course. Their only excuse was it hadn't figured prominently in the search so far.

Marjorie stretched her hand across the table and Clarence clasped it. This quiet show of affection had him blinking back tears. Though he'd always taken the quest for Joseph seriously, it now took on a deeper significance. He doubted they'd solve the mystery in less than two weeks. But he vowed to do his best.

CHAPTER THIRTY-TWO

The Silverberry Book Club members had come up trumps. Not only had everyone agreed to attend Marjorie's bridal shower, but they'd turned out in full force to help with decorations and food.

Friday evening, Aubrey surveyed her living room with satisfaction. Helen and Nathan were putting the final touches on the silvery streamers and lavender balloon bouquets which cheerfully disguised the peeling trim on the windows and the blotchy, faded paint on the walls. Stephanie and Terrance were sitting on the dinette chairs borrowed from the kitchen, which they had draped in white fabric and tied with purple bows, transforming them from trashy to tasteful. The day before, Phillip had lugged over an upright upholstered chair from her condo and it now sat in pride of place, festooned with clusters of paper rosettes and shiny ribbons. Penta and Lynn had surrounded it with gaily wrapped boxes and gift bags frothing with tissue paper. Now they were spending much of their time distracting Lynn's son Oscar from the display, the toddler understandably fascinated by the presents.

"Thanks for letting me bring him." She dragged her son away yet again. He laughed delightedly at this new game. "Benjamin's doing an all-nighter on the crisis line."

"It's wonderful to have him." It wasn't just the decorations that made her heart glow. The Silverberry Book Club members had been strangers only weeks ago, and it still shocked her that they had accepted her as one of their own so quickly and easily. Maybe making friends wasn't the torture she thought it was. Maybe all you had to do was be open to new experiences.

Natalie popped up at her side. "I think we're set. The food is laid out in the kitchen and the punch is chilling in the fridge."

"Thank you for everything. You and all the Silverberries. This is amazing." She wrapped one arm around Natalie's shoulders and squeezed. The brown eyes behind her glasses widened, her mouth opening in an O. "What? I'm not allowed to give my friend a hug?" Was she really so much of a cold fish that Natalie was shocked by such a small show of affection?

"Of course you can." Tentatively, she patted Aubrey's back. "And you are welcome. We had a blast. When will Marjorie get here? I can't wait to meet her."

"Phillip's bringing her by any minute. He's taking my dad out for a dignified bachelor night, so we used that as an excuse for her to spend the evening with me."

Clarence's attitude toward his ex-son-in-law might have softened slightly over the last weeks, but he was nowhere near ready to accept a casual invitation. In the end, she had told him outright what was planned and demanded he go along and play nice. He'd acquiesced with barely a grumble. She wasn't sure whether she should be worried or pleased about that, so had decided to simply accept it.

"Any news on the baptismal record search?"

"I wish, but no. When we talked to the parish secretary yesterday, she told us it would probably be a few days before she could look into it."

During one of their many recent conversations while organizing the bridal shower, she'd updated Natalie on the progress she and Phillip had made on the Joseph front. She hadn't revealed anything about the new state of their relationship, though. They hadn't discussed it, but she was certain he felt the same way she did—that no one needed to know about their liaison.

She wasn't sure she'd succeeded in her subterfuge. Especially given what Natalie said next. "I guess that means you won't be seeing Phillip anytime soon. Not until there's more to do about the search."

Her innocent tone had a shrewd edge that warned Aubrey to word her reply carefully. "We need to come up with a Plan B. In case we don't find anything out from Nipawin. So, I might be seeing him this weekend."

"Of course you might." Natalie's eyes twinkled, but she didn't prod any further. It was clear she believed they were well on their way to rekindling their long-ago marriage, but she couldn't confront her friend's hints and innuendos without giving away her own thoughts.

Natalie took a seat beside Stephanie, who'd been in a laughing discussion with Penta, and Aubrey stationed herself next to the window overlooking the street so she could keep an eye open for the guest of honour.

Though Phillip had said nothing overt, she knew he was waiting. For what, she wasn't entirely sure. Since the weekend they'd spent together, they'd made love twice more and had dinner together three times. He had made no mention of the future, friends, or family, for which she was extremely thankful. How could they tell anyone there was something between them, if they didn't know what that something was? Keeping the secret for now was best for everyone. Then, if it all fell apart, they wouldn't have to endure any sincere sympathy or smug I-told-you-sos.

And yet, the compulsion that had made her obliquely confide in Natalie grew stronger everyday. Did that mean her confidence in what she and Phillip were building was also growing? And if it was, did that mean she was willing to chance, for the third time in her life, a committed relationship?

She dropped into the nearest chair, dizzy and breathless.

What she felt for Phillip now was not what she'd felt for him at eighteen. And it wasn't what she'd felt for Oliver, either. She'd barely survived when those marriages had shattered, each in their different ways.

Could she survive having her heart crushed a third time?

Phillip cast a stealthy glance at the watch on his wrist. 9:27pm. In about half an hour he'd be able to suggest it was time to end the evening without appearing too eager to wrap it up.

He could survive another thirty minutes.

Aubrey had promised to bring Marjorie home once the shower was over. He hoped they were having a better time than he was. Given the surprise and pleasure on his aunt's face when she'd realized the party was in her honour, he was certain they were. Even though the room had been full of strangers, they'd welcomed her warmly and appeared determined to give her a wonderful evening.

Clarence, on the other hand, had remained morose throughout the drive to the restaurant and had only lightened up when his law cronies had joined them in the small, private room. Asher and Zeke had rounded out the group, making Phillip the fulcrum between the eighty-somethings and the twenty-somethings. He'd had to stay on his toes to keep the conversation going during the meal. Now they were all settled in with after dinner brandies, beer, and coffee, he could relax a little.

The three lawyers were in the middle of a heated discussion regarding a recent judge appointment. Clarence was seated at the end of the table, his back to a wall, and Phillip had made sure the other elderly guests had taken the chairs nearest his soon-to-be uncle. With their attention drawn away, he finally had a chance to focus on his sons.

"Thanks for coming." He leaned toward Asher and

spoke quietly under the debate on his right. "I really appreciate the support."

"No problem, Dad," Asher said while Zeke shrugged in agreement. "Since I can't make the wedding, I'm glad to do this much."

His son's fizzing excitement at the new job he was starting next week had sparked off and on throughout the evening. Phillip couldn't begrudge his joy in the new adventure, but that didn't mean he had to share it.

"I'm going to miss you. And so will Marjorie." He'd finally had everyone he loved together in one city. Now it was splintering again, and so soon. Hiding how deeply his dismay went might account for the low thrum of pain behind his left eyeball. "But we'll give you a proper send-off tomorrow." Jeanette was hosting a big family dinner. He had flirted with the idea of asking Aubrey to come along, but didn't think she was ready to field all the questions and comments such an invite would provoke.

Soon, he promised himself. Soon things would be out in the open, and they could start making plans.

Zeke spoke just loudly enough for Asher and Phillip to hear. "Are you sure Marjorie is doing the right thing? He's a cranky old bas—" Phillip kicked him under the table, and he stopped short.

"It doesn't matter what I think. And if you want to question her decision, feel free. You'd be a braver man than I am." He smiled. "She might be eighty years old, but I'd still bet on her in a bar fight."

"What does Aubrey think about this?" Asher asked. "It's kind of weird, having Marjorie marry your ex-father-in-law. It must be just as odd for her."

"To be honest, I don't think the marriage part bothers her at all. The affair and the baby given up for adoption really rocked her, though. I'm still not certain she's forgiven Clarence for cheating on her mother or reconciled to the fact that she has a half-brother out there somewhere. I've seen her struggling with it."

Despite their differences, the twins occasionally shared expressions that gave them an uncanny resemblance. He was confronted by a pair of identical looks now. "What?"

His sons glanced at each other, and Zeke nodded. At this signal, Asher said, "Is there something going on with you and Aubrey?"

He stared. He'd discussed the search for Joseph with each of them as an interesting topic of conversation, nothing more. Any mention of Aubrey he'd kept easy and casual.

At least, he thought he'd been casual.

"Why do you ask?" He didn't think he'd be able to divert the coming tide, but he had to try.

"You mention her. A lot. And are spending a lot of time with her. We were just wondering if there's something we should know." Asher's journalistic training gave his simple statements the weight of an interrogation.

How much should he say? He couldn't lie to his sons and telling them he felt no connection to Aubrey would be exactly that. Though she was still leery of the potential shimmering between them, he knew what he wanted.

Aubrey. As his significant other. His life partner. His wife. He didn't care what it was called, but he wanted her by his side.

Zeke let out a bark of laughter. "He's speechless, Ash. We've finally made him speechless." He lifted his beer bottle in salute. "We're okay with it, you know."

He gaped. "You've talked about us?" He waggled a finger, pointing from Asher to Zeke and back again. "The two of you? Together?" Maybe all his work over the years to keep the twins connected had paid off. Too bad that success meant they were now discussing his love life.

They ignored his shock. Zeke took up the charge. "Mom's happy with Robert. You deserve to be happy, too."

His heart swelled. His boys had grown into strong, confident men who knew the importance of family, no matter how that family was fashioned. They deserved the truth, without prevarication or dissembling.

"I love her." In the end, it was that simple. And that complicated. "I love Aubrey, and I intend to build a life with her. If she'll let me."

It was only after the words were out of his mouth that he became aware the conversation on his right had stopped. In the sudden, ringing silence, he turned and met Clarence's fixed stare.

The older man's face was a battleground—shock, anger, and annoyance vying for dominance. "You what?" The words cut like diamonds through glass despite their quietness.

The gazes of every man at the table were focused on Phillip, but he didn't let his eye contact with Clarence waver.

He had often looked back on his marriage with Aubrey and wondered two things.

If she hadn't become pregnant, would she have defied her father and married him anyway?

If he had had the courage to stand up to Clarence, could he have saved their marriage even after Samantha's death?

One thing was certain—if he truly meant to woo her back, it would be as the man he was now, not the man he had been then.

"I love your daughter." The awkward quiet grew even more tense. "I plan to ask her to marry me again, when the time is right. And this time you will give your blessing without any fuss."

CHAPTER THIRTY-THREE

Clarence stood, pushing back from the table so fiercely his cane, hooked on the back of his chair, clattered to the floor.

"Aubrey is old enough to know her own mind." The old man glared as his colleagues gawked, eyes wide in astonishment. "I trust her to make the right decision without my input. And that decision will be to keep her distance from you."

Phillip rose as well, keeping his movements deliberate in an attempt to check his soaring temper. "You poisoned our first marriage from the start," he stated flatly. "I won't let that happen again."

Fury flushed the old man's cheeks with unhealthy colour. "Aubrey was too good for you then, and she's too good for you now. She has a brilliant, inquisitive mind that would have been wasted as the wife of a labourer."

Trust him to completely ignore everything Phillip had achieved. He was now a highly successful businessman, but to Clarence he'd never be more than the punk who got his daughter pregnant and planned to support her by mowing lawns.

"You're right about Aubrey." It gave him bitter, burning satisfaction to agree with the older man. "She *is* smarter than me in so many ways. She has one major blind spot, though—you. She let you guide her life for too long. But she's torn through the curtain now and seen what you've been hiding all these years. She's finally realizing what a controlling, selfish old man you are." He snapped his teeth together before he could mention the affair and the adoption. Even in his rage he knew that would be going too far.

The red fled Clarence's face, leaving it pale and stark and he pressed his palms on the table as if needing to brace himself. Remorse stabbed Phillip with icy shards. He might have spoken the truth, but this was neither the time nor place.

"I'm sorry." He bit out the apology. It was hypocritical to meddle in the relationship between Aubrey and her father if he didn't want her father meddling in theirs. "I shouldn't have said that. But I love your daughter, and I won't let you ruin our chance to be together this time."

The server bustled in at that moment, cheerfully oblivious to the undercurrents swirling about the room with hurricane force. Her presence broke the gathering storm, but no one was eager to extend the evening. He called for the check, the twins furtively finished the last of their beers, and one of Clarence's friends made a half-hearted offer to drive him home. He refused with scant politeness and an abstracted air.

Meaning Phillip would be forced to take him back to Riverbend as planned—now an even more dubious pleasure.

Asher and Zeke gave him one-armed hugs, shooting sidelong glances at Clarence as they did so.

"Don't get me wrong," Zeke murmured in his ear. "I'm glad you married Mom, otherwise we wouldn't be here. But if being with Aubrey will tweak that old geezer's tail, I say you go for it. He deserves it."

His remorse deepened into guilt. He had made Clarence vulnerable to such scornful remarks, which hadn't been his intention. But before he could remonstrate and try to repair the damage he'd done, Asher and Zeke were gone, the law colleagues had said their goodbyes, and they were alone.

"I do apologize." His tone was as stiff as the cane he

retrieved from the floor and handed to Clarence. "That was a discussion we should have had in private, not in front of your peers and my sons."

"Yes." He took the cane absentmindedly. He had said nothing but the bare necessities since Phillip's last scathing words.

He took two halting steps toward the door leading from the dining room to the main restaurant and then stopped. Leaning heavily on his cane, he looked over his shoulder. "Is that really what she thinks of me?"

He wouldn't lie, but he could try and heal the wound he'd cruelly inflicted. "She loves you. But she does see you differently, since learning the truth about Marjorie and Joseph."

"It started before then, though, didn't it?"

The words were so quiet he could pretend he hadn't heard them, so remained silent.

"Even before she lost the election, she wasn't happy." Clarence turned away, his shoulders stiff and rigid, betraying a desperate, never-before-seen vulnerability. "I told myself she was still mourning Oliver, but that was a lie, wasn't it?"

"You should talk to her." Phillip gripped the car keys in his pocket, feeling the metal bite into his palm. "I spoke out of turn, and I truly regret it. Now, let's get you home."

Aubrey drove a contented Marjorie home just before ten o'clock and parked in a visitor's stall by the main entrance. Opening the trunk, she hefted out the box in which they'd packed the now-opened gifts and carried it inside.

"I hope you had a good time." She used her elbow to push the button for the elevator. "I'm sorry more of your own friends couldn't be there."

"I had a *lovely* time." Marjorie still glowed from the attention bestowed on her by the Silverberries.

"Clarence and I aren't having a typical engagement, and I doubt we'll have a typical marriage. Why should I have a typical bridal shower? Especially when I never expected to have one at all. I can't thank you enough for thinking of me."

"You're very welcome. You're a bride. You deserve to enjoy all the traditions." The elevator pinged as it arrived. "I hope Dad is enjoying his bachelor night, too." *He'd better be.* If he'd ruined the gesture Phillip had made—albeit reluctantly—she'd be *very* put out.

The door slid open, and they entered. Marjorie selected her floor. "I liked your friends. Maybe I should join the book club, too."

"You would fit right in." She shifted the grip on the box. "I can ask if you like. I'm too new myself to offer the invitation. I don't know all the rules yet."

"From what I gather, the only rule is there are no rules." They exited the elevator and walked down the hall. Marjorie unlocked her apartment. "After decades following medical protocols and social expectations, that sounds like fun."

Aubrey placed the box in the living room, kissed Marjorie's cheek, and headed home. Red Cat greeted her as she walked through the yard, and she crouched to give him a quick scratch. He grew more and more comfortable in her presence, but still wouldn't come in the house for longer than it took to eat a meal.

The Silverberries had spent the time she was gone cleaning up. With grateful thanks she waved them on their way, promising to see them all next week at the mixology class that was their next official meeting. Then she collapsed onto her couch and revelled in the silence.

Marjorie was right. It had been a lovely evening. For the first time in a long time, she had been completely comfortable in a room full of people—blissfully unconcerned about making a good impression, free to say and do what she wanted without worrying about putting a foot wrong.

She had felt like she was *home.*

Even seeing her father's name light up her phone's screen didn't disturb her serenity. Everything was going so well. Maybe he was calling to thank her for making him go to his own party. *Well, that might be expecting too much.* Smiling, she connected the call.

"Hi, Dad! How was your evening?"

"When were you going to tell me you and Phillip were getting married again?"

She heard the words, but her brain couldn't decipher them. "W-what?"

"Phillip announced that he plans to marry you. I assume this does not come as a surprise. What I'd like to know is when you intended to discuss it with me." Clarence's voice was sharp and brittle with anger. But did she hear *hurt* in it as well? She had to be wrong about that.

"I don't know what you're talking about." She scrambled to catch up, her thoughts a kaleidoscope of fractured images.

"Maybe you've forgotten, but your first marriage almost ruined your life. You weren't yourself for a long time after it ended. Your mother and I were extremely worried. Why would you even think of risking that again?"

"Shut up." The words shot out of her mouth. "Just be quiet for a moment."

A hiss of breath revealed his shock at her disrespectful command, but she didn't care.

She fastened on what was echoing with the greatest clarity in her mind. "Phillip told you we were getting married?"

"Yes." He added a grudging clarification. "I don't think he meant to. He was talking with his sons, and I overheard what he said."

"He told Asher and Zeke?" Her confusion welled into bubbling panic.

"Daniel and Harold heard, too."

Her heart beat in a frantic pace and prickles washed up her torso to her cheeks, making her lightheaded. A suffocating claustrophobia enveloped her. She was just starting to figure out what she wanted from life. How could Phillip do this? She didn't want to get married, certainly not now, maybe not ever. She'd spent too much time letting other people make decisions for her. If he thought he could join that crowd, he had another think coming.

Her father was talking but she interrupted him without compunction. "I have to go, Dad. We'll talk later."

CHAPTER THIRTY-FOUR

Phillip answered his door at seven o'clock Saturday morning, bleary-eyed from a restless night disturbed not only by his contretemps with Clarence but also Asher's impending departure. He'd barely managed two lifegiving sips from the cup of coffee clutched in his hand before the repeated peal of his doorbell sent him stumbling down the stairs.

The sight of an incandescently furious Aubrey kicked him awake harder than any amount of caffeine could.

Dark circles shadowed her eyes, lines cut deeply into the corners of her mouth, and she quivered with barely restrained emotions. She regarded him with the same disgust he'd seen when they'd uncovered scurrying centipedes while working in her yard.

"You've been talking with Clarence." Resignation overlaid his skittering feeling of alarm.

"He called yesterday. Which you did not have the decency to do."

Oh, god. He'd told Clarence to talk to her but hadn't dreamt he'd do so last night. As for himself, he'd been unable to decide whether he should call to warn her or plead his case, and the window of opportunity had slipped by. Not usually one to bury his head in the sand and hope troubles would simply disappear, he'd taken the ostrich route last night and wasn't proud of it.

"Come in." He stepped back and she stalked past him and up the stairs. He followed with a dragging

253

reluctance and the knowledge he deserved her condemnation.

In the living area she whirled around, catching him precariously balanced with one foot hovering over the last tread. He gripped the handrail and took the final step, feeling rather like a pirate's victim walking the plank.

"What were you thinking?" Hands planted on her hips, she stared, chin jutted with aggression. She wore jeans with a dirt-smeared knee, a loose T-shirt, and mismatched flip-flops. It appeared she'd been in such a hurry to tear a strip off him she hadn't bothered to dress properly.

"I'm sorry." He'd done a lot of apologizing to the Windts lately and he wasn't enjoying it. "It was an accident."

"You *accidentally* told my father we were getting married?"

He'd expected her scorn, but it still made him wince. "No! That's not what I said. I said I was going to *ask* you."

"That's not what he told me."

He had an answer for that, at least. "He's always had it in for me. Any chance he gets to twist my words or make me look bad, he does. Who are you going to believe, him or me?"

"Don't make this about *you.*" She snarled the words. He'd never seen her so livid, and if he hadn't been the focus of her fury, he would have been proud to see her so roused. She'd finally learned to stand up for herself, and it was an awesome sight.

If only he didn't have the sinking feeling he'd screwed everything up.

"How do you think I felt when Dad told me you'd announced to the world we were getting married again? You of all people should know how I feel about men making decisions without consulting me. You know how my father has treated me over the years. I thought you understood. Yet here you are, doing exactly the same thing."

Ice trickled down his back. He edged past her and placed his coffee mug on the counter, surprised to see his hand trembling. "I'm not. I didn't. I promise, Aubrey."

"So, you don't want to marry me?"

She launched the grenade so quickly he could only react by instinct. "No. I mean, yes, I do. But only if you want to marry *me*."

This garbled answer didn't appease her. Her eyes narrowed. "I have sex with you a couple of times and you think I'll marry you again?"

He'd thought they'd shared something deeper than just sex. Had he been wrong? His heart clutched. "I said I'm sorry. I know it's too early to talk about the future."

"You mean with me, I guess. Because it's apparently not too early to discuss it with my father. Or your sons. Or perfect strangers."

He forced out words through his rising fear. "What do you need me to do? I can't take back what I said. I want to be with you, and to me that means being married. I'm afraid that's just who I am. But we don't have to make the decision today, or this month, or this year. We can wait until we're ready."

"*Now* you say *we*." The spark of fury faded from her eyes. "If you'd only thought of that sooner."

A calm, rational Aubrey was scarier than the virago that had invaded his home. "What do you mean?"

"It's been all about *you*. All what *you* want. I've lived that life too long. I'm not going back to being the collateral in someone else's dreams. It's time for me to be the selfish one."

He stretched out his arm and she took a quick step back, out of his reach. "Don't do this, Aubrey."

She shook her head. "It's over, Phillip. Whatever we had or might have had. I won't put up with being told what to do any longer." She walked slowly down the stairs, so slowly he could have easily caught her. Pleaded with her. Begged her not to go.

He remained rooted to the floor, frozen in a miserable silence, and watched her leave.

She wanted to make her own choices. He could respect that.

Now. When it was too late.

Aubrey sleepwalked through the weekend, her sense of wellbeing and joy shattered by Phillip's perfidy. Nothing broke through her gloom, not even discovering Red Cat had taken advantage of the habitually open back door and curled up on her couch, as if he'd been doing it all his life.

She should have been proud for standing up for herself. Phillip's silence through the hours was evidence he had accepted her decree, but she could find no pleasure in it, no matter how she tried. However, she stood firm each time her father called, refusing to let him browbeat her.

"Tell me you are not marrying that man," he had demanded more than once.

While that was her fixed intention, something held her back from giving him the satisfaction. "That's none of your business, Dad. Whether I do or don't is up to me. I am not obligated to give you assurances either way."

He blustered and hectored, but she held her ground.

It was exhausting.

Monday afternoon, she tried to distract herself by studying paint colours, kitchen tiles, and new flooring. The contractors had submitted their quotes last week and she'd made her choice. A few formalities needed to be confirmed, but she was close enough now she could start thinking about specifics.

If only she could *think*.

She was having so much trouble concentrating that,

when her phone signalled a text, she snatched it up, eager for the interruption, no matter who it was.

With mixed relief and trepidation, she read Phillip's terse message. *News from Nipawin. I'm going to call in a minute. Please answer.*

She took a deep breath. She'd known this would happen sooner or later. It would be impossible to avoid him. Even after the wedding was over and the search for Joseph concluded—either with success or in failure—there would be times they'd have to be in the same room and be civil to each other. It might as well start now.

Still, she let the phone ring twice before she picked it up with sweaty fingers and swiped to answer. "Hello, Phillip."

"Aubrey."

She closed her eyes at the sound of his voice, the deep timbre sparking the longing she'd been suppressing into flames. "Did you hear from the parish secretary?" There. That sounded calm, unemotional. She couldn't betray how flustered she was. If he sensed her weakening, he might take advantage of that to convince her to give him another chance.

And she didn't trust herself to say no.

"One boy was baptized between August 4 and September 30, 1960. Four girls, but only one boy. His parents gave him the name Eugene Joseph Schubert."

She wasn't so caught up in her own turmoil that she missed the connection. "Joseph?"

"Yes. Now, it has always been a common name, but it isn't beyond the bounds of imagination to believe the adoptive family knew what the birth mother had chosen for her son and decided to honour her wishes this way."

"And only one boy?"

"There were more in the latter months of the year, but I don't see the family waiting that long to baptize the child. If this lead doesn't pan out, though, we can certainly check the others."

His tone wasn't exactly unfriendly, but it certainly

held none of the intimacy she'd grown used to during the last few weeks. She swallowed down her regret. "Did the secretary know anything about the family? Do they still live in Nipawin?"

"There's no Eugene Schubert in the parish register, but there are two others with the same last name. She wouldn't give me their phone numbers, but she was willing to call herself and ask them to get in touch with me. That was half an hour ago. I figure we have to give her at least a day before following up."

"Yes." The enormity of what she'd just heard struck her with a suddenness that left her breathless. "Have we found him, Phillip? Do you think we've found our Joseph?"

Phillip gripped his phone tightly. Talking with Aubrey was a pleasure so painful he was glad he was sitting down. "I think we have." He stared blindly out the window of his office. "I really think we have. But if not, we'll keep looking."

It was hateful of him, but he almost hoped this would be another dead end. The search for Joseph might be the only reason he had to speak with her for the foreseeable future. Which meant it was the only way he could attempt to atone for his stupidity and claw his way back into her life.

Though Clarence hadn't been meant to hear his intentions, he knew he could have handled it better. He could have shut the conversation down by insisting they speak in private. Or better yet not speak at all, since it truly had nothing to do with Clarence. Instead, he had exacerbated the problem by mentioning marriage.

Aubrey had every right to be furious. It hadn't occurred to him until she'd pointed it out on Saturday just how highhanded his actions must have appeared. He cringed every time he thought of it.

Thank heaven she couldn't shut him out completely,

not with the link between their families. And he had little compunction in using Joseph to further his own aims.

A small silence had grown between them, and he took heart that she hadn't disconnected as soon as she'd heard his news.

"Have you heard from Asher?"

At her quiet question, his faint flare of hope grew even brighter. "He made it to North Battleford last night and is doing the rest of the trip today. He should arrive in Winnipeg late this evening." Phillip had managed not to cry until after Asher's car had disappeared down the road the day before, but tears welled each time he thought of his son travelling to his new life. He thumbed the moisture from his eyes as he cleared his throat. "Thanks for asking. But back to Joseph. The area around Nipawin is scattered with small farming communities. If these Schuberts don't know Eugene, we can do a search of phone books or voter lists or property registers. And if *that* doesn't work, we'll think of something. I promise you, I won't give up."

She replied, but her words were drowned out by a buzzing in his ear. "I have another call coming in. Let me see who it is." He glanced quickly at the screen, froze, and then lifted the phone back to his mouth. "It's the same area code as the Nipawin parish number."

"Answer it then!" Her voice was pitched high and thin. "I'll wait."

He swiped to switch to the new call. "Phillip Church here."

"I understand you're looking for my cousin, Eugene," a man said.

CHAPTER THIRTY-FIVE

Four hours later, Phillip stood inside the vestibule at Riverbend and watched Aubrey stride toward him, beams from the early evening sun glinting off the scattered silvery strands in her hair. He thought back to their first meeting a few weeks ago. Sometime between then and now she'd gained a new confidence, a new swagger. He could read it in her swinging arms, her firmly held shoulders.

She was amazing. And he wanted her back. Badly. But he had to re-earn her trust first.

He pushed open the outer door and held it for her. She swept past, close enough he caught the citrus scent of her shampoo, acknowledging him only with a regal nod.

"Do you mind if we take the stairs?" He wanted a few moments alone with her. They were less likely to meet residents in the stairwell than the elevator.

She remained silent but adjusted her direction toward the heavy fire door at the far end of the hall.

Their footsteps echoed in the hollow chamber as he paced at her shoulder while they ascended. "All I told Marjorie was that we had an update on the baptismal records and that we wanted to meet with her and Clarence. This didn't feel like news that should be given over the phone."

"I agree." She didn't look his way, but at least she was speaking to him. He didn't think she was afraid to make eye contact—it was more that she didn't believe he *deserved* her consideration. For the moment, he was only a conduit of facts, not a friend. Not a lover.

He wondered uneasily if he'd done the right thing by not revealing the full scope of what he'd learned. He had told her about the cousin's phone call, but for the same reason they'd agreed it was best to tell Marjorie and Clarence in person, he hadn't told her *everything*.

He hoped she'd see his side when she heard what he had done.

They exited the stairwell and were steps away from Marjorie's door when it opened, and her curly grey head poked out. "I saw you coming from the deck. Clarence is here already."

He greeted her with a quick kiss on her cheek. Aubrey squared her shoulders and stepped in, chin lifted, and they joined Clarence in the living area. He sat, tense and alert, his gaze tracking Phillip with serious intent. Marjorie, too, gave off an aura of anticipation in her rapid speech and bright cheeks.

He should have known they were both far too intelligent to miss the import of this meeting, no matter what he hadn't said on the phone.

Once they were settled in what were becoming their usual spots—Clarence and Marjorie in their matching upholstered chairs, he and Aubrey on the sofa placed at a right angle—Marjorie clasped her hands and gazed at him expectantly. "You found him."

"Yes." The weight of her stare was a physical touch. Clarence drew his feet in, as if preparing to rise, then froze. "His name is Eugene Joseph Schubert. He was baptized in Nipawin, Saskatchewan on September 4, 1960."

"They kept his name." Tears filled her eyes, and she reached out blindly. Clarence leaned over and gripped her hand, his own eyes clear but his expression as soft as Phillip had ever seen it.

"His parents were Lydia and Oswald Schubert." Aubrey took up the tale, repeating what he had told her.

"They'd been married ten years with no children when they adopted him. As sometimes happens, shortly after they took Joseph in, Lydia became pregnant. With twins. He grew up with a brother and sister."

"You learned all this in the church records?" Clarence's words were skeptical, but his tone was gently seeking.

"No." Phillip drew in a long breath. "I spoke with one of his cousins, Hector. He told us those details."

"Oh, my." Marjorie's whisper was so soft he could barely hear her. "You spoke to his family?"

He explained how his conversation with Hector had come about. Beside him, Aubrey sat tense and quiet. As he talked, he risked a quick glance. She watched her father with no attention to spare for anyone else.

Clarence cleared his throat before asking his next question. "Did this Hector know why you are looking for Joseph?"

"I told the parish secretary I was doing a family tree, that the Schuberts were a distant connection to my grandparents, and that's what she told Hector. I didn't want to mention adoption, not yet."

Clarence's fingers flexed around Marjorie's. Then he asked the question Phillip was waiting for. "Where is Joseph now?"

Aubrey felt a jolt of surprise at Clarence's question. Not because he'd asked it, but at the way he'd framed it. When Phillip had told her about Hector's phone call, she'd blurted "Is he alive?" Clarence had been much more circumspect and altogether more positive.

Even after they'd determined—as best they could—that Joseph had survived long enough to be adopted by a new family, the possibility that he was no longer alive had nagged at her. Not that sixty was that old, but life was that uncertain. Illnesses and injuries plagued everyone. While the chances were good Joseph was still around, she hadn't been able to shake the tiny burr of worry.

Presenting Marjorie and Clarence with the news their son was dead was *not* the wedding present she wanted to give. Thank god that wouldn't happen.

"He lived in Nipawin until he was sixteen years old." Phillip was brisk, businesslike, keeping the emotions swirling through the room at a low simmer. "Then his family moved to British Columbia. They resettled in the Fort St. John area and began farming there."

"He's here? In British Columbia?" Clarence's eyes widened.

"As far as I can confirm." Phillip turned to her, a troubled look in his eyes. "I didn't tell you everything Hector said, Aubrey. I thought the three of you should hear it at the same time."

Her heart stuttered. "You told me Hector had lost touch. That the last they'd spoken was five years ago at Joseph's moth—Lydia Schubert's funeral." Marjorie may have given up her child, but she was still his mother. It felt odd to give the title to anyone else.

"And that's true." Lines creased between his brows. "What I didn't tell you is that he gave me Joseph's phone number. I called it to see if it was still active and reached voicemail." He took her hand in his, his grip warm and enveloping, and turned to Marjorie and Clarence, who were staring, mouths open in identical shock. "I hung up right away. But the man's voice on the message said it was Eugene."

"You mean we could call him? Right now?" Marjorie's voice was still soft, as if speaking loudly might shatter the spell cast by Phillip's words.

"We could." He heaved in a breath, let it out slowly. "But I don't think we should."

"Why on earth not?" Aubrey's brain buzzed, anticipating a joyful end to their quest. "The very thing Marjorie and Clarence want is right here, within reach. Why wait any longer?"

"For one, we can't be completely certain Eugene Schubert is Joseph." He released her to smooth his palms on his knees. "All the evidence is circumstantial. If there had been more information in Duncan Truble's file, maybe we would have no doubts. But there isn't."

The guilt-filled, haunted glance Clarence slid toward Marjorie was impossible to ignore. "Dad? Do you know something about Truble's files?"

He remained silent and scowled repressively, but she was no longer cowed by its fierceness.

Before she could demand answers, however, Marjorie withdrew her hand from his clasp and narrowed her eyes. "Clarence? What do you know?" It had taken her a few minutes to regain her composure after Phillip's announcement, but she sounded in fine form once more. Her voice snapped with command.

"I don't know anything about Joseph that I haven't told you." He hesitated a moment longer but appeared to realize he wasn't going to get away with any further prevarication. "Though if I'd known this day would come, I might have made different decisions."

"What decisions?" She pinned him with a glare.

He sighed and shifted in his seat, as if trying to block Phillip and Aubrey from the conversation with his shoulder. She considered giving the older couple privacy but rejected the thought. Her father had no compunction interfering in her life, and he'd opened the door to this scenario when he'd agreed to search for Joseph.

"About a year after Aubrey was born, I—" He paused, bowed his head briefly, and then straightened and continued. "I contacted Duncan and asked him to tell me what had happened to Joseph."

"You what?" Marjorie raised a hand to her lips. "You mean, you've known, all this time?"

He shook his head vigorously. "No, I swear. I didn't. Duncan refused to tell me. He said even though our agreement had been one friend assisting another, and that he wasn't bound by attorney-client privilege, he couldn't reveal the adoptive family. He said it would be unfair and cruel, to both them and us."

"If he had told you, what did you intend to do?"

"Alice and I had given up hope of having children together. I tried not to think of Joseph, but I began to believe he would be my only child. The urge to contact Duncan started then. But when Aubrey came along—" He held out his hand to Marjorie. When she didn't take it, he let it drop heavily back onto his knee. "Aubrey was a miracle. It made me realize what I'd asked you to give up. I thought maybe I could fix that."

Aubrey's throat burned and she gripped Phillip's hand tighter. Her father had called her a miracle. It didn't matter that she was more than fifty years old. Inside she was still a child...a child now vindicated in her belief in his love, despite evidence to the contrary.

Marjorie's interrogation hadn't paused. "How? How could you have fixed it? He would have been about eight years old. I would never have taken him away from the only parents he'd ever known, especially since you—" She broke off, tears brimming.

"You're right." Clarence swallowed, thin tendons tightening in his neck. "I would never have left Alice and Aubrey. I thought his family might agree to send pictures, let you know how he was doing. Even if they never told him about being adopted, they might have done that much. But Duncan wouldn't let me see the file, flatly refused to tell me anything that might lead to Joseph. I'm guessing he destroyed the documents that finalized the adoption. Either he missed the letters to Father Murray, or he didn't think they would provide any useful clues."

Marjorie seemed at a loss for words. Her mouth opened and then pressed closed. One tiny tear tracked down her powdered, wrinkled cheek.

"Our friendship faded after that." Clarence now appeared eager to get the full confession over with. "I was angry with him, and I don't think he trusted me anymore. It was impossible to get past that."

The room fell silent. The grumble of traffic on the street seeped through the window that looked over the parking lot. When the air conditioner kicked in it sounded as loud as a jet engine.

"You silly, silly man." Marjorie rose and took the two steps necessary to stand over him. She cupped his face in her palms and bent to kiss him gently on the lips. His hand came up to wrap around her wrist. Their foreheads rested together.

The scene was unbearably intimate. Aubrey leaned her head against Phillip's shoulder, closing her eyes. Moisture burned the back of her nose, and she sniffed. He embraced her waist, his chin brushing her crown.

Several seconds of silence passed. Then she heard Marjorie say, "So, if we're not going to call Joseph, what *are* we going to do?"

CHAPTER THIRTY-SIX

Phillip stood on the pedals and coasted down the slope and through the mud puddle at the bottom of the dip in a swooping rush. Dirty water spattered his back and bare calves as he powered up the hill. Dexter's whoops of joy echoed from behind as they wound through the narrow, rustic trails on their way to the lookout over the linked ponds.

When they reached their destination, they propped their bikes against a couple of trees and sat on the tabletop to take in the view over the marshy water below.

"Heard anything from the lawyer yet?" Dexter offered a bag of trail mix.

He waved *no, thanks*. Between his break with Aubrey and the Joseph situation, his appetite had been off for days. "Nothing. It's driving me crazy. I can't imagine what Marjorie and Clarence are feeling."

He had kept Dexter up to date on the search for Joseph. Once Marjorie, Clarence, and Aubrey had absorbed the fact he had Eugene's phone number, it had been decided he would contact a lawyer in Fort St. John, explain the situation, and request they get in touch with Eugene in the hopes of confirming he indeed *was* Joseph. No one was sure exactly how that could be done, though if he knew he was adopted the probability increased dramatically. If he didn't, they were hoping the lawyer would convince him to take a DNA test, which could then be compared to theirs.

Either way, it was going to be a shock. He hoped going through a third-party might soften both the potential blow to Eugene's life and his rejection of Marjorie and Clarence if he chose not to meet them.

He had duly made the phone call, and since then they'd been waiting. For three days. It was late Friday afternoon and there had been no further contact. He doubted they'd hear until Monday at the earliest, now.

Dexter took a long chug of water. The July day was hot, even under the heavy canopy of trees. "What about Aubrey? How's she holding up?"

"I'm not sure." A woodpecker's assault on a nearby tree rattled through the forest stillness. "We haven't talked since Tuesday, when I told her I'd found a lawyer in Fort St. John."

"Really, dude? What are you waiting for?"

He raised his eyebrows. "Dude? What are you, twelve?"

"You're the one pouting like a kid. Are you just going to give up or are you going to work for her?"

"I am *not* pouting." He yanked off his cycling gloves, crumpling them in his fist and squeezing them like a stress ball. "I never should have told you she broke off with me."

"Speaking as your friend and not a medical professional, I get why she was angry with you. But it doesn't seem like something that should completely end a relationship."

"I don't know if she will ever forgive me. I didn't mean to, but I did exactly what her father has been doing all her life. I took control away from her."

"And she took it right back by kicking your ass to the curb." Dexter punched him not-so-lightly on the shoulder. "Means you're even, right? So, what are you going to do about it?"

"I don't know."

"Do you love her?"

"Yes." Damn it, he did. There had been no hesitation

in his reply. He knew it, in his head and his heart. He loved Aubrey. And he didn't want to lose her, not again.

"Well, then, go get her," Dexter said.

If only it were that simple.

"I had fun last week. Did Marjorie—" The maniacal buzz of a blender drowned out Natalie's next words. She waited until Stephanie finished crushing ice and began again. "Did Marjorie have a good time?"

"She *loved* it." Aubrey sipped her Moscow Mule. She wasn't big on mixed drinks, but she was finding this one rather tasty. It went down easy—maybe too easy. Given her current, rather fragile, emotional state, she'd have to be careful. They might be learning to mix drinks, but that didn't mean she had to sample all of them.

The mixology class was taking place at the local bartending school. The brightly lit room had an extra long, glass-topped, dark wood bar down one side, and the Silverberries were lined up between it and the shelves of bottles that covered the wall at their back. The instructor paced up and down in front of them, explaining, correcting, and encouraging.

Natalie filled a cocktail shaker with ice. "I was looking forward to meeting Phillip." She reached for an egg in the bowl at her elbow. "How come you didn't introduce him when he brought Marjorie?"

She had hoped no one had noticed how she'd hustled Phillip on his way. She had been worried he might say or do something that would tip off the Silverberries to the fact he was more than just her almost-stepmother's nephew. Which was ironic, given how he had blurted things out at the bachelor party that same night.

She really didn't want to talk about him.

"I'm not so sure I want a cocktail with an egg in it." She watched Natalie carefully separate the yolk from the white, and then pour the white over the ice cubes in the shaker.

"Trying new things, remember? That's what we're all about at the Silverberry Book Club." She poured an ounce of white rum into the shaker, followed by an ounce of white wine. "And you haven't answered my question. I thought you were being civil to each other, but it looked like you couldn't get rid of him fast enough."

She glared into the copper mug that held her nearly depleted drink. "We had no problem being civil." *Is that what the kids are calling it these days?* She hiccupped a slightly intoxicated giggle.

Natalie's concentration on measuring the simple syrup and lemon juice that went into her drink next didn't keep her from catching the past tense. "*Had* no problem? Did you have a fight or something?"

"Or something." She tossed back the last of her drink and threw caution to the winds. "He told my father we were getting married."

That halted Natalie in the act of adding orange juice. She stared from behind the heavy frames of her glasses.

She hoped her silence meant they could change the subject. "Exactly what kind of drink are you making?"

"Punch Romaine. They served it on the Titanic the night it hit the iceberg. But never mind that." Natalie secured the lid of the shaker, her eyes never leaving Aubrey's face. "He told your father *what?* And *why* would he do that?"

"He says it was an accident. He was talking with his sons and my dad overheard. Which doesn't make it any better, as he was *telling his sons*." Her voice trembled. With anger, she assured herself. Not pain. Not regret. "If I could, I would never speak to him again. Unfortunately, his aunt marrying my father will make that impossible."

Natalie handed her the shaker. "Here, mix this. You

look like you need to burn off some steam."

It was rather satisfying to agitate the container violently while the other woman mounded crushed ice in a wide-mouthed glass. Her heart didn't feel any less bruised and battered, but she did feel calmer by the time she returned the shaker so Natalie could strain the liquid contents over the ice.

"You can explain how things went from being civil to announcing your engagement later." Natalie's voice was as deliberate as her actions as she topped the drink with two ounces of champagne. "If he's telling his sons about it, he must be serious about marrying you."

"It doesn't matter if he's serious or not. He isn't allowed to make decisions for me. And telling my father we are getting married is *my* job, not his."

Natalie paused in the act of cutting a thin slice of orange. "Um, did you hear what you just said?"

Aubrey blinked. Why was she staring like that?

Telling my father we are getting married is my *job, not his.*

Her mouth fell open.

"Do you love Phillip, Aubrey?"

She couldn't speak, but every fibre of her being reverberated *yes*. *That* was why she had been so upset. Because she loved him, and he'd hurt her in the worst way imaginable.

Natalie garnished the drink and placed it in front of her. "You don't have to say anything. The answer is written all over your face. Drink up, and we'll figure out a way to fix this."

CHAPTER THIRTY-SEVEN

Phillip didn't know how to heal his relationship with Aubrey. Words alone wouldn't be enough to convince her she could trust him again. He needed to make a grand gesture, something dramatic that would prove his love, assure her he would support her, not try to control her.

So far, he'd come up with nothing. He consoled himself that he had time. Thanks to Marjorie and Clarence, she wouldn't be able to avoid him, couldn't disappear entirely from his life. He just had to come up with exactly the right way to express his feelings.

Tuesday morning, he climbed into his truck and headed to work. It had been a week since he'd talked to the lawyer in Fort St. John. She had warned that rushing the process would benefit no one, and he'd agreed, but he had rather expected she'd keep him updated even if there was nothing new to report.

He couldn't do anything about Aubrey right now, so chose to do something about Eugene.

As none of them were familiar with any lawyers in the small northern city, Clarence had asked a colleague who was still practicing for recommendations. Hope Fenton had been on the list, and Phillip had chosen her partly because of her name. He hoped—haha—it was a lucky sign.

Using voice commands, he called her office, and the receptionist put him right through.

"Mr. Church! You were first on my to-do list today."

He clenched the steering wheel. The light turned green, and he released the brake slowly. "Does that mean you have news?"

"The day after you and I talked, I called Mr. Schubert. I explained that I been approached by a distant relative who was looking for information about his family, but didn't mention anything about adoption. We scheduled an appointment for Friday afternoon, which was when I revealed the true nature of your inquiry." A rumbling and beeping almost obscured her last few words. "Just a minute, let me shut my window. They're picking up the dumpster."

His faith in the lawyer suffered a minor blow. Not that he'd imagined her sitting in a corner office on the top storey of a lofty high-rise, but he hadn't exactly envisioned her sharing a wall with an enormous wastebin, either.

The growling lessened. "There, that's better," she said.

"What happened on Friday?" *Get on with it already*. He could barely swallow around the bundle of nerves where his heart used to be. "What did Eugene say?"

"I think you've found the man you are looking for. Mr. Schubert has known most of his life he was adopted. Your story matches what little his parents had told him."

Relief—possibly still premature—made him dizzy. A loud honk drew his attention back to the road and he quickly changed lanes, turned into the parking lot of a strip mall, and pulled into a space. "Eugene is Joseph? You're sure about that?"

"As sure as we can be without a DNA test. In fact, his daughter gave him one for Father's Day last month, and he's been working up the courage to take it."

"Working up the courage? That doesn't sound promising." What would they do if he refused to meet Marjorie and Clarence? What *could* they do? The

273

possibility burned like bile at the back of his throat.

"Those are my words, not his. But you must see what a huge step it would be. He told me he'd been thinking about looking for his birth parents for a while now, but didn't want to do anything while his adoptive parents were alive. He felt it would be disloyal. His father died almost ten years ago, and his mother about five. Since then, the idea has been buzzing around. That's why his daughter bought him the test."

"You found this all out on Friday?"

"Most of it. He asked for the weekend to think about everything, talk to his wife and children. After all, this affects them, too. He called me late yesterday, told me he'll submit the DNA sample, and gave me the go-ahead to call you."

Just because Eugene was willing to take the test and have Hope reach out didn't mean he was willing to meet his biological family. He scrubbed his tingling palms on his thighs, his brain whirling. "What do we do now? Do we wait for the DNA results?"

"We can, if that's what you and your family want."

He heard a *but* at the end of that statement. "What does *he* want? We've tossed a grenade into his life. It is his call."

"He wants to meet," Hope said. "He wondered, if he drove down to Prince George this weekend, if you might be able to arrange something."

Aubrey thought she might vomit. Marjorie and her father, on the other hand, appeared calm and collected. When she looked closely, though, she could see Marjorie was pale under the sharp red of her blush, and her father's mouth was an even tighter line than usual. But those were the only signs they were nervous about meeting their long-lost son.

Phillip came and took a seat next to her. "They'll bring our drinks over in a minute. When Joseph, I mean, Eugene, gets here, I'll go order his."

It was quarter to three on Saturday afternoon, and the four of them were at Café Voltaire, waiting for Eugene to arrive at the top of the hour. Hope Fenton had confirmed the meeting on Wednesday, and since then the wait had been excruciating. Aubrey had been unable to settle to anything. Not even the final preparations for the renovations at Cedar Street had been able to hold her attention.

The server brought their drinks and Phillip leaned to give access to the table. His shoulder brushed against her, and she shivered at the brief touch.

She was in love with Phillip Church. Whether again or still was a moot point. She loved him and may have shoved him away one too many times. Natalie was certain she could win him back, but by the time she'd worked up the courage to approach him, the news about Eugene had broken. Maybe it made her a coward, but she'd decided to wait until after the meeting.

She wouldn't put it off any longer. She was going to talk to him today. Come hell or high water.

A man wearing a crisp, clean, green and yellow John Deere ball cap appeared at the door of the café. She stiffened when she spied the agreed upon signal. "He's here." She stood, her chair screeching on the floor. Phillip did the same.

Marjorie gripped Clarence's hand. For a moment, the elderly couple stared at each other. Then as one they rose, turned their backs on Aubrey and Phillip, and faced the newcomer.

Their son. Tears pooled in her eyes and her breath sawed raw in her throat.

Eugene's step hitched. He removed his cap and, swallowing so hard his Adam's apple bobbed, took the final steps to reach them.

"I'm Eugene Schubert. You must be—" He faltered, twisting his cap in his fingers. "I'm not sure what I should call you."

The hesitation before her father held out his hand was so short as to be almost unnoticeable. "I'm Clarence." He managed a reasonable imitation of his usual decisive manner but couldn't hide all evidence of the turmoil bubbled under the surface. "This is Marjorie."

"We're so happy to meet you." Marjorie's voice quivered.

A tear escaped and trickled down Aubrey's cheek. She brushed it away. The look on his face—wonder, curiosity, and anxiety—was a hopeful sign this meeting meant as much to him as it did to his birth parents.

For long seconds, everyone remained frozen in their positions, until Phillip thawed the tableau by offering Eugene a drink. He asked for a black coffee, and Phillip left to put in the order, indicating a chair at the end of the rectangular table. "Have a seat. I'll be right back."

She didn't know about the others, but she was relieved to sit down, her knees weak with nerves. Another silence threatened, and she began babbling to avert it. "That was Phillip. He's Marjorie's nephew. Hope Fenton might have mentioned he was the one that called her. I'm Aubrey. Clarence is my dad." She clacked her teeth together before the word *too* could pop out.

Eugene shifted in his seat, his expression awed yet wary. "You're my half-sister."

She nodded. Her half-brother was right here, within arm's reach. A sense of unreality enveloped her. Despite the clatter and chatter from the café around them, the table was in its own private bubble.

"And you're my cousin," he said as Phillip returned with the requested coffee.

"Yes." He took his seat next to her.

Marjorie's gaze hadn't left Eugene's face. She wondered if she was seeing the similarities between Eugene and Clarence that had immediately struck her. Both were tall and lean, and Eugene's nose arched just like her father's—and her own. He had Marjorie's eyes, though, warm and brown, and something about the way he held his head was eerily familiar.

Once again silence stretched, threatening to grow uncomfortable. This time Marjorie broke it. "Did you have a good drive down? What time did you leave?"

The polite pleasantry eased the atmosphere, and his posture softened. "Actually, I came to town yesterday. I had business to take care of. I'd been planning a trip to Prince George this weekend even before—" He broke off again, but no one had trouble filling in the blank.

"Ms. Fenton mentioned you own the John Deere dealership in Fort St. John." Clarence also hadn't looked away from his son. The intentness of his pale gaze held yearning, sorrow, and soft amazement.

More tears welled in her eyes, and she took a sip of her drink to hide her reaction.

"Yes." Eugene went on with an account of how he'd had enough of farming by the time he was out of high school and had tried several jobs until purchasing the dealership about twenty years ago. "I worked the oil patch and drove truck and a few other things, but nothing took. Then I started working at John Deere and when it came up for sale decided to take the plunge. Haven't regretted a moment. My wife keeps asking when I plan to retire. I keep telling her never."

"You have children?" Marjorie's hands clasped her coffee mug, but she seemed unaware of its existence.

"Four. Two boys and two girls. Well, men and women now. Our youngest is twenty-five. Six grandkids, too." He smiled crookedly at Marjorie and Clarence. "I guess that makes you great-grandparents."

She smothered a laugh at the comical expression of horror that creased her father's face. But the mention of their genetic connection brought the conversation back to the reason for the visit.

"You probably have some questions for us." Marjorie's gaze fluttered away from her son for the first time, but she brought it back with a courage that almost broke Aubrey's heart. "About why we did what we did."

He nodded slowly. "A few. But nothing that can't wait. I think it's best we get to know each other a little before we dive into the deep stuff." He leaned over and peered past Aubrey toward the glass counter loaded with baked goods. "Those scones look pretty good. How about I treat everyone?"

CHAPTER THIRTY-EIGHT

Phillip's emotions at seeing Marjorie and Clarence with their son were so overwhelming, so mind-blowing, he felt like he was vibrating. Jumping out of his chair and yelling *yahoo* as he ran around the café was out of the question, but taking Aubrey's hand and holding on for dear life was a reasonable second choice.

She gave a tiny jolt when he first touched her under the table, but didn't tear her gaze away from Eugene for an instant. Hidden from view, her fingers closed around his and squeezed.

Tentative at first, the conversation flowed easier as time went on. Reunions like these were fraught with peril, and Phillip was thankful this one appeared to be missing painful drama, at least for now. Eugene came across as a practical, prosaic man, one who took things in stride, and his knowledge of his adoption and his own nebulous intentions to seek out his birth parents had obviously smoothed the way.

After an hour or so, it was decided that Marjorie, Clarence, and Eugene would meet for supper that evening. They invited Aubrey and Phillip along, but they declined. He wasn't sure of her reasons, but he thought it best to give the three time alone now that the initial greetings had taken place. It was their story, not his or Aubrey's. They needed to discuss it without an audience.

In the parking lot, he kissed Marjorie's cheek, shook hands with Clarence and Eugene, and watched them drive their separate ways before turning to Aubrey, who had remained at his side.

"How are you doing?" She'd been quiet for most of the meeting. This had been difficult for her, too, and he marvelled at the strength and grace she'd shown.

"You know, I'm doing okay." Her lips curved in a small but sincere smile. "He seems like a nice man, and it sounds like he's had a good life. That makes it a lot easier."

"Yes."

"Do you think he'll come to the wedding?" Marjorie and Clarence had extended the invitation just as they were leaving the café. Eugene had been stunned they'd chosen his birthday for the ceremony and had asked for time to consider.

"It seems fitting. But it might be a bit soon for him." It was only eleven days away, after all.

Her car was parked a couple of stalls before his truck. She stopped next to it yet made no move to get in. He waited, wondering if now was a good time to ask when they could discuss what had happened at the bachelor party.

She beat him to it. "Would you like to come over? I think we need to talk."

Not the most reassuring of sentences, but it was better than her cold silence of the preceding days. "I've been thinking the same thing. I'll follow you."

They drove in convoy to her neighbourhood, separating when she turned down the alley to access the back and he took the next turn to park on the street in front. The yard was still in disarray, and he wondered when renovations would start on the house. Since their relationship had crumbled, he had avoided checking on the progress of her contract with Twin Rivers, feeling it was an invasion of her privacy. It didn't look like he'd missed anything.

He went round the side of the house and in through the open back door. She stood in the junction of the hall and living room. "I'm just going to use the washroom. Have a seat."

He nodded and she disappeared. In the living room, he stopped short. Red Cat lay like a twisted pretzel in the corner of the couch, his fur sleek and shiny and his belly plump. "Well, hello there. You look like you finally figured out what side your bread is buttered on."

One orange ear twitched and he unfurled in a smooth motion. Phillip sat on the other end of the couch. He liked cats well enough, but this one had been feral not that long ago.

The creature padded across the cushions and onto his lap. After punching dough on his thigh, needle-like claws poking painfully through his trousers, he settled down and began to purr.

He scratched between Red Cat's ears, and the rumbling, reverberating song grew louder. Comforted, he waited for Aubrey to return.

Aubrey used the toilet, not because she had to but because she needed time to prepare for the next few minutes. Today had already been stressful and emotional, but she couldn't postpone this encounter. She had to clear the air, and the longer she waited the harder it would get.

After washing and drying her hands, she rested her palms on the counter and stared into the black-speckled mirror. "This is your call." Her reflection looked dubious but determined. "*You* are deciding to do this. What ever happens next is up to Phillip, but you will have done what you needed to do."

Heaving several deep breaths through her nose and expelling them through her mouth calmed some of her nerves. But the butterflies returned the moment she saw him in her living room.

His elbow was propped on the arm of the couch, and his head rested on his clenched fist, his eyes closed. Red

Cat sat chicken-style on his lap, purring under the long, sweeping strokes of his hand.

She took a moment to study him. He looked tired, with creases she hadn't noticed before around his mouth. His hand moved rhythmically on Red Cat's spine, but she had the impression he was half asleep. It seemed a shame to interrupt his peacefulness.

Then his eyes opened and his gaze met hers and the butterflies in her belly zoomed up into her throat. She couldn't think, let alone speak.

"You said we needed to talk." He didn't pause in petting Red Cat. Ridiculous jealousy surged through her. She wished it was *her* back he was stroking.

"Yes." She took a seat on the low stuffed ottoman she used as a coffee table, their knees only inches apart. She'd worn a dress to meet Eugene. In this position, it rose a little too high on her thighs. She tugged it down, trying to be discreet. Given the heated amber spark in his brown eyes, she wasn't successful. But maybe his reaction boded well for what she had to say.

"About last week. What you said at my dad's bachelor party." She licked her lips. "And the next day, when I went to your house."

"You don't know how much—"

She interrupted. "I owe you an apology."

His hand paused in its movements. An instant later he hissed and unhooked Red Cat's warning claw from his leg before resuming his strokes. "For what? I was the one who screwed up."

"Yes. You should have talked to me before saying anything to anyone. And I mean *anyone.* Your sons, my father." She narrowed her eyes. He had to understand this. If he didn't, it was all for naught. "It wasn't what you said, so much as that you said it to *other people first.*"

"Hold on." He stared at her. "You didn't have a problem with *what* I said?"

She waved that off. "That's not important, not right

now. You have to understand it was leaving me out of the decision that was wrong."

He looked like he wanted to argue her first point but left it alone. "I know it's not a good reason, but my sons backed me into a corner. They made me realize how much you mean to me. And when Clarence overheard me telling them I love you, I wanted to reassure him I was serious. The marriage thing just popped out."

I love you. The present tense sounded sweetly in her ears.

"To be clear. I'm not apologizing for being furious. I'm apologizing for not listening to your side of things. It was just"—she drew in a lungful of air, let it out again—"for a while I was so hurt, so crushed, that I could barely breathe. I trusted you, thought you knew how I felt about being a puppet in someone else's dreams. Then you did what you did, and I realized I was wrong. Or thought I was."

"I get that. Do you realize, though, that I have felt the same way, more than once?"

She frowned. "The same way as what?"

"Powerless to control my own life. Not all the time, and maybe not as often as you, but certainly at times. The worst was after Samantha died. I would have given *anything* to bring her back. But I couldn't. Then you left me, and I realized just how little control I did have."

The mention of Samantha punched her so hard she gasped. "What happened to Samantha wasn't your fault."

"I know. But what happened after was. You blamed me once for not fighting hard enough to keep us together. You were right. I thought I deserved to lose you. I didn't think I was worthy of you."

The sheen of his tears undid her. She slid off the ottoman and knelt between his knees, disturbing Red Cat, who lithely jumped over the arm of the couch and flounced away, tail in the air. "We were a pair of fools, weren't we?" She cupped his jaw in her palm, resting her other hand on his leg. "Let's not be fools again."

He tilted his head and let his lips brush her skin. "What are you saying, Aubrey?"

"I wanted control of my own life." Joy blossomed within her, bright and hot and exuberant. "I'm taking it. I love you, Phillip. Will you be a part of my life? Of my days and nights and every moment between?"

"For as long as you'll have me." His tone was fervent, his eyes flaring with sincerity. "And I hope, this time, that's forever."

Her arms slid around his neck as he hauled her into his lap. His kiss was heated and frantic, welding the last cracks in her heart shut. Without letting her lips leave his, she squirmed around to straddle his thighs, and then set about proving to *him* that she'd meant every word, that she meant to fight for him, that she was never letting him go again.

CHAPTER THIRTY-NINE

A week and a half later, Aubrey stood next to her father and watched him pledge himself to Marjorie. The older woman wore a simple sheath dress of palest lavender, with a matching fascinator clipped to her freshly permed hair. She glowed with a bride's heartfelt joy, and Aubrey had to keep blinking back tears during the age-old words of the Catholic ritual. Her father wore a new black suit. While his face reflected none of the softness of Marjorie's, his voice was firm and strong, and it was impossible to deny he cherished her.

On the far side of Marjorie, Phillip was dashing and handsome in his own neat black suit. His tie complemented her dress, and the emotions Aubrey saw crossing his face echoed her own feelings.

Despite her initial misgivings about the small guest list, the intimacy lent a depth and richness to the ceremony she hadn't envisioned. If she ever decided to marry Phillip again, she'd have to keep that in mind.

Marry Phillip. A tingle of anticipation riffled in the pit of her belly. As if he knew exactly what she was thinking, he caught her eye and mouthed *I love you*. The tingle threatened to flare into full on lust, and she broke the connection, but not before a blush heated her cheeks.

She did her best to concentrate on her father and Marjorie as the rites wound to a close. This was their day, and they deserved her full attention. It wasn't until everyone was back at Riverbend and enjoying the light treats and drinks that made up the mid-afternoon reception menu that she was able to draw him aside for a semi-private moment.

He pressed a kiss to her forehead in a casual, loving gesture that made her breathless. "I think it went well, don't you?"

"Yes." Her father and Marjorie were surrounded by well-wishers and looked pleased and proud. "I think they were disappointed Jos...Eugene didn't come."

"I'm kind of glad he didn't."

She looked at him, surprised. "You are?"

"If he had, the focus would have been on him. His presence would have detracted from the main reason we're here—Marjorie and Clarence."

She hadn't thought of it that way. "Do you think that's why he didn't come?"

"It's certainly possible. He seems a pretty astute guy. And his invitation for them to spend a week with him and his family after the wedding was very thoughtful. I know Marjorie thinks it will be the perfect honeymoon."

"I hope so. There's still so much that can go wrong."

"That's true for everything in life. We know that."

She laid her head against his shoulder in tender acknowledgment. His arm came around her waist and she sighed with contentment.

Chatter and laughter filled the room. Asher had watched the ceremony from Winnipeg via video chat, but Zeke had taken the day off work in order to attend. He stood talking with Sophie, who had made the trip from Toronto to see her step-grandfather married. Helen and Nathan were there as last-minute representatives of the Silverberries, and various other familiar faces shone with friendship and happiness. She felt connected to these people in a way that brought nothing but pleasure. Her life was so much different than it had been just four months ago.

And it was time to make another change. She turned

to Phillip and waited for him to look at her. "I've been thinking."

Maybe those words should have worried him, but the last several days had been so wonderful Phillip couldn't drum up an ounce of anxiety. "What have you been thinking?"

"As much as I've loved this sabbatical, it's time to go back to work."

"Really?" He drew her out of the room. The double doors were wide open, the cheer spilling into the hallway. They took seats on a low, upholstered bench on the far side of the hall—still able to watch the party, but far enough away to speak quietly. "Back to the law?"

She nodded. "Yes. And not just because it's all I know, or because my father is assuming that's what I'll do. I've started to miss exercising my brain on difficult problems that affect people's lives. Being a lawyer—my kind of lawyer, anyway—is more about mediation than litigation. I want to focus on that. And when I think of all the lawyers that had a part in finding Joseph..." She shrugged. "Maybe one day I can help someone like those people helped us."

"Have you talked to your old firm?"

She shook her head. "I'm not going back there. It's too easy to get caught in the rat race working for a large company. I'm going to go independent." Her lips pinched, revealing some nervousness, but her eyes were clear.

"I think that's perfect." He stroked her cheek and pulled her into a one-armed hug. "I'm proud of you."

"I'm proud of me, too. I'm not in any hurry to start, though. I want to concentrate on Cedar Street first. Red Cat and I want to get home as quickly as possible." The renovations had begun last week, and he had helped her and the cat—ferociously yowling and squalling from inside a carrier—move to her condo, where they were living in the meantime.

Her face glowed with a serenity he hadn't seen in a long time, if ever. She was no longer the slightly scatty teenager, nor the brittle politician, nor the broken, lost woman she'd been just weeks ago. She was an amalgam of those overlaid with a new confidence, new power.

She took his breath away.

Listening to Marjorie and Clarence say their vows had made him determined to make his relationship with her official. Call him old-fashioned, but it was a step he really, really wanted to take. He thought she did, too, but they could wait to discuss it. For now, he'd promised himself he'd enjoy what each day brought, without demanding a plan for the future.

"I've been thinking about work, too." He would never be less than honest with her again. "I never told you, but I considered selling Twin Rivers."

She jerked up from her cozy position snuggled on his shoulder. "You what? Why? You love that company."

"I do. But I'd stopped *enjoying* it. I've changed my mind, though. I'm not going to sell, but it's past time I put a succession plan in place. I'm going to train someone to do my duties, which will free me up to get out of the office, get my hands dirty. And with Asher halfway across the country, it will give me more time to travel." He'd already started mapping the process, though he hadn't made the decision public, even within the company. "I can't walk away cold turkey, so weaning myself off slowly seems the only option. I hope it isn't a mistake."

She laid her hand on his thigh. "It doesn't sound like one, but if it is, we'll figure it out."

"We?" He took her hand and played with her fingers absently while meeting her bold, direct stare. "I like the sound of that."

"I do, too." She kissed him softly, tenderly, but with such promise he grew dizzy. "I do, too."

ACKNOWLEDGEMENTS

Families can be made by blood or love. I have three siblings, two of which are adopted. In fact, on my mother's side, my grandparents had as many adopted grandchildren as those related by blood. And it didn't make a darn bit of difference to any of us.

In *Turn the Next Page*, I send my characters virtually to Nipawin, Saskatchewan. My father was born at the hospital there, while his family was living in the even tinier nearby community of Love. Yes, you read that right—Love. When he was ten his parents moved to British Columbia, as many Saskatchewanians have done before and since. When I learned having Joseph adopted outside his birth province would make the search more difficult, it seemed a logical place to send him.

Many lawyers feature in this story. I'd like to thank Garth Wright, a personal injury lawyer here in Prince George that I worked with in my career writing and producing television commercials. While not his area of expertise, he certainly was able to guide me away from the most egregious mistakes I had plotted out. I should also thank The Creative Academy for Writers (https://creativeacademyforwriters.com), who invited lawyer Shawn Jones to present at one of their Expertpalooza events. He reinforced what Garth had already warned me about and encouraged me to adjust the plot to what you read here.

While *Turn the Next Page* is not based on any true events, I do want to draw your attention briefly to the character of Father Murray Athol. While searching for Saskatchewan schools where Duncan Truble might have met the priestly friend he asks for assistance, I came across Athol Murray College of Notre Dame, a private, independent, co-educational boarding high school located in Wilcox, Saskatchewan. I didn't feel right stealing his name, so made the switch of first and last, and hope I haven't offended anyone in the process. I won't tell you any more about him but can't leave the subject without sharing Father Athol's most famous quote: "I love God, Canada, and hockey—not always in that order."

I have two other quick thank yous to make. When Aubrey states that life was too short to read anymore depressing books, some of you may have recognized a quote from Susan Elizabeth Phillips. I wholeheartedly agree with this sentiment—and it's one of the reasons I write romance! And I would be remiss if I didn't give credit to my daughter, Larissa, for Terrance's magnificent statement that he is "a maestro at proactively conserving my energy reserves by the considered delegation of meaningless tasks." When I'm in need of multisyllabic words, who better to ask than someone with two Masters degrees—one in History and one in Library and Information Studies?

As always, thanks for reading. And for those of you interested, the recipe for Punch Romaine as made by Natalie is on the next page. It really was served on the Titanic the night it hit the iceberg.

Punch Romaine
(recipe courtesy of Saveur.com)

1 egg white
1 oz. white rum
1 oz. white wine
1/2 oz. simple syrup
1/2 oz. lemon juice
1 oz. fresh orange juice
2 oz. Champagne or sparkling wine
Twist of orange peel, for garnish

Fill cocktail shaker with ice. Add egg white, rum, wine, simple syrup, lemon, and orange juice. Shake vigorously until frothy. Mound crushed ice in a large coupe glass and pour drink around it. Top with champagne, and garnish with orange peel.

Thanks for reading
Turn the Next Page.

Reviews and ratings are a great way to help other readers discover new authors. Just a line or two is all that's needed—or simply click the number of stars you think it deserves. I encourage you to post your honest opinion at the retailer where you purchased your copy, on GoodReads and BookBub. Thank you so much!

Visit my website to discover more titles in the Silverberry Seduction Seasoned Romance Series.

I'd love to stay in touch. Subscribe to my newsletter and you'll immediately receive *Margin of Risk,* a companion short story in the Silverberry Seduction world. You'll also be able to tag along with my dog-walking adventures, find out what I'm reading when I should be working, and other randomness...along with all my writing news, of course! Find the sign-up form at www.brendamargriet.com.

ABOUT THE AUTHOR

Brenda Margriet writes savvy, slow burn, contemporary romances with ordinarily amazing characters. In her own ordinarily amazing life, she had a successful career in radio and television production before deciding to pilfer from her retirement plan to support her writing compulsion.

Readers have called her stories "poignant," "explicit and steamy," "interesting, intriguing and entertaining," and "unlike any romance you've read before" (she assumes the latter was meant in a good way).

Join Brenda on social media—she is most active on Facebook and Instagram. And you can always discover more about her and her books on her website, brendamargriet.com.

ALSO BY BRENDA MARGRIET

SILVERBERRY SEDUCTION SEASONED ROMANCE
Secrets Under the Covers
Loving Between the Lines
Turn the Next Page
Strictly by the Book
Too Good for Words
The Complete Silverberry Seduction Series
(e-book only)

TIMELESS SEASONED ROMANCE
After Words
Richly Deserved

THE BENDIXON SISTERS SERIES
Allegro Court
Gateway Crescent
Crossroads Corner
Taking His Measure: The Complete Bendixon Sisters Series
(e-book only)

STANDALONE READS
Mountain Fire
Reserved for You
No Life But This
When Time Falls Still
The Promise of Frost

Read excerpts and find buy links at
www.brendamargriet.com